SKELETON KEY

SKELETON

KEY

Lenore Glen Offord

With an Introduction by
Sarah Weinman

FELONY & MAYHEM PRESS • NEW YORK

SKELETON KEY

A Felony & Mayhem mystery

PRINTING HISTORY
First edition (Duell, Sloan, & Pearce): 1943
First paperback edition (Dell): 1945
Felony & Mayhem edition: 2015

Copyright © 1943 by Lenore Glen Offord
Introduction copyright © 2014 by Sarah Weinman

ISBN: 978-1-63194-032-3

Manufactured in the United States of America

Printed on 100% recycled paper

Library of Congress Cataloging-in-Publication Data

Offord, Lenore Glen, 1905-1991
  Skeleton key / Lenore Glen Offord. -- Felony & Mayhem edition.
    pages ; cm. -- (A Felony & Mayhem mystery)
  ISBN 978-1-63194-032-3 (softcover)
  1. Widows--Fiction. 2. Murder--Investigation--Fiction. I. Title.
PS3529.F42S57 2015
813'.52--dc23
                    2014041226

To Joyce, Katie and Jane

CONTENTS

The icon above says you're holding a copy of a book in the Felony & Mayhem "Vintage" category. These books were originally published prior to about 1965, and feature the kind of twisty, ingenious puzzles beloved by fans of Agatha Christie and John Dickson Carr. If you enjoy this book, you may well like other "Vintage" titles from Felony & Mayhem Press.

———◆———

For more about these books, and other Felony & Mayhem titles, or to place an order, please visit our website at:

www.FelonyAndMayhem.com

Other "Vintage" titles from

FELONY&MAYHEM

SKELETON KEY

INTRODUCTION

Out of the Shadows: The Suspense Novels of Lenore Glenn Offord

THE SHEER BREADTH and depth of crime fiction allows for expertise in a particular sliver of the genre. A reader obsessed with solving intricately plotted crimes may be unable to start a conversation with a lover of modern-day cozy mysteries focused on niche topics. The *noiristes* might engage in awkward conversation with the spy-thriller aficionados. Those keen on psychological suspense might look down their noses at fans of plot-driven action adventures.

Partly by accident, equally by design, the corner of knowledge I've carved out over the past few years centers around what I call domestic suspense: namely, novels by women published roughly between the dawn of the Second World War and the onset of Second-Wave feminism. They aren't quite hardboiled—at least, not if you compare them to books published by Hammett, Chandler, Cain, and the like—but they aren't exactly cozy, nor do they fit into the "had I but known" school of ladies-in-peril invented by Mary Roberts Rinehart.

Instead they are somewhere in between, featuring independent career women like the titular heroine of Vera Caspary's

Laura; housewives on the edge protecting their families like Lucia Holley in Elisabeth Sanxay Holding's *The Blank Wall*; and new mothers desperate for relief from crying babies, demanding children, and condescending husbands like Louise in Celia Fremlin's *The Hours Before Dawn*. I've discovered a whole host of wonderful, needlessly neglected authors, many of whom now have a new generation of serious readers. But flash-lights on earlier generations tend to miss a few spots, the dust of time concealing other forgotten names and literary gems ripe for discovery.

Lenore Glen Offord was new to me until quite recently. But once I delved into her not very large body of work – twelve novels between 1938 and 1959, eight of them mysteries – I discovered a writer of utterly delightful tales that mixed a strong sense of fair play, a wry wit, and a shrewd sense of domestic relationships that were, for their time, quite innovative, even subversive. How near-modern to trip across a mystery with a blended family in the making, where the murder-solving gets equal time with mother-daughter bonding. Here is crime fiction without airs, thunderous moralizing, or ponderous prose. The touch is light, even sprightly. It's perhaps not surprising to learn that Offord herself wore multiple hats, as a novelist, a literary critic, a passionate theatergoer, and a mother.

Lenore Frances Glen was born on October 24, 1905 in Spokane, Washington to Katherine and Robert Glen, the latter a longtime newspaper editor in the city. She lived on the West Coast for her entire life, making ample use of Pacific Northwest and California settings in her fiction. She moved to Oakland, California for college, received a B.A. (cum laude) from Mills College in 1927, and after marrying Harold Offord in 1929, migrated to Berkeley, CA, ostensibly for graduate work at the city's University of California outpost. They remained in and around Berkeley for nearly sixty years, with Offord giving birth to a daughter, Judith, in 1943.

For a time the Offords lived in the San Francisco neigh-borhood of Russian Hill, which provided the setting and title of her first novel, *Murder on Russian Hill*. That book introduced Coco Hastings, a voracious reader of mystery novels who, with her antiquarian husband Bill, gets embroiled in an actual murder in her own proverbial backyard. The pair returned for their second and final engagement in *Clues to Burn* (1942).

In between Offord ventured into more mainstream territory with *Cloth of Silver* (1939), about a girl reporter at a local newspaper contemplating love and marriage (she dedicated the book to her father: "To Pops, who told me so"); *Angels Unaware* (1940), a family drama where the arrival of unexpected guests exposes long-dormant fault lines; and the standalone thriller *The Nine Dark Hours* (1941), more in the classic domestic suspense mode of an ordinary young woman caught up in increasingly sinister events. (Offord's superior standalone thriller, *My True Love Lies*, set in the San Francisco art world, was published in 1947.) Yet mystery/suspense was always Offord's favorite genre, as she explained in a 1949 interview with the *Oakland Tribune*. "It is the first, and sometimes forgotten commandment for any novelist that he have a story to tell...I think [mystery novels] are sound discipline for the writer."

With *Skeleton Key*, published in 1943 by Duell, Sloan & Pearce, Offord mixed a smart, curious heroine, her own insider's knowledge of California, and a deft hand with the foibles of domestic conflict—and fashioned the start of her most artistically successful works. *Skeleton Key* introduces Georgine Wyeth, a twenty-seven-year-old widow, with a small child, whose personality emerges, fully-formed, in a descriptive paragraph early on in the novel: "one glance...left you with no more than a vaguely pleasant impression. A second proved unexpectedly rewarding; those who troubled to take it saw her eyes and thought 'lonely,' her mouth, and thought 'sweet'; and then this increasingly sentimental gaze, having reached her chin, was brought up with a round turn. The set and tilt of the jaw spoke of stubbornness and humor, and more than hinted at a peppery though short-lived temper."

It is a dangerous thing to underestimate Georgine Wyeth, especially if the person doing the underestimating is Georgine herself. She is wont to do that, convincing herself (here and in subsequent books) that she is paralyzed by her fears: of the unknown, of heights, of strange situations. In fact, her *modus operandi* is very practical: it's the height of World War II, she has to support her seven-year-old daughter because there is no husband around anymore to do it for her, and she'll take any job that suits. The search for that suitable job proves frustrating and protracted, but perseverance finally wins out as Georgine finds a position as a typist for a fearsome European scientist and moves into a *cul-de-sac* on Berkeley's Grettry Road.

Mystery arises not long after her arrival, as the small Grettry Road community is shaken by the death of an air-raid warden during a blackout, courtesy of a runaway car. (Blackout regulations on the West Coast were considerably more stringent and comprehensive than in other parts of the country: on a dark night the entire neighborhood might be all but pitch-black.) His death, first declared an accident, soon appears to have been something a lot more sinister.

Grettry Road is, understandably, riveted by the murder, but Georgine is somewhat distracted: it takes some convincing for her to realize it, but little Grettry Road is offering a glimpse of her future, of a face that "stood out like those of a bold carving: eyes deep-set between sandy brows and high cheekbones, flat planes of cheeks, firm jaw. The face looked as if it would be hard to the touch...he looked from one person to another, with such a total lack of expression that she'd thought he must be inwardly amused."

Georgine's glimpse, like the reader's, is the first of Todd McKinnon, professional pulp writer ("hack work, but I can live on it") with a weakness for playing the harmonica late at night (quietly, if you ask him nicely) and a nose for unsolved mysteries that add *gravitas* to his fictioneering. His declarations of love are understated, but when he utters a line like "You're a nice woman, Georgine. You're one of the nicest women I ever met. Don't take anything second-rate; you can have the best, you know," she understands Todd's full, passionate meaning. In Offord's hands, Todd resembles the kind of romance hero more prevalent in Preston Sturges comedies like *Palm Beach Story* or *Christmas in July,* capable yet a little befuddled, inquisitive but silent when the situation calls for it, and often enmeshed in the thick of strange adventures, especially those of his own making.

The two make a good sleuthing team, what with Todd's methodical, laconic investigative acumen and Georgine's intuitive understanding of people. Nevertheless *Skeleton Key* is primarily Georgine's story of rolling with the punches, contending with her many fears, trying to provide a home for her daughter, Barby, and knowing "she could do only one thing: save herself." Despite her belief in her own phobias, Georgine looks problems square in the face and deals with them, however unpleasant. She is a worthy antecedent to the crime-solving heroines of the 1970s, like Marcia Muller's Sharon McCone or Maxine O'Callaghan's Delilah West, and the very opposite of the fluttering Rinehart prototype.

Where *Skeleton Key* is clearly viewed through Georgine's eyes, *The Glass Mask*, published in 1944, is more of a group effort. Barby, now eight, "lights up like a pinball machine" over Todd's twenty-one-year old nephew, Dyke, during a trip to his part of California. Barby's crush makes it impossible for her mother and Todd to refuse Dyke's suggestion that the three of them—a soon-to-be blended family—visit a particular house on their way home. They stay overnight, and then another night, until it's clear that *someone* (perhaps a relative of their increasingly peculiar hostess?) plans to keep them there indefinitely.

The Glass Mask is as much cloistered country-house tale, the walls constricting with a Poe-like metaphorical flourish, as it is about Georgine facing her fears, most notably of marriage to Todd. There's little reason they shouldn't tie the knot, especially when Barby loves her "Toddy" so. And yet Georgine can't quite shake off the niggling worry that she won't be able to handle the dangers that can find a writer of pulp tales, especially when that writer is devoted to basing his fiction on fact.

Her concerns are not for herself. As she tells Todd, "If you have anything to do with crime, even just writing about it, you're bound to get mixed up in horrors every so often. I could accept that for myself, if I tried. I could take it for you; it's your life, you have a right to risk it." The trouble for Georgine is she "never thought of its touching Barby. How can I let her in for that sort of thing? She hasn't the choice. I have to make it for her." Despite these eminently practical doubts about whether to go ahead with the marriage—doubts cast aside amid the whirlwind of solving yet another crime—the matter-of-fact way in which she brushes off queries about traveling with a man not (quite) her husband is most refreshing. There's little in the way of histrionics; Georgine merely listens, and goes about her day.

Once the mystery sorts itself out, the answer to Georgine and Todd's domestic conflict does the same. Married several years by the time of the events in *The Smiling Tiger* (1949), they find new mysterious adventures in the midst of a neighboring religious cult that does more harm than good. Beyond-Truth, as the cult is called, opposes marriages that will produce children: the end of the world is coming, after all, and what's the point in procreating? Todd doesn't want to write about this unpleasant group, but as he's in a writing rut, the lure of the paycheck trumps all—as does a more overt threat to Georgine. *The Smiling Tiger* is a fun read but the bite of the earlier two books isn't quite as pronounced. It would be another decade before Georgine, Todd, and Barby made their next, and last, appearance.

Offord's output slowed when she was named the full-time mystery critic for the *San Francisco Chronicle* in 1950, her column given the cracking title "The Gory Road." During the Second World War she shared the column with her friend Anthony Boucher, the famed critic, novelist, essayist and anthologist, but she continued by herself when he decamped for the "Criminals at Large" column at the *New York Times*. Offord's work at the *Chronicle* won her the Edgar Award for Best Criticism in 1952, and she remained the paper's critic until 1982, making her one of the longest-serving reviewers of mystery fiction in the country.

In addition to *The Marble Forest* (1951), a serial novel that included a chapter by Boucher, Offord published three more books. *Enchanted August* (1956), is a work of young-adult fiction set at Ashland, Oregon's famed Shakespeare Festival, which Offord attended frequently, along with her daughter Judy, who may have been the inspiration for the protagonist and who acted with the company as a child. *The Girl in the Belfry* (1957), is a true crime account co-written with Joseph Henry Jackson. Her final novel, *Walking Shadow*, also set at Ashland, continues her series but with a focus shift: the main character is Barby, all grown up and now a costume assistant on a summer production of that famous "Scottish play," *Macbeth*.

Despite being the nominal heroine, Barby is more of an Eve Arden character, resigned to playing second fiddle to the beautiful, mysterious Margaret Lenox. Winsome, red-headed, and blazingly talented, Meg attracts many but keeps most at a distance. Might it have something to do with a recently discovered corpse back in Berkeley? The tenuous connection puzzles Barby enough to call in the cavalry, i.e. her stepfather Todd, still plying his trade in crime writing and still capable of deducing the truth, even after several missteps of misdirection. The solution is a surprise, but what elevates *Walking Shadow* to Offord's most accomplished novel is her utter familiarity with Shakespearean drama, the politicking of summer stock, and her love of it all. Theatrical settings have a special place in mystery fiction, inspiring a number of novels by classic writers like Ngaio Marsh, Margery Allingham, and Edmund Crispin, and more recent works by Joyce Harrington, Pat Carlson, and Jane Dentinger, and the "Scottish Play" has been a particular favorite.

After *Walking Shadow*, Offord stopped publishing novels. "Every mystery story published in the U.S. was mailed to our house," says Offord's daughter, "and she read each one, at least enough of it to decide if it was something she wanted to review. I think that as she got older, a lot of her writing energy went to the reviewing. I think she felt that she'd accomplished what she set out to do in the novel form."

But she didn't abandon fiction or creative writing altogether. In addition to her perch at the SF *Chronicle*, Offord published short stories and poems, most notably "Memoirs of a Mystery Critic" in *Ellery Queen's Mystery Magazine*, a wonderful rhyming verse that catalogs the many, many plot and character tropes of crime novels and closes:

> By now, for these plots
> I could fill in the dots
> With one hand behind me
> And a blindfold to blind me.
> And yet I keep reading them,
> Greedily needing them.
> Don't think of them,
> Just keep on printing them!

Offord was also active within the world of Sherlock Holmes fans, most notably as the first female member vested into the Baker Street Irregulars, the premier fan club for all things Holmes, Watson, and their creator, Arthur Conan Doyle. New members are given special nicknames, and Offord's was "The Old Russian Woman," a hat tip to *Murder on Russian Hill*. But Offord never attended a BSI event. Those were in New York, and she stayed on the West Coast. The other contributing factor? She was the sole female Irregular (it would be another 20 years before another woman was invested into the club). "I don't believe in forcing my way into a group that is all-male and has kept to itself," Offord explained in a 1984 interview with the *Times-News*.

"I wouldn't want a male trying to force his way into a group I belonged to if it were all-female."

In 1988 Offord and her husband, Harold, moved to Ashland, Oregon to be closer to their daughter, who had become a choreographer for the Shakespeare Festival. In doing so Offord became a year-round resident of the place she immortalized in *Walking Shadow*. She died, at age eighty-five, on April 24, 1991. (Harold passed away the following year.) Her life was clearly one of love, laughter, and literature, where words on the page carried tremendous meaning, as an author, a critic, or a play-goer. Lenore Glen Offord deserves the much wider audience that these new reissues will undoubtedly bring, a contemporary audience certain to enjoy her novels.

—SARAH WEINMAN

CHAPTER ONE

The Mad Professor

THE STREET SIGN appeared first, like a ship's mast coming over the horizon. *Grettry Road*, it read, in black letters on a strip of yellow-painted tin. The larger sign below it came into view next, line by line: NOT A—THROUGH—STREET.

The young woman toiling up the hill took in the whole unencouraging message, paused, looked at the steep slope behind her and spoke aloud, indignantly. "My pals!" she said, presumably referring to the city fathers, who might have let her know earlier.

A few more steps, however, brought her to the crest, and the fathers were exonerated. Avenida Drive continued to the right along the edge of a canyon, and the blind street curved downward to the left. Best of all, beneath the signs at the intersection was a convenient flat rock. The young woman made for it and sat down, panting.

She was footsore and warm and on the verge of discouragement. The miniature briefcase she carried was full of magazine-subscription blanks, and as Georgine Wyeth knew too well, they all remained obstinately true to their name.

Again she spoke aloud, bitterly; but this time to herself.
"You!" she said. "You couldn't sell water to a desert tank
corps."

This was undeserved. There had been other June days
as warm and lazy as this one, on which housewives had
answered their doorbells and listened to her sales talk, and
sometimes even fallen for the Magnificent Combination
Offer, or the Three Year Subscription for the Price of Two.
Today, a sudden wave of sales resistance had nearly over-
whelmed her.

Oh, well, thought Georgine philosophically, *probably
like everything else it could be blamed on the war*. In a
season when Japanese forces roosted on the Aleutian Islands,
and when the ocean outside the Golden Gate was muffled
in a fog-bank supposed by many Bay residents to be solidly
packed with enemy aircraft carriers, a slight sense of imper-
manence might well be felt. She squinted her blue eyes
against the glare, and looked at the western horizon. There
was the notorious fog-bank. You had a fine view of it from
this perch.

The view also comprised the soaring towers of San
Francisco, two bridges and a number of islands, and almost
all the cities on the east side of the Bay. Across the canyon
to Georgine's left squatted the red dome of the Cyclotron
building, and far below it lay the campus, blocked out in
fawn and green, tile-red and white, like a section of modern-
istic linoleum. Georgine surveyed the miles that were spread
soft-colored and glittering within her vision, and thoughtfully
nodded. She had lived in Berkeley long enough to realize
the paramount importance of this view in the minds of hill-
dwellers. It explained the existence of the isolated group of
houses that was called Grettry Road.

A faint wind was stirring, gratefully cool on her face
and neck. She took off her old Panama hat and ruffled the
short brown curls of a war bob, and sighed in relaxation. Her
round curly head looked like a girl's, and so did the slim figure

in the blue cotton suit and saddle oxfords, but her face was more mature. It was a bit too thin and anxious-looking for her twenty-seven years.

One glance at Georgine Wyeth left you with no more than a vaguely pleasant impression. A second proved unexpectedly rewarding; those who troubled to take it saw her eyes and thought "lonely"; her mouth, and thought "sweet"; and then this increasingly sentimental gaze, having reached her chin, was brought up with a round turn. The set and tilt of the jaw spoke of stubbornness and humor, and more than hinted at a peppery though short-lived temper.

Little by little, as at the moment she sat resting with her attractive legs stretched out before her, her face lost its anxious determination and took on a look of soulful thought. She was wondering if she'd ever get used to cotton stockings. This important question occupied the forefront of her mind; another part was lazily deliberating whether to go home now or to ring just a few more doorbells. The short blind street to her left seemed a poor prospect for sales. It was too quiet, half asleep under the summer sunlight; more than likely nobody was at home.

From the Campanile, far below, drifted the notes of a chime: three o'clock. By sun time, of course, it was only two; mid-afternoon, that little zero hour when the shadows forget to change, when a woman alone in the house becomes suddenly aware of a dripping tap, the tick of a branch against the window. The air was full of the sleepy shrilling and humming of insects. Somewhere across the canyon eucalyptus leaves were burning, and their aromatic smoke, sweeter than incense to Californian nostrils, came floating across the hill. Georgine sat on, dreamily inert. Gradually all conscious thought left her mind, until it felt clean and empty as a house ready for new tenants.

She heard it then for the first time: that thin little thread of music, lonely as a shepherd's pipe on the quiet air. It wasn't mechanical music, for the reedy notes wavered a little on the run in the fourth bar, and stopped and were repeated. So, there was somebody at home in Grettry Road. She found herself wondering what odd sort of person would play Schubert's *The Trout* on a mouth-organ.

It caught the imagination, somehow; mental adventures like this were distinctly to her taste, which was lucky, since as a mother and wage-earner she could hardly afford to seek any other kind. Maybe, she thought, it would be worthwhile to try that street after all.

Georgine Wyeth stood up, looked at the sign that said NOT A THROUGH STREET, and shrugged. Then, quite willingly, as if enchanted by the tune of the Pied Piper, she stepped into Grettry Road.

There was no telling how far away the music had been when she heard it. She rang first at the two well-built, unpretentious houses that faced each other across the mouth of the street. The doorbells burred unheeded in their quiet depths. Nobody seemed to be at home.

From her resting-place the larger part of the road had been out of sight, curving away behind a high outcrop of rock that took up most of the eastern side. She left the porch of the first house on the west and went downhill, scuffing through the dry sickle-shaped leaves that carpeted a vacant lot shaded by a fine stand of eucalyptus. At the outer curve of this lot she paused, looking down the steep slope of Grettry Road, which could be seen in its entirety from this point alone. At the far end, where the road flattened and widened, a low white-painted fence kept cars from plunging into the canyon. There was only one house on the east side, three-quarters of the way down; but on the west there were four.

Three of them were small, differing so aggressively in detail and ornament as to make it obvious that the same hand had built them all. Their front walks, on three descending levels, led straight onto the street—there were neither curbs nor sidewalks—and their narrow side yards were separated only by thin straggles of hedge. They had a comic look, like white puppies peering over the edges of adjacent stair-steps. Presumably their lower floors were built down into the first slope of the ravine.

The door of the highest one stood ajar, and Georgine could hear someone moving about inside, just out of sight. She rang the bell; its tubular chime sounded so close to her ear that it made her jump.

Whoever was walking around that inner room completely ignored the sound. The footsteps were quick but sounded heavy enough to be a man's. She found herself peering through the screen in an effort to see him. She rang again, and waited; waited a full two minutes.

She stood frowning at the screen for a moment, and then retreated rather slowly to the street and stood gazing up and down its empty length. The technique of ignoring agents had certainly been brought to a fine point in these hills; the residents might as well come out and kick you downstairs!

She was irritated, and found herself rather fostering her annoyance. For a moment there she'd had a decidedly queer feeling, *As if*, thought Georgine, *I'd died and didn't know it, and everyone looked right through me.*

Well, there were other houses. She walked fifty feet downhill and tried the next one. Surely someone ought to answer here, for as she came up a door closed audibly in the depths of the house; but nobody came, and she could not even hear the doorbell.

How quiet this street was! There was no sound now except that of her rubber-shod feet, and its padded echo from the rock wall. Generally in mid-afternoon you'd expect to hear children playing, but there could scarcely be any living in this remote, steep dead-end. The silence gave it a sleeping-beauty quality, for the breeze had dropped and the striped shadows of eucalyptus lay motionless on the buckling asphalt of the pavement. She still hadn't found a sign of her mouth-organ player. The music had stopped just before she entered the road, and now it seemed as if she'd never heard it.

She turned her head suddenly, catching in the tail of her eye a movement in one of the upper houses, as if a curtain had been twitched aside and as hastily dropped into place. So that was it; she must have *agent* written all over her, somehow, and the people along this street were playing possum. She'd done that herself in the past. The realization gave her an obscure sense of relief.

At the lowest of the triplet-houses the bell gave off that indefinable echo that tells you the place is empty. Georgine's lower lip folded softly over the upper, and she glanced about her once more. If she had any sense, she'd go home now, but honor must be satisfied. She compromised by not crossing the street; there was only one more house on this side, the big one at the end, and she would probably draw a blank there, too. If not—she prepared to hand out a sales talk that would fairly batter the listener into acceptance.

The big house had no doorbell. She grasped the knocker with unnecessary violence, intending to shatter the echoes; and before she could let it fall, felt it twitched from her fingers.

The door swung open. A majestic Negro woman, in a black dress and white apron, stood benignly gazing down at her. "Come right in," said the apparition softly. "We been waitin' fo' you."

The well-known sensation of walking down a step that isn't there was as nothing to the effect of this welcome. For a moment Georgine could do nothing but gasp. A reasonless feeling of terror touched her, and was swiftly gone. Then she opened her mouth to say, "You can't mean me!" and caught herself just in time. *Why not?* she thought; *there were characters who simply yearned to subscribe to magazines, and it would be crazy to give up the chance of meeting some.* In dazed silence she stepped into the dimness of a square entrance hall.

The dark lady retreated before her with a stately tread, reminiscent of the chorus in *Aïda*. "P'fessah! P'fessah!" she boomed in her velvet voice, into the rear of the house. "She got here." A far-away shout answered, unintelligibly, as Georgine followed her guide into a small, hot, drab living-room that looked as if nobody ever lived in it.

The African Queen gestured nobly toward a chair. "There's been so many disappointed him," she remarked, "I was right glad to see you comin' along the street, ringin' do'bells. You lose the address?"

There must be a catch in this, Georgine thought. "I—yes," she said vaguely. "People were at home, I heard them, but no one answered the bell."

"Maybe you tried Frey's." The deep voice was respectfully soothing. "He's stone deaf. And the Gillespies, next to him, they unhitched the do'bell because Mr. Gillespie works nights."

So that was it; simple, normal, only Georgine hadn't happened to think of it. Yet she gave a nervous start as another voice spoke from the doorway, "That's all, Mrs. Blake," it said, and the housekeeper strode magnificently out.

The Professor was tall, bald and sixtyish. His sharp black eyes, narrowed in the hot glare from the window, looked Georgine over; once up, once down, He nodded, came briskly into the room and sat down on a straight chair. "Your name?" he snapped out.

Georgine's fingers moved toward the clasp of the little briefcase. She usually began by giving her name, though few forestalled her by asking. "Mrs. James Wyeth," she said. Jim Wyeth had been dead for seven years, but to give her Christian name made her sound like a divorcee.

"Mine is Pah-eff, P-a-e-v," said the Professor, adding angrily, "—the last young woman managed to misspell it in four several ways. Accuracy is my one desire.

"Now; I'll tell you at once that I pay by piecework. There are less than three hundred pages, and I will pay one hundred dollars for the job; one ribbon copy, two carbons. You must work here. Not one page, not one line is to go out of this house. Is that understood?"

Out of this speech, delivered in a furious staccato, Georgine really heard only three words: *one hundred dollars.* Around her floated a vague impression that there had been a mistake after all, that Professor Paev wanted some typing done, that there were certain conditions; but that sum of money loomed in her mind like a glittering promise. She could type; she could earn it.

One hundred dollars. It might be hay to some people, but it wasn't to her. It was more than her entire monthly income from Jim Wyeth's insurance, ten times as much as she earned in her best weeks at the subscription business. It would pay off almost all the debt owed to Barby's doctor since last October, and Barby could have a new winter coat after all, and she, Georgine, could draw a few free breaths. With scarcely a pause, she said, "I understand."

It wouldn't take more than ten days, surely. And she had ahead of her two weeks free of responsibility, for that morning she had seen her little girl start off with the family of a kind neighbor for her first vacation away from home. Georgine firmly believed that no child, however delicate, should become wholly dependent on its mother. It had startled her no little to find that the seven-year-old Barby shared this view, but that was beside the point. Everything was falling into place.

Her shock of disappointment was therefore all the greater when she heard the Professor demanding, "Describe your knowledge of chemistry."

Bang went the doctor's bill. "I had it for a year, in—in high school," Georgine murmured.

"How much of it do you remember?"

She sought wildly for some recollection. "There was an experiment where you put sodium in a tank of water, and it ran around. Mine blew up," said Georgine unhappily. "I'm afraid that's all I—"

"Any physics? Bacteriology?"

Bang went the winter coat. "None," she admitted.

"You're hired," said Professor Paev, briskly rising.

Georgine blinked at him. There was something odd about these requirements; but again, for a moment, the hundred dollars seemed to flutter within her reach.

And then the Professor flung over his shoulder, "I will call the Acme Agency and tell them that if you prove reasonably accurate, I shall be satisfied." He was halfway to the hall before her voice stopped him.

"Professor Paev, I'm not from the Acme Agency."

The man stopped short. Then, with a curious deliberation, he closed the door and came across the room to her chair. "Who sent you here?" he said harshly.

"Nobody. It just happens that I can type. I'm slow, but I'm accurate. And if it isn't taking the bread out of somebody's—"

"*Who hired you to spy on me?*"

"Nobody, I tell you!"

"It's diabolical," said the Professor, breathing rapidly, "but I might have suspected it. Somehow, they must have figured that my experiments were nearly complete. They'd know how much I needed a typist. They should have prepared you better." The high bald head swooped down at her. "You might as well tell me who it was, I'll pay for the information!"

"I think you're crazy," said Georgine, and thrust herself to her feet. "Do I look like a spy? I came here to sell you some magazines, and before I got the words out of my mouth you offered me a job that it just happens I can do! Who wouldn't take it? I need the money, you need a typist. And what on earth would I be spying *about*?"

"Ah," said Professor Paev with a mirthless smile, "you would like to know, would you?"

They stood glaring at each other. Neither moved, but Georgine had a fantastic mental picture of two cats jockeying for position before a fight. If she held this pose much longer she'd burst into laughter.

"This is absurd," she said crisply. "I didn't intend to cheat you. It's a shame, too, when so many typists have disappointed you—but I see why, now."

The Professor's eyes narrowed. He said nothing.

"Before I go, could I interest you in any subscriptions, renewals, gift offers? I was afraid not. Well, good-by."

She heard an odd rusty sound. It seemed that Professor Paev was chuckling. "Wait," he said. "We might come to an understanding. Perhaps—an exchange of references?"

"Did you say exchange?" Georgine paused on the verge of a step. "That's more like it."

"Ah, yes. Someone whom we can both trust. I live alone here, you see, though Mrs. Blake is always present during the day. But perhaps I should tell you one thing: the consensus of the neighborhood is that I am perfecting a Death Ray in my laboratory."

Georgine gave him a penetrating look.

"I admit," he said blandly, "that I may have given them that impression myself. Indeed, in one sense it is not far from the truth. But you needn't feel any alarm, Mrs. Wyeth."

Dear me, she thought; *that gasp of mine must have been obvious.*

At five o'clock that afternoon Georgine was still at 82 Grettry Road, the home of Professor Alexis Paev; and she was still slightly dizzy and incredulous.

What an afternoon; up, down, up again in spirits; luck handed her, luck snatched away. The voice on the telephone, that of the President of the Parent-Teachers Association of Emerson School, who had fortunately remembered Mrs. Wyeth; the voice saying, "He's quite mad on the subject of science, but harmless every other way. We've known him for years, long before he resigned from the Faculty." From such a respectable source, this should be completely reassuring; but the words *mad professor* carried inescapable overtones: that laboratory in the basement, walled in glass brick, probably full of evil vapors and steaming flasks, and long tubes glimmering with unearthly lights... A death ray, indeed. The old gentleman's jokes were ponderous, he looked odd when he smiled, as if it didn't suit his face... And he'd wanted someone who knew nothing about science, so she was actually sitting here in a hot little south room on the top floor, with one window that looked off into space across the deep canyon, picking away letter by letter, figure by figure, at a seemingly endless stack of work.

Culture medium Penicillium (spp.), she wrote, *adsorbed by norite. Elute with chloroform, distil, take up in ethyl alcohol and reppt.*

Oh, DEAR, Georgine thought; *I can't do this... Yes, I can. I've got to.*

Ten or twelve days of it...the bill, Barby's coat...something to take up the slack of her loneliness while Barby was away. The stubborn insistence that it still came under the head of mental adventure...and the pay to be counted not in nickels and dimes, but in dollars; a hundred dollars to come... At five minutes after five it came, in a lump. The Professor tapped on the door, whisked in and inspected the three pages she had laboriously finished, nodded and got out a check book.

"Not all at once?" Georgine said, frowning at the check.

"All at once. Postdated, you will observe," said Mr. Paev.

She raised grave blue eyes to his. "You're convinced that I'm honest, or will be three days from now?" The long bald head nodded. "And you want to make sure I'll keep coming back until the job's finished?"

"I believe I've read you correctly, Mrs. Wyeth," said the Professor, his gaze doing its best to penetrate her skull.

"I think it's goofy," said Georgine, reaching for the typewriter cover, "but I'm game." The last words fell on empty air. The Professor was already halfway downstairs.

She had to stop work, but she couldn't go home yet. At four o'clock the African Queen had brought up a message; the block air-raid warden was to hold a meeting for all the residents of Grettry Road, even the temporary ones, at five-fifteen, at his home. Would Mrs. Wyeth be good enough to join them?

Mrs. Wyeth supposed she would. After the illogical sensations and unexpected developments of the last two hours, she felt that she could be neither surprised, irritated nor alarmed.

Having got her hands thoroughly inked in the struggle with an unfamiliar typewriter, she now went in search of a bathroom, without bothering Mrs. Blake for directions. There was one on the southwest corner of the house. It was obviously the Professor's own, but he could scarcely object to her drying her hands on one of his paper towels.

How like a lone man immersed in science to build such a house; all the furniture drab, hideous and far from inexpensive, most of the rooms an inconvenient shape, and the best view in the place from an upstairs bathroom! She raised the window and leaned her arms on the sill. You could see all of Oakland, shimmering under the heat-haze of late afternoon; you could see the lion-colored flanks of the bare hills to the south, and the plantations of trees nearer to Grettry Road, and the canyon that fell sheer from the fence at the end, and grew shallower as it swept around to the north past the back yards of the Road, dark with manzanita bushes, blue-green with bay and young gum trees.

And just below the window, you could see a thicket of flowering shrubs, and a spot right up against the house wall where, it seemed, the Professor had begun a garden.

That was a curious place for a flower-bed, hemmed round with bushes so tall that it could be seen only from this spot directly above. There were no other windows that overlooked it, for the living-room wall below was blank at that spot. There wasn't even a path leading to it.

It was a cleared space of earth, recently cultivated so that no weed marred its slightly mounded surface, and it was about six feet long and three feet wide. There was just one thing it resembled: a freshly made grave. The old man couldn't have *meant* that, about the Death Ray?

He was joking, I know he was! Georgine told herself fiercely, clutching the window-sill, unable to avert her gaze from the spot below. *People simply don't murder other people and bury 'em in the back yard. They don't! Probably if I were down on the level ground, that patch would look quite different. It's just being so far above it that makes the thing look so uncanny. That must be it.*

She withdrew slowly from the window. Her fingertips ached from digging into the sill, and it took an effort to erase the frown that tightened her brows.

CHAPTER TWO

Everyone on Edge

IN THE LATE AFTERNOON, it seemed, Grettry Road came to life, for the living-room of the block warden's home, thirty yards up the street, was respectably full ten minutes before the meeting began. Mrs. Blake, who had walked up with Georgine, withdrew in great dignity to an isolated corner. "Hired help," she explained serenely, "ought to sit by itself."

"Doesn't anyone else have help?"

"They used to," said Mrs. Blake. A look of melancholy pleasure came over her ebon face. "They had Japs."

The warden was not yet on hand. Georgine had gathered that he was a bachelor; the woman with the genuinely golden pompadour, who was arranging blinds and showing people their seats with a proprietary air, was only the next-door neighbor, Mrs. Gillespie; her husband, a large, handsome, sleepy-looking man, was also on hand and rather sulkily assisting her.

The golden lady must have been ravishingly pretty, ten years before. The beauty was still there, but beginning to go soft around the edges like an ice-cream shape left too long on the plate. Georgine thought she looked wistful, as if anxious for people to like her; and this impression was carried out when Mrs. Gillespie, sitting down beside Georgine on a large chesterfield, was distantly greeted by the woman on the other end.

"Couldn't you call me Mimi, Mrs. Devlin?" she asked with rather touching shyness. "I mean, all we neighbors know each other so much better, now there's a war on."

Politely, but with no enthusiasm, Mrs. Devlin repeated "Mimi," and thereafter returned to the formal mode of address. She was a large bony woman with the face of a saintly horse, and for the first few minutes she was surprisingly cordial to Georgine.

"You're the Professor's temporary secretary, Mrs. Wyeth? How very interesting. Rather eccentric, isn't he?"

The check rustled in Georgine's pocket. She felt constrained to say nothing, but to smile vaguely.

"How boring for you," said Mrs. Devlin, "to be dragged to this utterly pointless meeting. We've been perfect martyrs to Mr. Hollister's whims. Don't you think this talk about air-raids is a pack of nonsense?"

"Not quite that," Georgine said. "If there really were an air-raid it'd be a big help if we knew what to do."

Mrs. Devlin lost interest in her at once, and turned aside to get the best light on a large square of needlepoint work. "Mrs. Wyeth, this is my little boy," she murmured.

The little boy, who was about six feet tall and looked at least seventeen, flushed painfully at this title. He hastily told Georgine that his name was Frederic, only everyone called him Ricky. "I'd just as soon get 'em started on Fred, or something like that," he added. "Ricky sounds pretty juvenile."

Georgine smiled up at him. She did like these teenagers, so nice and easy without being fresh; they simply acted their age. And what a handsome young sprig this was; he must resemble his father.

Ricky Devlin, having impressed her with his maturity, now suddenly looked about twelve years old. "Are you typing the Professor's stuff, Mrs. Wyeth?" he demanded, his eyes shining. "Gee, listen, is it really a Death Ray?"

"Ricky," Georgine said, "between us, I don't understand a word of it."

His face fell. Probably he was still secretly devoted to Superman comic books. He was about to say something more when a clear, languid young voice sounded at the door, and his head involuntarily turned. "Hi, Claris," he said, elaborately offhand.

"Hi, Rick," the slim creature answered, lowering extravagant lashes over hazel eyes. She might have been sixteen or twenty-two; there was just one word to describe the red-gold hair in its long bob, the little swing of the skirts, the soft mouth as brilliant with lipstick as an enameled cherry on a hat: *luscious*, Georgine thought. What was her name, Claris Frey? Well, Claris was a dish, and no mistake. Somehow, Georgine's generalities about young people didn't quite fit, here. The child looked as if she were trying to be older than her age, an attitude which Georgine thought had died with the post-war flapper.

Just behind her came a tall, graying man with curiously intent eyes and a gentle, deprecatory smile. He might at one time have resembled the gorgeous infant he had fathered, but something had drawn deep lines of patience in his face, pulling it into a brooding mask.

"Claris," Mrs. Gillespie called, "bring your dad over and introduce him. This is Mrs. Wyeth, who's going to be with us a few weeks."

"Just in the daytime," Georgine explained, as the man crossed the room with a graceful light step, and held out a hand with a smudge of green paint near the wrist. Claris had stood directly in front of him, speaking softly but with great precision, and Georgine realized that this must be the "stone deef" gentleman who had not heard his own doorbell; but it scarcely prepared her for the loud bellow with which he greeted her. "I am glad to welcome a new neighbor," bawled Peter Frey, into a sudden silence.

Georgine was horrified to hear herself shouting in return, though she knew it was useless. She wasn't moving into the

Road, it was only by chance that she—in fact, she'd rung Mr. Frey's bell that very afternoon—

His eyes followed her lips with desperate concentration, and halfway through her stumbling speech he began to shake his head. "I'm sorry," he said, this time almost inaudibly. "I started too late to learn lip-reading. You have to go very slowly for me—or maybe you'd write it?"

He was actually pulling out a pocket pad when Georgine's violent head-shakings stopped him. She was crimson and smiling with embarrassment. Peter Frey also smiled, slowly and painfully. He made an abortive gesture, bowed, and left her, standing with his back to the room and looking out the window.

Mrs. Gillespie at once began to talk airily about something else. "Aren't we a funny lot, up here? I'd always wanted to live in one of these hill houses, with a view, you know, and where there were nice people so we could sort of neighbor back and forth." She cast a dubious glance at Mrs. Devlin, and lowered her voice. "They don't seem to do it as much as I'd thought, though. We've been here for nearly a year and a half, longer than Roy Hollister or the Freys, but I never got to know any of 'em except Roy until these meetings began. My brother Ralph that lives with us, he says they're just a bunch of dopes, but I think," said Mrs. Gillespie courageously, "some of 'em would be real nice if you got to—"

She broke off and sat with parted lips, listening. The buzz of general conversation died; from the open street-door down the hall a man's voice sounded, strident, authoritative: "What in the hell have I got to do with it? I pointed out your position, and that was all."

"That's all?" The answer came in a higher key, unsteadily. "You—you keep me on the rack, you won't lift a finger to—"

Mrs. Gillespie half rose from her seat. "Ralphie!" she breathed, and then caught her husband's eye and sank back reluctantly.

"Shut up," said the first voice, in a lower tone, "and come on in to the meeting. If I think of anything I'll let you know, so you can quit doggin' at my heels."

"Ralphie," Mrs. Gillespie whispered again, her hands twisting nervously. "Oh, why will he—"

Abruptly a man appeared in the living-room door, and stood surveying the company. You knew at once that his was the strident voice; he was a stocky man with a florid, unremarkable face, the felt armband of Civilian Defense prominently displayed on his sleeve. It was a good entrance, effective as the sharp rap of a gavel. The audience froze to attention.

Warden Hollister opened his lips to speak; and, sudden and loud as a gunshot, the front door violently slammed.

Everyone in the room gave a nervous start, and Peter Frey swung round from the window. That shattering noise had had in it all the fury that taut nerves could produce.

Mr. Hollister recovered himself and laughed shortly. "Come in and sit down, Stort," he said over his shoulder. After a moment a lean man, somewhat resembling Mimi Gillespie, passed him with averted, twitching face. He sat down wordlessly in a dim corner, beside a man whom Georgine hadn't yet identified, and remained throughout the meeting in the same position, gazing down at his knees, a lock of blond hair falling over his eyes.

"Now," Hollister said, looking around swiftly, "Are we all here? Where's Devlin?"

"Out of town," said Mrs. Devlin shortly. Her son added, "Sure, didn't you notice the Jeep was off the street? I can't keep her in the garage when Dad's home."

"The Carmichael ladies?"

Several voices told him that the ladies were in Carmel, opening their cottage so they could go down for the weekend of the Fourth.

"When they knew there was to be a meeting?" Hollister scowled. Somebody chuckled softly. "Well, damn it, I don't hold these get-togethers for my health, you know! I've got information to pass on, and you're supposed to come here and listen, all of you."

"Heil Hitler," said Mr. Gillespie, just audibly.

The Warden ignored this with an effort, and glared into a corner. "Is Professor Paev absent, *again?*"

Mrs. Blake's organ tones answered him. She would pass on anything important, having been sent as deputy for an employer who never left home if he could possibly help it. "Anyhow," she added, "come some bombs, it'll be my job to attend to 'em. I guess the P'fessah couldn't be bothered." She retired again into her dignified silence.

"Maybe you're right," said Hollister with a grudging smile. He flipped open a notebook. "Now, will you all attend carefully, please. There's a new method of treating incendiary bombs—"

Mrs. Devlin sighed audibly.

The meeting progressed with remarkable efficiency. Georgine found herself thinking that these hill-dwellers were making very heavy weather of their defense measures. In her section, the householders perfected their preparations and then relaxed; up here, everyone was in a state of tension, as if expecting a bomb to drop.

It was the warden himself who was producing the tension. She became increasingly sure of that as he talked. The man was terribly in earnest, everything he said was quite true, but he was scaring people instead of reassuring them. "I want to speak about carelessness in leaving lights on," he said heavily. "You have all been asked to remove the bulbs from your illuminated street numbers. Don't you know that those can be seen for miles in the air, and that an enemy airman is instructed to bomb any light that's showing? If Grettry Road is blown to bits, it might be the fault of just one of those numbers."

"Well, why tell us about it?" said Harry Gillespie defiantly. "We've all fixed ours. It's the Carmichaels you're talking about, as we—"

"The Carmichaels?" Peter Frey burst in obliviously. His eyes had been going from face to face, desperately trying to catch up with moving lips. "Are you talking about them? They're to be away for a few weeks, and they asked me particularly to see that their flowers were all picked; so please take any you want, everybody."

"Daddy!" Claris shook his arm and he subsided, lowering patient eyelids. "If the Professor doesn't have to come," she added, "I don't see why Dad should."

"I appreciate it," said Hollister sharply. "Anything that's done in the way of coöperation is a little bit of help to me. Lord knows I don't get much. Now I've got to watch for the old ladies to come back, and go speak to them about that light. I'm the fall guy. I'm the only one available up here to do the dirty work, and I'm rushed to death as it is."

"Listen, Mr. Hollister," Ricky Devlin said eagerly, "you could use me any time, you know I told you that."

"Now, son," said Hollister impatiently, "we've been over that before. The grown men would all have to be out of the way before they could use you." He added slyly, "You've got business of your own at night, anyhow." Ricky gave him a swift look.

"Yes, Ricky darling," said Mrs. Devlin fondly, "you're far too young, you're just a baby yet."

An agonized silence followed this remark. Everyone mercifully avoided looking at Ricky, but from the corner of her eye Georgine saw his clasped hands tightening until the knuckles glistened. He caught his breath sharply as if to say something, but Mrs. Devlin, all unaware, went on, "And certainly it won't ever be necessary. We haven't even had a blackout for months, and I do think this hysteria is bound to die down soon. We work ourselves up over something that can't happen at all!"

"But it can, Mrs. Devlin," said Hollister grimly, "That's what I keep tellin' you—any night, any minute. What's more, the next blackout is like as not to be the real thing. And let me tell you, when it comes I want every one of you to get in his refuge room and stay there. None of this hoppin' out into the street to look up at the pretty planes, none of this standin' by uncovered windows where you can get glass splinters through your eye."

Without lifting his head from his chest, Ralph Stort said, "Oh, for Chri*sake*, Hollister."

Roy Hollister's face grew a shade more florid. "Good God, what you people need is to have a few bombs dropped on you! I hope they do fall. You'd obey orders fast enough then. And we've got to be ready. Lord, we're not half covered, up here. We ought to have a day warden, and there's nobody to serve; Gillespie needs his sleep after he's been at the shipyards all night—"

"Damn' good of you to be so considerate," said Mr. Gillespie, in a tone so nasty that Georgine was startled. She began to ask herself, *What goes on in this place?* Wasn't there something more than war nerves—?

"I could serve temporarily, if you like," said the quiet voice of the man sitting beside Ralph Stort. He bent forward as he spoke, and his face came into the light so that its angles stood out like those of a bold carving: eyes deep-set between sandy brows and high cheekbones, flat planes of cheeks, firm jaw. The face looked as if it would be hard to the touch. During the minutes just past Georgine had been watching him as he looked from one person to another, with such a total lack of expression that she'd thought he must be inwardly amused. At this moment their eyes met briefly, and she was sure of it.

"Well, thanks, McKinnon," Hollister said dubiously. "You're night warden in your own district, aren't you? That might do, for as long as you're up here. When are the Cliftons coming home?"

"I don't quite know," said Mr. McKinnon. "I'm not hurrying them, it's very convenient for me to work there daytimes."

"See me after the meeting, then. I guess that's all, folks. If you'd stay a minute, Mrs.-uh-Wyeth? Like you to fill out one of these slips."

Ricky Devlin lingered beside Georgine; she saw that his color had returned to normal, and was no longer afraid that he might burst into tears of shame if anyone noticed him. "Is it you who plays the mouth-organ, Ricky?" she asked. "I heard someone practicing this afternoon."

"Not me," Ricky said. "It musta been Mr. McKinnon over there. He's the old bearcat on the harmonica."

"The one who was just talking? Not *really*?"

Mrs. Gillespie, preparing to go, bent over her. "He's a little queer, anyhow," she said anxiously. "I don't know if he'd be a very responsible warden. You know what he told somebody? They were talking about draft numbers, and he said he'd never be called, the Army didn't want him because he was a Japanese spy. He said they'd fixed up his face with plastic surgery."

Georgine's lips twitched, and she glanced once more at the transformed face, which would have looked perfectly at home under a Glengarry bonnet. "Of course I knew it was a joke," Mrs. Gillespie added, "but he must have a funny kind of mind to say a thing like that."

The living-room was gradually emptying; Mrs. Devlin folded up the embroidery to which she had given her attention throughout the meeting, and looked for her son. He was speaking to Claris Frey. The sight of the two young things standing in a glow of afternoon sunlight brought a queer pain to the heart, but they behaved like no more than casual acquaintances. "New dress, Clar?" Ricky said politely. "Very solid set of threads."

"Thanks," said Claris languidly, turning away to follow her father. Mrs. Devlin gave a little sigh, in which relief and satisfaction were plain. "Coming home with mother, Ricky dear?" she said triumphantly.

It was at that moment that Georgine conceived a violent partisanship for young Frederic Devlin. Anyone could have forgiven him if he had snarled at his mother; but he did not. With a curiously adult resignation he stood back to let her precede him, and there was nothing in his boy's face but courtesy.

Hollister had gone to the door with some of the party, and Mr. McKinnon came strolling across the room to stand by Georgine. The light struck a spark of copper from his sandy brush of mustache. "As one temporary resident to another, Mrs. Wyeth," he said, "let me tell you that all wardens aren't quite as zealous as this one. He does a conscientious job, but maybe we're not so near to dissolution as he makes out." The casual quiet of his voice made light of everything from the war downward.

"I'd gathered that," said Georgine. "This block seems to be organized within an inch of its life."

This innocent remark caused an explosion that made her drop her pencil. From beside the door Ralph Stort shouted, "God, yes! That's a sample of what the authorities do for you, they're not contented with getting us into this goddamned war, they give someone the power to get us in here once a month and torture us. We might as well all be dead. I wish I *was* dead!"

Mimi Gillespie, who had been waiting for him in the hall, now popped back into the room, "Oh, brother, don't say that," she began ineffectually, laying her hand on Stort's arm. At the same moment Harry Gillespie said harshly, "Skip it, Ralph, and come on home. Can't we get through a day without one of your nerve-storms?"

Stort turned on him furiously. "You great hunk of flesh, you don't know what I go through."

"Well, go through it somewhere else," said Mr. Gillespie, vigorously pushing his brother-in-law into the hall. Mimi trotted after them, hopelessly murmuring, "Harry, don't, please. Now, Ralphie, you just need a drink."

"Impassioned," said Mr. McKinnon mildly.

"Right in tune with the rest of the meeting," said Georgine rather crossly. "I never saw a bunch of people so set on annoying each other, or getting embarrassed. And heaven help me, I did my share. Did you hear me in that yelling contest with Mr. Frey?"

Mr. McKinnon nodded, very gravely, but with the twinkle reappearing far back in his eyes.

"Look here," Georgine murmured, "is he as deaf as all that, or is it just convenient?"

"Why?"

"When the door banged he jumped, just like all the rest of us. Were you here then?"

"Yes, I was here. But I think Frey's affliction is genuine. You ever hear of sound perception? The totally deaf can't distinguish words, but they can feel vibrations."

"Oh," Georgine said. "I'm glad to know that; I was just ready to get mad at him all over again, for ignoring his doorbell this afternoon."

"Was that you, ringing at house doors about three o'clock? H'm. I'm sorry I didn't answer, but I was working." He sat down beside her, his light voice flowing effortlessly along. "The morning was one long list of callers: the Fuller Brush man, the last one in captivity probably; and two ladies trying to find out how many extra beds I had, but not with any ulterior motive I believe, and"—he chuckled suddenly, and Georgine looked up—"a little tike about two feet high asking it I had 'any skwap wubbah.'"

Why, she thought, *he's attractive when he talks about something he likes; that kind of amused tenderness makes his face come alive. Funny how much more affectionate the word "little" sounds in a Scots accent that takes the t's out of it.* "Li'le," Georgine murmured inaudibly.

"And so," McKinnon continued, again looking impassive, "I planned to ignore the doorbell from then on. But if I'd known what I was missing…"

He didn't finish, but it was obvious that he was one of those who took second looks at Georgine.

"Maybe it's as well for you," she said. "The way I felt then, I'd have sold you a Magnificent Combination Offer before you could get your breath."

"Sold him a what?" said Mr. Hollister genially, coming in to receive her completed dossier.

"Magazines," she told him. Mr. McKinnon looked over the warden's shoulder and read her address aloud. "Right down in my home district," he observed pleasantly.

"Magazines?" Hollister said, "You're not a secretary?"

"Only temporarily. Professor Paev happened to be looking for one, and I grabbed at the chance."

"Well, well. That must have been what that mousy little gal was after; the one who went in there last week."

"Didn't see her," Mr. McKinnon said.

Hollister kept his eyes on the printed form he held. "Sure. I guess she found the old Prof was too hard to get on with—or something. I only saw her going in that one time. Come to think of it, I never saw her again."

He looked up suddenly, with a jovial chuckle. "Seemed like she just disappeared."

Georgine had thought of Grettry Road as situated at the other end of nowhere, but after all it didn't take so long for her to get home. She could walk it in half an hour, by using the short cut which dropped through the Gillespies' back yard and through the brush and dry grass of the canyon, ending in a breathless scramble up the far side. From then on the streets were steep, but inhabited.

She was tired; she felt thankful for once at the sight of her landlords' house, a job of remodeling which had changed an honest old dwelling into a pseudo-Spanish monstrosity. It was only a few feet from the sidewalk, and Georgine lived in a yard cottage at the rear of its spacious lot. It was lucky that the landlords were elderly and didn't drive, since her house had once been the garage. The approach to it, though now closed by a stucco wall and a very artistic gate, had been the driveway. She went through the gate, under the overhanging balcony lavishly ornamented with pendent baskets and standing pots of petunias, and cast an unhopeful glance at the mailbox. Too early to expect a letter, of course. Barby had been gone only since this morning.

She looked at her check, frankly gloating. In the face of its written figures, she could forget her absurd fancies, the eerie stillness of Grettry Road in the afternoon, the tensions of the warden's meeting, even the curious gardening habits of her new employer.

A year ago she might have regarded the residents of Grettry Road as a queer crew; now, she was aware that they were no more peculiar than the inhabitants of any block in Berkeley—perhaps than a cross-section of a university town anywhere. The know-your-neighbor campaign must have brought surprises to a lot of people.

Georgine put off until after supper the pleasure of endorsing her check and putting it in the mail, addressed to Barby's doctor. The late sunset had died when she slipped out in the warm June night and posted the letter. "There," she said aloud as the green metal flap of the box clanged.

She should have felt triumphant. Instead, an inexplicable feeling seized her; quite against her will, she found herself remembering a horrible story she'd once read. In it, a man had lost the object which could have saved him from doom, and a voice, audible to him alone, kept repeating in his ear, "You can't give it back now. You can't give it back now."

Well, how foolish! Why should she want to give back the check? What if it had passed out of her keeping, almost irrevocably? *You can't give it back now.*

That odd chilly feeling on her shoulder-blades must be due to the fact that she'd run out without a coat. Nobody was abroad on this quiet, respectable street. There was no reason for her to hurry back to her cottage, and close the door behind her and turn on an extra lamp.

But in spite of forcing herself to a moderate walk, she was breathless when she reached the house. Her living-room waited for her peacefully, the same as always in its shabby, comfortable furniture, its brown and tawny colors, the familiar smells of redwood and starched curtains and whole-wheat toast.

She leaned against the door that shut night out, and felt her world swing back to its normal state. This was home, this was sanctuary.

CHAPTER THREE

The Rising Tide of Alarm

More THAN ONCE, in the days that followed, Georgine Wyeth noted with amusement how much Grettry Road, in its semi-isolation, resembled a village. There was a little more tolerance, not quite so minute a knowledge of other people's affairs; but it had most of the other traditional elements, the self-elected grande dame, the eccentrics, the restless youngsters, the village siren. "All we need," Georgine told herself, "is a Safeway store at one end and a movie at the other, and we could hole in for the duration. Maybe we'd need a hairdresser's, too—No, they're using me to talk to instead."

It was even more entertaining to find herself in the role, not exactly of confidante, but of a fresh mind on which everyone was eager to stamp his own impressions. She had sought no further acquaintance with the Road's inhabitants, but it was forced on her. In her brief outdoor rest periods at noon and mid-afternoon, and in the times of arrival and departure, she managed involuntarily to collect an astonishing amount of knowledge about the neighbors.

On the day after the block meeting Mr. John Devlin, at No. 18, returned from his sales trip through California and Nevada. He was on the lawn with his son when Georgine started homeward after an industrious and uneventful day. Ricky, friendly as a puppy, greeted her.

"Hello, Mrs. Wyeth! Look, here's my dad. He just got in about an hour ago."

Georgine's first glance at the elder Devlin gave her a small shock. The descriptive word that sprang to her mind was— *haunted*. The next minute, as he smiled politely, she thought she must have imagined it. John Devlin was dark-haired, gray-eyed, an older and more worn edition of his attractive son, but obviously several years his wife's junior. Georgine had a wholly indefensible thought about the union, for which she had to reprove herself.

In the midst of this she realized that Ricky was trying to enlist her as an ally. "*She* thinks there'll probably be some bombings, Dad," he said eagerly "And gosh, look, they'll need me if there are. If you'd just insist that I could be a messenger or something... Don't you think I could do it, Mrs. Wyeth?"

"Ricky, really, I can't take sides, when your parents feel they don't want you to serve." The look in his face made her add, "You do seem very strong and—mature."

"Old enough to go into the Navy, if I could get Mother or Dad to sign a permission," Ricky muttered.

"Now, Rick, that's enough," John Devlin said irritably. "You know how y'mother feels about it. You're needed at home. We can't both go off and leave her alone."

"There are lots of jobs around here." His voice was low.

"I have to do what I'm doing. You don't know anything about it," Devlin snapped back at him.

Ricky looked at him hopelessly. "Well, if I'm old enough to be the man of the house...! No, please don't go, Mrs. Wyeth, I kind of hoped you'd talk to—"

"I can't, Ricky. Don't you see I can't?" Georgine had begun to edge off toward the intersection, but the voices followed her.

"Y'mother's a fine woman, she's devoted to us both," said the elder Devlin. The words flowed perfunctorily past his lips, as if he'd learned them years ago. Ricky retorted, "Well, I know it. But doesn't she know I'm a man now? Heck, if I could find some way to prove it, kind of in public—"

"That's enough," his father cut in loudly. "For the Lord's sake get the Jeep out of the garage so I can park my bus under cover. You know how y'mother feels about caring for the cars."

Georgine was several yards down the road when a series of snorts and rattles made her turn. Ricky had proudly brought his jalopy to rest on the curve of the vacant lot.

Good grief, thought Georgine, *the one spot where it's visible from every point in the street! I suppose he thinks it'll be a treat to us.*

Mr. Roy Hollister passed her in his car, with a genial wave. He slackened speed in front of No. 18, to lean out and yell, "Hullo there, Devlin! Home again, hey? How's the wide-open towns of Nevada?"

In an astonishingly surly voice John Devlin called back, "All right, I guess. What's it to you?" He turned angrily on his heel and made for the house.

Georgine wondered what made him so haggard and uneasy. The war, maybe; it got everyone down more or less. And yet the haunted look seemingly had nothing to do with the problem of bombings, nor with Ricky's desires. He'd been thinking about something else, had John Devlin, even as he argued.

She began to reflect that Grettry Road showed a very low percentage of contented residents. There, was, of course, the cheerful Mr. McKinnon, at home during the day in the house near the intersection; his mouth-organ music floated constantly onto the still air, and now and then the musician himself emerged to call at the various homes up and down the road, presumably in pursuit of his duties as a day warden. (At the home of Professor Paev, she knew by auditory evidence, he made no headway whatsoever.) There was also Mr. Peter Frey, who, insulated by his deafness from the alarms of the world, daily set up an easel in the canyon below the Gillespies' back yard, and painted untutored but pleasing landscapes.

Georgine, traversing the short cut on Tuesday evening to the great detriment of her stockings, forgetfully greeted Mr. Frey when his back was turned. He painted steadily on, the look of patient endurance quite gone from his face.

There, she thought, *is a happy person; he's made himself a full life in spite of his handicap. But as for the others…*

Maybe she was offering herself for the sacrifice, by coming out onto the level space at the foot of the road for her rest periods; but a girl had to have a breath of air now and then, and—well, it was rather interesting to see what topic of conversation appealed to each of the neighbors. "Mental adventure," Georgine told herself on the afternoon when she met Ralph Stort coming out of the Carmichaels' garden with an armful of flowering branches.

He seemed to feel that he must defend this action; he looked at her sulkily, and remarked, "Mimi sent me over to pick some of these. We were supposed to, you know. The two old Tories left for Carmel this morning. You see 'em?"

"I must have been at work," said Georgine. "Otherwise I can't think how I missed the departure. It's about the only event I have missed, so far."

"God!" said Ralph Stort violently, running a shaking hand through his lank blond hair. "I try to fix my mind on little bits of neighborhood gossip, just to keep from thinking. Sit around here and think—it's driving me mad!"

"You don't, uh, have a job to do?"

"Job?" Mr. Stort looked at her with bitterness. "What chance of a decent job does a man have in a country like this?"

"Plenty," said Georgine with spirit. "And what's wrong with this country?"

Stort said, "And I thought you looked intelligent! It's going to hell, that's what's wrong." His voice took on a plaintive cadence which sounded as if he talked like this from habit, to himself if no one else would listen. "Talk, talk, talk about freedom, and at the same time let a man be hounded and tortured…"

With a rather startling effect his eyes ceased to focus on her. "If I just knew what to *do*," he muttered just audibly. "If I could get away from here, if I only dared to—"

The rest of this was lost in the roar of a plane, swooping low over the hill and streaking toward the Bay. The noise seemed to recall Mr. Stort's thoughts, for he addressed Georgine again, most of his speech being drowned out. She heard nothing but the last words. "Lost Generation," said Mr. Stort, touching his own breast tenderly.

Georgine had considerable ado to keep from grinning. She had a strong feeling that Ralph's mysterious problems could be solved by someone like a drill sergeant, who would be glad to tell him what to do. Without that, however, he'd never get out of his muddle, whatever it might be. Not guts enough, she thought robustly.

Then his face changed, an ugly flush coming up under its blond skin. Mr. Roy Hollister had just emerged from his front door, a letter in his hand.

"Hollister! Wait a minute," Stort called out. "I've got to see you." Absently he thrust the flowering boughs toward Georgine. "Here, take these in to Mimi, will you?"

"Certainly not," said Georgine crisply. "I must get back to work, I'm behind schedule as it is."

Yet she lingered for a moment outside Professor Paev's door, watching the two figures climbing through the stippled sunlight in Grettry Road: the stocky back of Mr. Hollister, the taut thin one of Ralph Stort. Stort was talking earnestly, gesturing with the bedraggled sheaf of branches. Hollister's head moved slowly from side to side as if reiterating, "No. No."

Gait and gesture gave her a curious impression that he was enjoying himself.

She had an inspiration. Hadn't somebody said that Mr. Harry Gillespie worked on the graveyard shift at the shipyards, and went to work at ten-thirty every night? If he'd give her a ride down the hill, she might stay in the Road through the evenings and get caught up on her work.

Mr. Gillespie was agreeable to this. She waited in his car on Wednesday night, observing the fervor with which he kissed his wife good-by at the door, and was astonished to have him start down the hill by the longest route.

Being not without an education in the ways of wolves, she had thought of Harry as strictly monogamous. Had she read him all wrong? If the road led into any dark canyons, she'd better be prepared.

"Flattering myself," Georgine reflected dryly when, after five minutes, Mr. Gillespie abruptly turned about and drove back to Grettry Road. He was purposeful, he offered no explanation, he looked narrowly at the lighted windows of Hollister's house, and then got out and went into his own home.

He came out almost immediately, looking obscurely satisfied and relieved. "Forgot something," said Harry, and drove off again, this time by the direct route.

H'm; funny. He hadn't—surely he hadn't expected to find his wife entertaining company at this time of night? Had he gone back in that hope, or fear?

He was very sociable now, chatting about the difficulties of night work. "Sure, like you say, it turns your life upside down. It's like walking around in a bad dream half the time. But hell," he added simply, "the job's there to be done and it's up to anyone who can, to pitch in and do it. 'Tisn't much when you think of what the boys took on Bataan."

He meant it, Georgine discovered with respect. You didn't often run across such candid patriotism.

"The toughest part," Gillespie went on, "is leaving Mimi alone, nights. Of course she's got that da—her brother Ralph with her. Not that he's much good," said Ralph's host with appalling frankness, "but he's fond of her, I'll say that for him."

His ensuing silence seemed to demand comment. "I thought he didn't look very well," Georgine ventured.

"Well!" Harry grunted. "He's prob'ly as strong as I am, they got him patched up good enough after that time his plane crashed, three-four years ago. But he feels pretty sorry for himself, seems like the gov'ment never has done right for him since he was old enough to vote."

"He, uh, suffers with his nerves, I gathered."

Mr. Gillespie gave a short laugh. "He's worried. Hasn't felt right for a month, since they sentenced his old pal Pelley. Hell, I oughtn't to 'a' said that, he wants it all forgotten about him being in the Silvershirt gang for a while; but I say, what's the odds if he's out of it now?"

I bet you never let him forget it, Georgine thought with a flash of reluctant sympathy for Ralph. "Oh, look here," she exclaimed as the car went round a familiar curve, "you're not to take me all the way home! Just drop me by the street-car line."

"Not on your life,' said Mr. Gillespie gallantly. "I got plenty of time. Say, if you're going to be working nights you ought to let Hollister know. He's death on knowing just who's at home in his block." His voice was heavy.

"Really," said Georgine, opening the car door. "I hardly think that's necessary. He's enough of a dictator already!"

"You said it," Harry Gillespie agreed. "Well, see you tomorrow night."

It was odd, she thought, how omnipresent this Roy Hollister seemed; he kept turning up either in person or in conversation.

And yet the man himself was so ordinary! If you tried to describe him, you'd start out, "Well, he's an air-raid warden"— and then find yourself stumped. You might also say he was bluff and hearty: a manner which did not appeal to Georgine, but which doubtless was well-meant. He had strolled out at noon to chat.

"Well, well, Mrs. Wyeth! Still with us?"

"For a few days more, Mr. Hollister."

"Not finished yet? How you gettin' on with the old boy's great discovery? He showed you the Death Ray yet?"

"That's only his joke," said Georgine coolly. "I don't know what he's working on."

"You don't?" The warden laughed heartily. "You're nearly through, and you haven't found out yet?"

"It's just words to me. I only copy, you know."

"Oh, sure," said Hollister vaguely. She thought, *What an empty sort of man he seems; a face like ten thousand others, and nothing but platitudes behind it... Or was that all?* He was looking searchingly at her, and for a moment something stirred and uncoiled beneath the idle sentences they had exchanged.

Georgine rose, and he laughed again and strolled away. "Got a call to make," he said over his shoulder; almost as if that remark were significant.

She thought, *Darn him anyhow, reminding me of that old yarn about the Death Ray... I never did look at the Professor's flower bed; I wonder what it's like from down here... I could step round this side of the house and find out...*

She had just managed to force her way through the outer layer of flowering shrubs when she looked up at the bathroom window. It framed a bald forehead, an ear-fringe of black hair, a pair of black eyes which were watching her steadily. The Professor appeared to be drying his hands. He was taking a long time to do it.

Georgine gave him a sunny smile and a wave, and with a falsely nonchalant air turned and waded off through the bushes, in quite another direction.

It was later that Thursday afternoon when she held brief converse with Claris Frey. Claris had emerged from her own front door, waving good-by to Mr. Todd McKinnon, resplendent in his warden's armband, who had seemingly been paying the last of his duty calls. Then she came wandering down the road, fetching up beside Georgine and gazing disconsolately out across the canyon. "Darn him," she murmured vaguely, "darn him, anyhow!"

"Who?" Georgine inquired, smiling, "Mr. McKinnon?"

"Oh, no. He's a good Joe; he dried the dishes for me, while he was waiting to call on Daddy, and then he never did get to. No, I mean Mr. Hollister. Did you see him come out of our house?"

"No, I just came out."

"I bet he was lookin' pleased with himself," Claris said, her soft hazel eyes bright with resentment. "He pinched me." She rubbed herself reminiscently. "As if it wasn't bad enough that he kept Dad until too late for us to go downtown! We were going to buy a war bond, and then get me a new sweater—Dad always thinks he has to choose the color—and now the banks are shut and it's too late. I broke a date, too, just so I could do something Dad asked me to, for once, and old Hollister has to come in and tell dirty stories for an hour first, and hold us up!"

"Dear me," Georgine said. "Dirty stories, to you?"

"Oh, no. I was in the kitchen, but I think that's what he was writing to Dad. On the pad, you know. Fact is, I'm almost sure, because the pages he'd written were burning in the fire-place when I went in—and I could hear him laughing while Dad read them."

"Always pleased with his own jokes," Georgine murmured. "Was your father amused?"

"How do I know? He doesn't laugh aloud, much. I could hear just about what he usually says when people are writing on his pad. 'No, I can't do that,' and 'what makes you think so,' and 'I see your point there.' Sounds absolutely dumb," said Claris languidly.

"Has your father been deaf long?" Georgine asked.

"Since I was little. My mother was living with us then. I don't remember much about it, but he told me there was an explosion in the factory where he worked, and he—well, he couldn't even talk for a couple of years after." Georgine clicked her tongue. "Oh, they paid him for it, we're still getting money from some kind of a fund they had, but—he learned to talk again, but he couldn't go back to work because he couldn't hear. He doesn't seem to mind, most of the time," said Claris with superb callousness. "Look, there he goes down into the canyon to work." She sighed, her lovely young face slack with boredom, and turned to depart. "Maybe I'd better see if I can unbreak that movie date, I haven't got a darn thing to do."

Georgine said something which sounded so arch that she immediately regretted it. "Isn't Ricky at home this afternoon?"

Claris twitched round as if startled, and looked full at Georgine. Then she moistened her lips and smiled, slowly. "Ricky *Devlin*? As if I had anything to do with him, except living next door!"

"I'm getting spoiled," Georgine told herself wryly; "when I'm in Grettry Road, I can't step outside the door without meeting someone, and then I have to come home and go into an empty house." She said thanks and good-by to Harry Gillespie, on this Thursday night, and went serenely through the gate and up the long walk to her garden cottage, and opened the door with her key.

The moment she stepped inside she knew that someone had been here during her absence.

In the next minutes, after a frantic survey of the small house and its contents, she was increasingly sure; and yet whoever had searched the place had tried to arrange that she should not know. There were only the few small signs, obvious only to a housekeeper's eyes: the rug that had been left straight and was now slightly awry, the sugar tin in the kitchen turned the wrong way, and the clasp of her miniature briefcase hanging loose as if someone hadn't been able to master the trick of its fastening; but stronger than anything was that sense of something alien. "Someone's been sitting in my chair, said the middle-sized bear."

"I don't like this," Georgine said half-aloud. She stood in the middle of the living-room and turned slowly, her blue eyes growing dark with perplexity as she surveyed it inch by inch. Her hands were balled into tight fists in her pockets, and her lower lip folded over the upper in that oddly youthful gesture which with her meant not temper but perturbation.

And, ten minutes later, "I might have expected something like that!" she said indignantly, dropping the telephone back into its cradle. What were the police good for, anyway? Her chin jutted out dangerously at the memory of that calm, reasonable voice at the other end of the wire. "Your house was entered in your absence. What makes you think so? Was the door open? Oh, it was locked. Any sign that the windows had been forced? They were all locked too? I see. Was there anything missing? I see…"

It had gone on for several increasingly uncomfortable minutes, during which Georgine had battled with the impulse to shout, "Skip it!" and slam down the telephone. At the last, she and the desk sergeant had seemed to agree perfectly; it was all, they decided, in her imagination.

"But it wasn't," she whispered, and darted another quick glance around the warm little brown room.

Well, there was one solace in Barby's absence. Georgine, not having to set an example, could leave the lights on. Only to her most secret self would she admit how much the dark frightened her.

Friday came with such brilliant sunshine, such a heartening air of normality, that she convinced herself the sergeant might, after all, have been right. The day continued well with the arrival of a postcard from Barby, amazingly legible. The hostess must have held her hand while she wrote. "I am having a good time, I feel fine, we went wading today, X X X X Barby."

Georgine took it into the house and read it some eleven times. Then, realizing that she was late to work, she told herself not to be sentimental, and started off.

She hadn't yet done with receiving confidences from the neighbors. Her first encounter came as she toiled panting along the last lap of her journey, through the adjoining back yards of Grettry Road. Mimi Gillespie was in her garden, attired in a slack suit which only shipyard wages could have bought; Georgine had observed that Mimi dressed with almost painful suitability for every occasion. Her demeanor this morning, however, was not as debonair as her costume. She seemed to have been crying.

"I guess I'm doing the gardening now," Mimi said in answer to Georgine's casual comment. She poked listlessly at a large milkweed. "My brother went away last night."

"Not for good, surely? Doesn't he live with you?"

"Oh, no," Mimi said. "He goes up to his ranch every so often. It's just a little stump farm out here"—she gestured vaguely northward—"with a couple of hands that help him work it on shares. I guess that's really his home. He—did Harry talk to you about him, any?"

Promptly and tactfully, Georgine lied.

"Well, they don't get on any too well. Harry doesn't understand Ralphie at all, and they don't feel the same way about the war. I do my best," Mimi went on with a rather pathetic look of helplessness, "and I do so want to have everything nice, and have quiet at home."

"Of course you do," said Georgine gently, beginning to edge toward the street. "I'll have to hurry, I'm late. Look, would you tell Mr. Gillespie I shan't have to impose on him tonight? I'm planning to get home by daylight."

She nodded to Roy Hollister, who had just emerged from the lower door of his house and was heading for the canyon path, and looked round to make sure Mimi had heard her. Mimi had disappeared into her own home, her thick-soled play shoes were even now clattering up the stairs from the basement game room to the street floor.

The second encounter came during the noonday recess, when the wiry figure of Mr. Todd McKinnon appeared, strolling down the Road. Georgine, perched on the low fence at the end, greeted him with reservations. "Have you come to find out what sort of stuff I'm typing for the Professor? Everyone else wants to know, soon or late."

"I hadn't thought of it," he said agreeably, sitting down beside her, "but I'll ask if you like."

She wondered fleetingly how old he was; somewhere in the early thirties, she'd guess, though those lean faces never changed much with years. "No, don't bother," she replied. "I don't know. I can see, though, why the old gentleman wanted a typist who could simply copy without understanding, because the neighbors are certainly curious. Do you think they really believe it's a Death Ray?"

"These days," said Mr. McKinnon, "people will believe anything. And why not? Take my invention, for example," he continued indolently, but cocking an eye at her. "It sounds impossible, but the Army and Navy have agreed that nothing could be more desirable."

"Do tell me about it," said Georgine, her eyes crinkling.

"It's a method of camouflage," said the inventor, "that makes a bomber not only invisible but inaudible. The citizens of Tokyo wouldn't know what had hit them."

"Remarkable. You've perfected this?"

"Yes, indeed. The Armed Forces got me a special deferment while I worked on it. I fixed up a bomber for them," said Mr. McKinnon, taking his mouth-organ from his pocket and hitting it violently on the palm of his hand, "and there was a demonstration. One and all were agreed that it was a complete success."

"That ought to revolutionize the conduct of the war."

"Well, yes, but there's been a li'le trouble," he said sadly. "We've never been able to find the bomber again—I'm afraid you think I'm not telling the truth."

"Oh, why not?" said Georgine. "My eldest son was the pilot. So that's how you spend your time, inventing in the morning and playing the mouth-organ in the afternoon? Must be a fascinating life."

"I'm the envy of all comers," Mr. McKinnon agreed. "The noise doesn't disturb you, I hope?"

"No, I like it. *The Trout* is one of my favorite songs. But I don't hear it often. I'm working at top speed these days. And that reminds me. I'd best get started again, on some more of those scientific terms that don't mean a thing."

"Slows you up, doesn't it, when you can't understand what you're writing." McKinnon was sympathetic.

"Yes. I wish the Professor'd let me take work home." A thought struck her as she rose to go into the house. "You don't suppose," she said softly, half to herself, "that someone believed I did just that, and was curious enough to—break into my house and find out?"

McKinnon looked at her quickly. His eyes were gray with brown flecks, like particularly hard slabs of Scotch agate, and so deeply set under his brows that the upper lids were all but invisible. It gave them a curiously searching expression.

"Someone's been in your house? Recently?"

"Since I came to work here." Georgine already regretted having mentioned it. "At least I thought so, it may have been my imagination. It's been running riot since last Monday."

McKinnon looked up Grettry Road, his eyes resting on one house after another; then the eyes smiled at her, as if to say, "Someone here? One of these ordinary people?"

"You and the desk sergeant," said Georgine cryptically, "must be brothers under the skin." She went back to work, feeling, for some obscure reason, more comfortable.

She got up a burst of speed that afternoon, sliding the carbons from finished sheets and shooting them between fresh ones with scarcely a pause, feeling efficient and proud of herself. A remote part of her mind heard the afternoon sounds of the Road: the majestic footsteps of Mrs. Blake moving about the house; the telephone bell; an occasional car whirring past the intersection; and through it all the oddly carrying strains of the harmonica, from far up the street. Possibly in compliment to her, McKinnon was again playing *The Trout*.

Toward mid-afternoon Georgine paused in her work for a moment, conscious of some difference in the air. It was cooler, and the light had a new quality. She got up to stretch, and looked out the window.

The fog-bank outside the Golden Gate, which had lain quiescent through all these brilliant days, was moving at last in response to some mysterious law of weather. Lazily it had shifted and uncoiled, rising, hollowing like an enormous shell to roof the City and the Bay, streaming gray and thick toward the folded canyons of the eastern hills. For a few minutes you could still see the confetti-colored houses on the flat lands below, with the fog's shadow advancing across them smoothly, without haste. Then they were blotted out, and the sun also disappeared.

Georgine shivered, congratulated herself on having prudently brought along a topcoat, and returned to work. She began to separate the typed sheets which she had flung aside as fast as they were finished. Ribbon copy, carbon, onionskin; ribbon copy—She stopped, appalled.

At least half of the second and third sheets were blank. She had been putting on too much pressure, and in her haste had turned the carbon paper backward.

There was only one thing to do about this. Georgine burst into tears, put her head down on her arms and howled heartily for three minutes. Then, much refreshed, she dried her eyes and powdered her nose and started to type the pages all over again.

But it meant she'd have to work tonight; she was still behind schedule, and this horrible mishap, unless repaired at once, would make it impossible for her to finish within the ten days she'd allotted. "Oh, dear!" Georgine groaned, now typing with exaggerated care. "If I make any more mistakes, I'm sunk."

She frowned in annoyance as a velvety voice sounded from below. "Mis' Wyeth! The P'fessah says could you step down to the lab'atory a minute, please?"

The laboratory? She'd never been allowed near it before, nor indeed into the basement story of the Professor's house. She found herself not unwilling to see it; she ran lightly down the stairs. Mrs. Blake had directed her to the door at the east end of the basement corridor, but there were two doors. Georgine tried one of them. No, this wasn't right; this was the garage, housing a well-preserved coupé of pre-depression vintage, also a remarkable collection of junk. The drive for "skwap wubbah" could not have penetrated this far, for Georgine saw lengths of hose, old gloves and at least three worn-out tires. Even the wedges that held the inner doors open were covered with rubber, so they would hold on the cement floor of the passage. Georgine grinned to herself, with a mental picture of the Professor's response to scrap collectors. If he had been approached by the little tike about two feet high, the luckless infant was probably still running.

She tapped at the door which was set at right angles to the inner entrance of the garage. "Come in," said the abrupt voice of Alexis Paev.

Georgine saw, with an absurdly let-down feeling, that the laboratory was very dull-looking. There were jars of colorless liquid on glass-enclosed shelves, but they were neither bubbling nor sending off mephitic vapors. The rest of the furniture consisted of a long sink and a discolored table with a few racks of ordinary test-tubes; a stool; an empty wire cage.

The only picturesque detail was the remote humming sound that pervaded the air. Georgine glanced about quickly, hoping against hope to find a sinister source for this. There was nothing but a set of four small slatted openings, slightly protruding from the wall in which the door was set. They were high up, near the ceiling. Those couldn't be a Death Ray; they'd been built into the house.

"Mrs. Wyeth," said the Professor, swinging round, "will you take down and type a list of figures for me, at once? I must have a statement of expenses, at least an approximate one." His black eyes burned. He looked more human than she'd ever seen him. "It's come, after all these years. I knew they'd see the light if I could hold out long enough."

"Good news?" Georgine was infected by his excitement.

The Professor laughed aloud. "I resigned from the University, several years ago," he said triumphantly, "because the Regents refused to give me proper endowment. Those blind idiots, they couldn't see how unimportant their little departments of arts and languages were beside a discovery like this! And now, after I've worked alone for six years, now that my research is all but finished, they want a share of the credit! I hold no grudges," said the Professor with a malicious grin that belied his words, "but if they want me back they'll pay. I'll pour it to 'em!" He looked at his watch. "Quick, Mrs. Wyeth, type up this list. I'm to be at the Regent's house in San Francisco at nine-thirty, and I must get down town and buy myself some new shoes and a tie, and have this suit pressed."

Georgine took the list of figures, but hesitated. "I'd meant to stay and work this evening, Professor Paev. Will Mrs. Blake leave at the same time as you?"

"She'll fix your dinner," the Professor barked. "Women —always preoccupied with food..." He snatched a handkerchief from his pocket, surveyed its ragged edges and cast it from him. "What's that? Nervous? Nonsense. You couldn't be safer, with neighbors only fifty feet away. Lock all the doors. I want 'em locked anyway. Will you finish that list, please?" He looked fiercely into space, muttering, "I'd best not try to drive. Car might break down. *If you please*, Mrs. Wyeth!" Georgine departed summarily.

"Will you shut off the air-conditioning?" he shouted after her. "There, behind the door, right outside!"

She tightened her lips in annoyance, and peered about the corridor wall until she found a plate embossed *Nuaire*. As the switch flipped over, the mysterious humming noise died away. "No romance left," she told herself sadly.

Of course the Professor was right about her having small reason to be nervous; nevertheless—*Indeed I'll lock all the doors*, thought Georgine, typing away at the astronomical figures of the Professor's estimate. *You bet I will lock myself in. I won't bother Harry Gillespie again—a taxi wouldn't cost too much just for once.*

For some reason she was reluctant to let the neighbors know that she was once more staying away from home this evening. If that tenuous suspicion of hers had any foundation, someone had too much interest in her and her household. She would feel safe here just so long as she was supposed to be somewhere else.

Therefore Georgine, going downstairs with the typed list and watching the Professor leap with flying coat-tails into a cab, stood well away from the door. Mrs. Blake always kept her own counsel with the other residents of the Road. Georgine saw her go off, too, at her usual time.

When the wind dropped, she imagined she could still hear the reedy, lonely strain of the mouth-organ from the house up the hill. Or was it in her own head? A tune like that got in your mind and wouldn't leave you.

Georgine ate the excellent cold supper which Mrs. Blake had left for her, and hastily washed the dishes. It was still light in the kitchen, with the pearly cold light of late sun. If she hurried, she might just get home before dark.

In the drearily furnished room upstairs, where she worked, Georgine glanced out the window for a moment before drawing the blind and turning on the desk lamp. "Fog comes on little cat feet" indeed. No cat ever galloped as fast as this was going: against the shaking plumes of eucalyptus at the canyon's head, the fog streamed gustily.

She had finished her typing and was painstakingly checking over each sheet, making small pencil corrections, when the last of the homecoming sounds died away in the

Road. This was the roll of Roy Hollister's garage door; funny how soon one learned to recognize those noises, to gauge their distance; the door seemed to echo more flatly tonight, the thick mist distorted its vibrations.

And now it was quiet, except for the muted roar of traffic rumbling from the city far below. The sun appeared for five minutes under the high fog, and then was sucked down behind the hills of Marin County, and into the sea.

She hadn't been quick enough. Now she could not get home before dark.

CHAPTER FOUR

Blacked Out Forever

DARKNESS FELL OVER the Bay cities, and lights pricked out in house after house, flowered in great bursts at the shipyards, and made glowing ribbons of the main streets. But into the lonely canyons, across the great stretches of ranch land in the middle valley of California, darkness came unchallenged except by a few misted stars, and here and there a farmhouse whose windows shone a feeble yellow.

Eighty miles to the northeast a little shack stood by itself on a knoll, miles from a habitation. A car was parked outside it, and not far away a long line of telephone poles marched, swinging their taut garlands of wire.

There were two men in the shack. Through the door that stood open to the summer night they could be seen bending attentively over a checkerboard. The light of a coal-oil lamp fell on them and struck out a luminous rectangle across the threshold. A dog lay beside one of the chairs, motionless, his head on his master's foot.

One of the men, lifting a checker for a move, paused with his hand in mid-air. He raised his eyes, listening, and the dog stirred. "Huh," the man said, smiling, "darned if my ears don't prick up just like Spot's, here."

"That's one," the other man said elliptically, nodding. He went outside, lifting his face to the night sky. A high long drone drifted down to his ears. "North," he said. "Headed southwest, I think."

His companion was bending over a telephone instrument. "Army flash," he said, and waited. Voices crackled in the receiver; presently, at a signal, he began unhurriedly, "Flash one, single, high, heard…"

"Hell," he said disgustedly, hanging up the receiver. "I jumped up so sudden I joggled the men out of place."

"Lucky they don't pay us for this job," the other man said. "If they did, we couldn't afford to do it."

They laughed as if at a well-worn joke, and replaced the checkers.

Twenty-five miles away a middle-aged couple paced nervously up and down outside a private garage on a hilltop. The woman said plaintively, "It's dark as pitch. I don't know how they expect us to see anything."

"We don't have to, Mother," the man said. "Now, just keep calm, you seemed to do all right when they were training us. This is the only way we can do our—Listen!"

"Go on," the woman said dubiously. "We've been caught that way before. It's the Sikes boy's motorcycle."

"I guess you're right." He cupped his hand behind his ear. "Yeah, there it goes up the hill—Say, I'm not so sure. Sounds awful high to me."

"You want to put it in?" His wife was still doubtful. "But what if it *is* the Sikes—"

"Can't do any harm. I bet there's plenty of us've reported motorcycles and such. They'd rather have a false alarm than miss a real one."

"Oh, all right. You do it. I'm never sure."

"No, Mother. You've got to phone sometimes."

The woman turned reluctantly into the garage. "Ar—army flash," she quavered into the telephone, and had to clear her throat several times before she could answer the crisp voice that said, "Army; go ahead, please."

"Unknown," the woman said, hoarsely, "unknown, and we just heard it, we can't see a thing; unkno—What's that? Oh, yes, the code number, wait a minute." She scrabbled among papers. "Victory forty-three. Direction unknown, distance unknown, we can't see where it's going."

"Thank you," said the crisp voice.

The woman drew a deep breath. "That's that," she said. "I don't see how it helps 'em much."

It seemed to make no difference to the score of women who sat about a huge table map. They spoke into their headset telephones, they reached out sure hands to lay small markers on the map, to set up odd little racks bearing slips of card. The checker-playing men had inspired the placing of one of those direction arrows, the nervous couple another; another came, and two more, and another, now only a few minutes apart.

There were more telephones on the glass-enclosed balcony above, where other women sat; and still more in the distant center to which they were reporting. Looking up from the floor of this second map room, you saw men in uniform and men in civilian clothing. You saw their lips move before the instruments, and their hands stretch out to make notations, to press buttons on the board before them. You saw several of them exchange glances, speak to each other, return to the telephones.

It looked very simple and leisurely; yet, within ninety seconds of the last report there had been a careful check and re-check, and a certain order had been given, and a civilian official had been interrupted while listening to his favorite radio program.

Within the space of a few more seconds the radio fell silent. The marking arrows on the huge map were pointing directly at San Francisco Bay.

Georgine Wyeth waited, none too patiently, in the one lighted room of Professor Paev's house, the southern workroom whose window looked over the canyon. The harried woman at the taxicab company had promised her that a cab would pick her up sometime. "It will be subject to delay," she had said. How *much* delay, for heaven's sake, Georgine wondered. It was a full hour since she had finished work and put in the order. It would serve the cab company right if she started out walking, and let the driver find an empty house when he came—if ever he came.

They had the drop on her, though. She was frankly unwilling to go walking through these deserted hill streets alone, and doubtless the cabman knew it.

She looked through her perfectly typed pages once more, and stacked them neatly, and decided to allow herself a cigarette. She had found the matches, and was about to strike one, when a far-off wailing sound struck.

Georgine's hands had begun to shake, and she put down cigarette and match quickly. "That's it," she said aloud in the empty room. "That's it…"

There was something in that endless wail that went, deeper than the ears, past the conscious mind, into a part of one that was pure instinct. It had been like that at the very beginning of the war, long before the sound became familiar. Blackout—alert—this is it.

What had Hollister said? "The next one may be real."

She flicked the switch of the desk lamp and felt her way to the window. If the sash were opened, it was supposed to minimize the danger of shattering glass. But, she thought suddenly, she needn't stay in this room; the Professor's refuge room was the downstairs hall, and those two small windows by its door had been permanently blacked out. Mrs. Blake had said that in case of a bombing, all those present in the house could crowd into the closet under the stairs. Georgine had had a vivid picture of herself, the Professor and the African Queen, all mashed together in the dark, and had quaked with inner laughter. She wasn't laughing now.

She might have thought of this; but there hadn't been a blackout for months, you forgot between times... The next one will be the real thing. "Barby," Georgine said, her lips barely moving. "Oh, God, I can't die while she's so little." *Oh, come, be sensible, who's going to die?*

The fog over the cities had stayed faintly luminous for a few minutes; now that white glow had died slowly, and it seemed that everything else had died with it as the roar of trains and traffic slackened and disappeared. Georgine had never before been in the very heart of silence, as she was now, alone in this black house.

She felt her way along the corridor wall to the upstairs window. In the stillness she could hear, very high and far away, a faint droning sound, and found herself peering upward desperately as if her eyes could pierce roof and fog and miles of night air. Then that sound was covered by a nearer, homelier one; Roy Hollister's front door opened, and his feet clacked briskly along the cement walk.

Almost at once there was a noise as if of stumbling, and the warden said "Damn!" loudly and heartily. Georgine ceased to shake, and found herself silently laughing. He must have tripped over one of the uneven places in the road's paving, where it had buckled badly in the summer heat. The footsteps were muffled now, and she guessed that he had taken to the edge of pavement for safety. The tiny blob of light from his dimmed electric torch was visible in this blackness, as it would never have been in an ordinary half-luminous night.

There was another minute glow, somewhere across the street; Georgine, straining her eyes, could almost make out numbers in its shape. *Dear me*, she thought, again grinning;

the Carmichael sisters didn't turn off their street-number light after all, and won't Hollister be furious! He hadn't seen it yet, for the Carmichael house was below his and faced southwest; and he had started methodically uphill toward the Devlins'.

Georgine's conscience smote her suddenly. People didn't do much to coöperate with the poor man. She might as well obey orders and seek the refuge room.

She got down the stairs deliberately, one at a time, and felt her way round the walls of the entry. Wooden panels, a space with woolly materials hanging: the coat closet, left open...more paneling, then rough paper over the windows that flanked the door; wood panels...the staircase.

She went round once more. It was no use; she couldn't find the light switch. "Don't sit in the dark," the authorities had counseled, "it's bad for morale." *They didn't know the half of it*, Georgine thought, clenching her teeth to keep them from chattering. She could feel morale draining out through the soles of her feet.

There was no use in imagining the things that might be coming at her out of the dark house. She sat down on the bottom stair, hoping violently that the blackout wouldn't last long. What time was it? Seemed as if she'd heard the Campanile strike ten, just before the siren went off.

There came the warden's footsteps, down the road, pad, pad, pad, very stalwart and reassuring. There was no other sound. Georgine knew just when he stopped at the sight of the flagrantly illuminated number. The timbre of the steps changed; he was going in the Carmichaels' gate, past their thick hedge, and a faint clanking bore witness to his attack on the metal holder of the number.

After several minutes the steps were retraced. They grew more audible, but slower, as he prepared to cross the street, angling down toward the Paev house. They had a cautious sound now, as if Hollister were feeling his way across the rough pavement.

Then the noise came.

It was only a rush and a rattle at first; then, before the ear could define it, a dull crashing impact followed the first sound; and then, with a terrifying bang in which wood seemed to be splintering, the noise rose to a crescendo of shrieking metal: crash, bump, crash, into the ravine.

Georgine found herself by the front door, her hand closed round the knob, her whole body clammy with terror. It must have been a bomb, the first of those bombs that had been expected for months. There had been no explosion, but maybe this was a different kind...

Her breath whistled through a constricted throat, her eyes stayed fixed as if to pierce the blackness. She ought to be finding the staircase and crawling under it, but she could not seem to detach her hand from this doorknob. *It's all that's holding me up*, thought Georgine wildly, over a host of other chaotic thoughts. *I've always wondered how I'd act if there were a real raid. Now I know; I'm so scared I can't move... How long have I been standing here? What's that funny noise in the street, not like the other one, more like someone groaning, or breathing?*

The knob turned silently under her fingers, and as silently the door swung inward. It was in defiance of all orders, but she couldn't stay alone here in the dark, not knowing what had happened. Let the warden scold her if he liked, he was here to reassure people. That padding noise sounded rather like his footsteps again, but softer.

"Mr. Hollister," Georgine said, her voice coming back with startling loudness from the echoing wall. "Is that you, Mr. Hollister?"

The padding noise stopped.

"Please, what was it? Is anyone hurt?"

There was no answer at all; no voice, no other steps.

Only, from the middle of the street came the sound of harsh breathing.

At a little distance across the road there was a dull glow, dim and tiny as fox-fire. It looked like the warden's torch, but if he was holding it, why didn't he answer her?

Somewhere a chime struck the half-hour. The wind came up again slightly, but the odd breathing went on. It sounded—painful. There were no more loud sounds.

"Someone *has* been hurt," Georgine whispered. She gritted her teeth and stepped out into the cool blackness, somehow darker even than that inside the house, because unconsciously one expected light from the sky.

She was halfway across the street, making for the dim torch, when her foot touched something soft. She froze instantly, and for a moment not all her will-power could make her bend over to feel what lay beside her.

In that moment all the sensations of the past week crystallized within her: the seemingly unfounded fears, the creeping uneasiness that she had tried so hard to overcome, the dream-like warnings of her unconscious self. It was something like this that she had expected; it was the worst horror of all that she was not surprised.

Yet to have it come at last was almost a relief. She bent over, and her hand found warm wet flesh. Whoever it was must be badly hurt, but not dead, for his hand beat weakly against the pavement as if he were trying to rise. Was it that sound she had heard, and mistaken for footsteps?

Her groping hands went farther, and felt the round metallic crown of a helmet.

The warden was hurt. That must have been blood she had touched. Georgine tried to recall her lessons in first aid, she felt gently for a spurting artery and found none that could be determined by touch. She thought, though, that there must be broken bones. How could one tell?

The small torch still glowed through its layers of paper, at the side of the road. It must have been flung from his hand at the moment of that impact, whatever it had been; doubtless the flashlight had fallen on the carpet of leaves beside the road. But what had hit him? What had made that frightful crash?

Her groping fingers encountered and held something small, hard, cylindrical, which she thought must be his whistle.

It was dry and clean to the touch; nevertheless, Georgine conquered a moment of shuddering repugnance before she put it to her lips and blew a long steady note. There was no shrilling vibration, only a melancholy hoot that seemed to mingle with the night like an owl's call. She blew it again. The man beside her stirred and moaned.

Far up the road a door opened. Georgine could see a sliver of light, instantly extinguished. A voice came quavering down to her, "Wh-what is it?"

With a tremendous effort she made her own voice come steadily. "I'll need some help. The warden's been hurt."

The other voice came in a little shriek. "A bomb?"

"I don't think so. Who is that—Mrs. Gillespie? Can you feel your way down here?"

"I—we're not supposed to come out," the voice floated plaintively down to her. "Can't it wait till the lights come on?"

"How do we know when that'll be? We ought to do something now! You come down here—he's breathing so queerly—" Georgine felt herself beginning to crack under the strain. She got up unsteadily, very slowly stumbled over to the flashlight and picked it up. If you held it close to the surface of the road, you could see where you were going. It took her back to the unconscious form in mid-pavement; as she regained Hollister's side she heard cautious steps feeling their way downhill.

Georgine held the light close to Hollister's face.

Three feet away, Mimi Gillespie stopped in her tracks and began to scream. "Oh, turn off that light! Don't! Don't shine it on him, I can't—"

It wasn't the bleeding from the scraped and lacerated face that was the worst; curiously, what made Georgine's head swim and weighted her stomach with cold lead was the mark of a tire-tread, clearly printed in dust across the man's jacket, across the white felt of his armband.

"How could it have been a car?" she said weakly. Mimi's screams had died to gasps, now. "Nobody would have been driving in the blackout. Nobody'd drive down here, anyway.

Mrs. Gillespie, get back to your house or find a telephone some-where, and call a doctor and the ambulance."

"You can't," Mimi wailed. "Nobody can get one, the tele-phones don't answer. I tried when the blackout began, and you can't even raise Central."

"Isn't there anybody?" Georgine said desperately. "An advanced first-aider, someone who can help?"

"Not up here, not tonight. The old Carmichael ladies—they might do it, but they're away," Mrs. Gillespie babbled. "*You* do something, can't you? Oh, poor Roy!"

"I don't know enough about it. And there's nothing to work with, I daren't move him; all we can do is cover him up," said Georgine dully.

"That's a good idea." Mrs. Gillespie's voice was stronger, as if all the problems had been solved. "I'll get a blanket, if I can—" She bent over suddenly. "Listen! Did he say something? Maybe he's not so badly hurt, maybe he was just stunned." Georgine, bending close to Hollister, put her ear down to his lips; Mimi leaned shudderingly over them both, gasping, "Oh, he said, 'I am dying. Come, I'm dying.' Wasn't that it?"

After a moment, Georgine said, "It sounded like that." And under her hand the body of Roy Hollister relaxed with a dreadful finality.

Now that it was too late, someone else was coming down the road. "What's the matter down there?" said a male voice, hoarse with anxiety. "Was that you screaming, Mrs. Gillespie? Where's the warden?"

"Oh, Mr. Devlin," Mimi cried, "I'm glad you came, we were all alone—the warden's here, something hit him."

"Hurt?" John Devlin said on a long groan. "How?"

The light shone once more, dimly, on the tire marks. Devlin said, "My God. Oh, God, so I was right about that noise. Ricky's car, his jalopy, isn't—isn't there any more. It must have got away, and—and plunged downhill, and Hollister was in the way." Through the darkness Georgine could hear him panting hoarsely. "Why don't the damned lights go on?" he shouted, startling her.

Mrs. Gillespie had begun to shuffle away. "I'll get that blanket," she said, almost cheerfully.

John Devlin knelt, and his hand went along Hollister's lax arm and found the wrist. "But listen," he said in a shocked tone, "he's—I can't find a pulse. He's *dead*."

"I'm afraid so," Georgine said faintly.

"We can't leave him like this, my God! Where's there a doctor—"

Mrs. Gillespie went once more through her explanation.

"Well, but the warden's own phone ought to work!" Devlin said. "I heard they'd made some arrangement about that, so it gets the switchboard when nobody else's does. Try that, Mrs. Gillespie!'

"In Roy's house?" Mimi said on a kind of shriek. "With him out here dead? Oh, I couldn't go in there!"

"I'll go with you," Georgine said.

"That's right. I'll stay with him. This is no place for women," Devlin's voice said gruffly. There was a jingling sound. "Here are his keys, in his side pocket, a whacking big bunch. You take that little torch, might need it to find the door key."

It was an incredible relief to Georgine to rise and move away from the limp form on the pavement. She thought vaguely, *How queer people are about death; Mrs. Gillespie was glad to be given an errand somewhere else—or was that why she sounded almost sprightly? And here's Mr. Devlin, cheerfully staying right here, feeling in Hollister's pockets. There's no accounting for reactions.*

The darkness still pressed about her like something tangible. There was the night breeze on her face, the sting of the fog, the tautness of eye-muscles straining to pierce the black air; the gray of pavement and cement walks did give off a faint sort of glimmer that helped her to find her way, but that was all she could see. Beside her, Mimi Gillespie pressed close, breathing quickly. Georgine could feel the soft fuzziness of a loose sleeve. "Were you undressed?" she said absently.

"I—no," Mimi faltered. "It was cold, I sat up reading but I put on a house robe over my clothes. And when the sirens went, I just turned off the lights and waited. We've got blackout curtains, but they take too long to fix."

The street was hard and uneven underfoot. Georgine felt for step after step, holding the light downward. She wondered for a moment if she could be dreaming all this. There was the front walk of Hollister's house; she went along it, Mrs. Gillespie in her wake; both women holding out groping hands toward the wall of the projecting garage. "Ricky's car must have gone right down into the canyon," Georgine said. Funny how you found yourself speaking in a whisper, as if a little noise mattered now. "Didn't you think it was a bomb when the fence splintered?"

"Oh, yes. It seemed like—as if I couldn't move. Here, don't bother with those keys, the door's unlocked."

Then why on earth, Georgine thought, had he carried that great bunch? "You know where the telephone is?"

"Yes. On a little table by the—here it is. What'll I say? You do it."

Georgine listened for the operator's voice, but nothing came except the hum of wires. Surely in just one more minute someone would answer? The light shone as if in a spot of phosphorescence on Mimi's white robe, moving slightly with her nervous breathing.

Then all at once the white robe wasn't there. Georgine heard a gasp and a rush, and felt wind coming through the open door. "Something in the house," a terrified murmur sounded from the path outside.

Was that someone moving in one of the rear rooms?

Georgine flicked off the light. If there had been a little glow under the living-room door, if she hadn't imagined that yellowish line, it was gone now.

Her heart was doing its best to thunder its way through her ribs. She could have turned on her torch again, and moved to the door and peered through the layers of darkness in that room—to see if anyone was there.

Probably that's what a really brave woman would do.

Instead, sheer instinct prompted her. "Police!" she said breathlessly into the dead transmitter. "Hello, operator, will you give me the police station?"

If there had been a rustling sound in that room, that too was gone.

She could not gauge the time, nor even guess how long it was she stood there, clutching the smooth vulcanite of the unanswering telephone. New voices sounded, hushed, in the street outside; she thought she recognized Ricky Devlin's tones, and heard him calling softly, reassuringly, to his mother. She would have given a great deal to rush out and join the others; but a stubborn sense of duty held her where she was. It could have been five minutes, or twenty, before an operator responded to her repeated jigglings of the connection bar. It was minutes later before a voice answered, "Emergency hospital."

Georgine's knees were weak with relief as she gave her message. She managed to remember the cross-streets nearest to Grettry Road, for help in location; she was switched to the police-station, after another long wait. As soon as the blackout was over, an ambulance and a squad car would start for the Road; perhaps sooner.

She wondered if she'd given all the right details. Her hand was cramped from its hard clutch on the telephone, the cool darkness seemed to press on her and make breathing difficult. She stumbled out into the Road.

From the campus, far below, came the notes of the Campanile, rising slowly and heavily. Eleven o'clock. And, as if that had been a signal, a long sustained note droned through the night, and the fog began to reflect light. The windows of Grettry Road flashed into illumination, and around the bend came a car on which shone the great red eye of the police signal.

"Stand back there, please, and let me get to him. Don't crowd... Did anyone see the car hit him?...Where was it parked?...His name—no, just one of you, please... Any family? Who got to him first?"

Questions, and voices answering them, sometimes singly, sometimes in chorus; the glare of the police-car's headlights, shining on the Road's inhabitants, some fully dressed, some in the odd combinations of clothing snatched up in the dark; the calm listening face of the young officer from the squad car, and the glinting top of his pencil as it moved back and forth over the pages of a notebook; voices, babbling in the street…

Sheila Devlin: "Ricky, stay right here near me, won't you, dear? You were certainly sleeping soundly, not to hear the sirens.—But you heard me when I called through your door, didn't you, dear? I was sure you answered."

Ricky (absently): "Yeah, sure I did. I must of thought it was morning, and rolled over again, until I—I heard that crash."

Claris Frey: "Oh, how terrible! How perfectly awful! Is he—is he dead?… No, I didn't wake Daddy, he went to bed ages ago with a headache. He's there now. Of course he hasn't heard a thing. Oh, what a shame about Mr. Hollister. It was just yesterday afternoon he was laughing so, with Daddy…"

John Devlin: "Hell, no. I didn't come out when I heard that crash. I thought it was a bomb, just like all the rest of you, and I was looking for something to get under so I wouldn't be killed. Lord knows Hollister himself pounded that into us often enough: stay in your house, don't look out the door."

"…bombs…" "…that awful crash…" "Alone in the house…"

They buzzed and racketed in Georgine's ears until she felt deafened. She went into the Professor's house to wash her hands and get a drink of water, only then discovering that she had left the door swinging wide. Fortunately, it had done no harm, and the Professor would never know.

The lights were perversely easy to find, this time. There was no one in the house, but—Georgine paused on her way to the kitchen, lifting her head and sniffing—there was a funny smell that reminded her of baking in an old-fashioned range. Had someone been burning paper?

She made a brief detour around the house, cautiously switching on the lights before she entered each room. She must have dreamed that, too. There was nothing in the fireplace but a neatly laid fire which would never be lit.

When she returned to the street the ambulance had come. The body of Roy Hollister had been left where it was, however, and the blanket had been drawn up over the lacerated face. She could see more clearly, now that the shock was wearing off; little details, magnified by the sharp contrast of darkness with the white glare of headlights, stood out in her vision. She saw Ricky Devlin and Claris Frey standing together, a little apart from the others, not looking at each other; their lips moved cautiously as if they were exchanging guarded words. Ricky moved away at a summons from the officer, and Georgine saw him reach down a hand to rub his knee, gingerly, before he went on. He was limping just perceptibly.

She saw a shadowy figure joining the group, and recognized Professor Paev. He had come up from the canyon, through the Gillespies' back yard. Presumably he had walked up via the short-cut, for burrs and foxtails clung to his trouserlegs. He was in a mood so brusque that it hinted at a crushing disappointment as well as annoyance. "I was only halfway home from the train," the Professor barked, "when the lights went out. I've been sitting on someone's front porch for an hour. On someone's front porch!" he repeated angrily, as if this were the last straw.

The keys that John Devlin had pressed into Georgine's hand were still in her coat-pocket. Perhaps the officer would want them.

She went slowly up to the young policeman, who was talking to Mimi. Mrs. Gillespie, with her golden swirl of hair and her curves noticeable even through the folds of a white chenille robe, was the sort of witness any man would like to question. "We heard him say 'Come, I'm dying,'" Mimi told the officer earnestly. "I guess he—he was conscious for just that minute. Don't you think so, Mrs. Wyeth?"

Georgine, who had already told her story, nodded thoughtfully. "Here are his keys," she said.

The young officer held out a hand for the heavy bunch, and bent over them. Georgine had not looked at them before; one or two were of an unusual shape, she thought.

The policeman looked up at her with sudden attention, and opened his lips as if to speak. Then he changed his mind. He was frowning slightly as he pocketed the keys.

"That car must have been smashed to bits," said Mrs. Gillespie, her eyes wide with pleasurable horror. "I'm going down to look at it, do you want to come?"

"I'd better take a look myself," said Ricky Devlin from behind them, rather huskily. The officer had already inspected the wrecked car in the canyon; nevertheless he accompanied the two women and the boy as they climbed through the gap in the low fence, and slipped and scrambled down the slope, following the trail of broken bushes.

"Gosh," said Ricky inadequately, turning the beam of his flashlight on the crumpled mass of metal.

There seemed to be little else to say. The four stood viewing the Jeep's carcass, tipped on its side in the brush. The windshield was gone except for a few shreds of glass, the steering wheel hung rakishly from a near-by bush, and the shabby leather upholstery was scarred and torn. Ricky started toward the car, and the officer said, "Don't touch it, sonny. We'll want to inspect those brakes."

"I wasn't going to do anything. And I told you fifty times I left it in gear, with the handbrake on and the wheels turned against a rock. I told you!"

"Sure," the officer said. "I know you told me."

Ricky swallowed. "Poor old Jeep," he said with fine carelessness. "Two of the tires gone, that's the real disaster." He scrambled round to the front and surveyed the crushed radiator. For a minute more he said nothing; then out of the dimness behind the torch his face looked at his companions, its lower lip hanging slack. "It—it killed someone. It killed a man," he said in an unsteady whisper, and suddenly dropped the torch and disappeared into the bushes. There were sounds.

"Poor kid," Mimi muttered. "Should we go and—"

"I'd leave him alone," Georgine said quietly.

The young officer looked at the Jeep and then up the slope, and shook his bead. "These hills!" he said soberly. "It's a wonder more people aren't killed just this way. There's hardly a month that a car doesn't get away and run into someone's back garden. This jalopp' could have got up a lot of impetus, tearing down that hill; hit this fellow near the bottom, knocked him for a loop and run over him—one wheel at least—and then bounced against this fence and somersaulted over. Crazy sort of accident, but it's not so unusual."

Ricky emerged from the bushes, very white, wiping his lips with a handkerchief. "Listen, officer," he said. "Am I supposed to be responsible? What'll they do to me?"

The young policeman resumed his official reticence. "There may have to be an investigation," he said.

Ricky looked at the two women. There was appeal in his eyes, and the most abysmal terror Georgine had ever seen.

CHAPTER FIVE

Not All Aboveboard

ON THE MORNING OF July 4, Georgine Wyeth walked downtown through almost deserted streets, and came to the handsome new building that housed the Berkeley Police Department, and hesitated only a moment before she went in. It had taken her the larger part of a restless night to make up her mind to this move.

Maybe it would be simpler just to find out where the offices of the Homicide Squad were. It proved to be easy; down the hall to the right, and through the door with its glass panel blacked out. She went in, glancing to her right into a glass-enclosed cubicle. A man in plain clothes was standing at the desk, his back to her. She tapped on the door, and he turned.

The Messrs. Walter Pidgeon, Gary Cooper and Ian Hunter paraded rapidly through Georgine's mind, and then vanished. No, not like any of them; but a hint of each face in the rugged, blue-eyed one before her. "Something I can do?" the man said courteously.

"Yes," Georgine said. "I have some—what might be some information about the death of that air-raid warden who was killed last night. I didn't know to whom to give it."

"Perhaps I'm the one you'd want to see," the man said. "I'm Inspector Nelsing. Will you sit down?"

She took the chair he indicated. Inspector Nelsing was looking at her in a disconcerting way, as if she were not a person at all, but a sexless entity labeled Bringer of Information.

"Do you know about that accident?" She made herself speak steadily. "It was a man named Roy Hollister. A car ran downhill in the blackout and killed him. The car belonged to a young boy who lived on his block, and I—the officer didn't say what might happen to him, but I thought if they decided it was his fault it would be called criminal negligence. There were one or two things I noticed that it seemed you ought to know."

"Just a minute," the Inspector said, and walked rapidly out and down the hall. Before he returned with a handful of papers Georgine had had time to reflect that he wasn't even approaching middle-age, with that unlined skin around his eyes; and she had inadvertently read the address of a letter tucked into the desk blotter. His first name was Howard.

He shut the door behind him and sat down, his eyes already devouring line after line of a typewritten report. "You'll excuse me if I read this?" he inquired, briefly glancing up. "The officer who handled the case isn't on duty just now."

Georgine said she'd excuse him. She had never in her life met with such devastating politeness as was practiced by the police of this city, even when they were making light of her fears. She wondered how they acted if they suspected you of murder. "Pardon me, madame, would you mind stepping into the jail?"

Inspector Nelsing put the sheets of paper on the desk, and meticulously evened their edges. "You are—?"

"Mrs. Wyeth."

"Oh, yes. You heard the impact, and after a time—how long? Several minutes?—yes; you went out to see if someone had been hurt."

"There was something else. I didn't tell the officer this, I wasn't absolutely sure I'd heard it, but—it sounded to me as if someone might have been tiptoeing off up the road."

"H'm. Near the body?"

"I thought farther up. You know, I may have imagined it," said Georgine in a hurry, forestalling him if he should think of this himself. "When I got to Hollister he moved once or twice, very feebly, and his hand struck against the pavement. It could have been that."

"Anything else?" He was serious, and very patient.

"Yes. He—said something before he died; or at any rate before he lost consciousness for the last time. Mrs. Gillespie heard it. She thought, and of course she may have been right, that he said he was dying. But I was nearer."

"What did you think he said?"

Georgine looked at him warily. "I worried about it all night, the words seemed to—well, sort of stick in my ears, and I couldn't convince myself that was all he said. I think the words were—*someone driving.*'"

"That would refer to the car that hit him?" said Inspector Nelsing dispassionately. "Was the engine running?"

"No, no. All I heard was a kind of rush and rattle, just the noise a car would make if it had started downhill by itself. It's perfectly possible that's all that happened, only I thought you should know. Please understand I'm not being a busybody, I'm—"

"Mrs. Wyeth," said Nelsing, "may I ask you not to apologize so much? Just tell me what facts you gathered, and let me decide for myself whether they're worth consideration."

"Oh. Yes, of course. Those are all the facts."

"Did you want to add any conjectures?"

"Are you *asking* for them? Well, I did have some, but they sound rather fantastic." She caught his eye, and hurried on. "If someone had got into that car, as the warden went down the road, I—I suppose it wouldn't have been impossible to wait till he was in the right position and then run him down?"

The impersonal gaze did not change. "Just a minute. The report says that no one was in the car when it went over the fence; at least, there were no signs of an occupant. It would mean that the person would have to jump out somehow before the crash."

"That—that might have been possible, too, if the car slowed up on the level part of the road. Ricky's car didn't have any doors. That made it like a jeep; he was very proud of the resemblance."

"Did you hear anything like a person jumping out?"

"No, but there are drifts of leaves along the road."

"It would have to be a very agile person. A leap like that, from a car going even at half speed, would spin you around hard; you'd be likely to fall. I don't suppose you noticed if any of the people who were standing around after the accident showed signs of having had a spill?"

Georgine hadn't thought this far ahead. She looked at him, frowning. "The—the only one—yes, there was one, but it couldn't have meant anything."

"Who was it, Mrs. Wyeth?" His handsome mouth tightened. "I presume you didn't volunteer this information with the intention of withholding part of it?"

Her eyes dropped. She said in a troubled voice, "Ricky Devlin, the boy who owned the car."

"I see," Nelsing said quietly. He waited for a minute before letting drop his next question. "Did you know the man who was killed?"

"Hollister? No. I met him only once or twice in his capacity as warden."

"What kind of a man was he?"

"The boss of the barnyard," Georgine said with a subdued laugh. "He wardened harder than anyone I ever saw. Otherwise, he was just ordinary, like—like all the men you see walking along the street smoking cigars. And yet—" she hesitated, wondering how to frame the next sentence. "He had a sort of *impact* on people that I couldn't define or explain to save me."

"Was he popular with the neighbors?"

"Well, no. On the contrary, I'm afraid," she said.

The question slid in casually. "Would any one of them want to kill him?"

"I don't know, Inspector. I thought if there was somebody driving that car, he might have come from outside."

Inspector Nelsing just looked at her, during a lengthening pause. She became aware of several things, one after another. A) She must have believed that someone in the Road had killed Hollister, but B) in the attempt to convince herself it wasn't true she had said exactly the opposite; and C) the detective was scornfully aware of this process of reasoning.

After a long time he spoke. "Everyone is immobilized during a blackout," he said wearily. Georgine made no response.

Nelsing arranged the sheets of the report once more. He seemed to be choosing his words carefully. "That isn't a great deal to go on, Mrs. Wyeth," he said, "but it so happens that there are one or two points of interest in this report. The officer said you had Hollister's keys for awhile."

"Yes. Mr. Devlin insisted that I take them, but the door was unlocked. And—while I was in the hall, using the telephone, it seemed to me that someone else was in the house. Mrs. Gillespie thought so too, and ran. But we might have dreamed that up too, you know, simply because we were scared. I was *awfully* scared," she added, defiantly.

"I see," said Nelsing. "Someone in his house. You didn't investigate?"

"Certainly not."

"Did you examine those keys at all? No? I wonder, Mrs. Wyeth, if you've ever seen a skeleton key."

She looked up at him again, silently.

Inspector Nelsing rose. "Yes," he said deliberately, "there were two or three on that bunch you had, and the Warden Service hasn't authorized the use of any such thing. I think I'll take a little run up to this Grettry Road. I wonder if you'd mind coming with me."

From a welter of thoughts and disturbing new ideas, Georgine expressed only one. "No," she said firmly.

Nelsing looked up from locking his desk. "No what?"

"No, I don't want to go up to the Road with you. I've given you my information, and now I want to go home. Soon or late I suppose I'll have to go back to the Professor's and finish my typing, but I've no desire to meet any of those neighbors again."

"Could I ask why?"

"No reason, only a silly feeling. I've been—well, uneasy, ever since I stepped into that place last Monday. And now that there's been a—" She broke off and swallowed. "You might as well know. I'm a terrible coward."

"Many women are," said Inspector Nelsing calmly.

Well!

It had cost her a good deal to make that honest admission. "But I asked for it," Georgine told herself; "what did I expect him to do, say, 'Oh no, not *you*, you're brave as five lions'?"

"And surely," he added, "if you've mingled freely with the neighbors during this week, if you talked with them and went in and out of their homes last night, you shouldn't be afraid of them now. If you kept your head enough to try first aid and call the ambulance when you found a man was hurt, surely you see that your fears can be overcome?"

"I was geared for a war, not for a murder."

Howard Nelsing stood by his desk, tapping it softly with a forefinger, looking down at her. "There isn't so much difference," he said seriously. "Murder is on a smaller scale, that's all, and it stems from the same things: greed, jealousy, fear, hatred. Somebody gets stabbed in the back, and justice demands that the stab be avenged. The ordinary citizen gets caught up in it just as he does in war. And have you thought that individual crime goes on just the same, century after century, no matter whether we're fighting other nations or not? If we could wipe it out, perhaps there wouldn't be any wars.

"Besides," his tone became suddenly more personal, "I'm afraid I'm going to need you, Mrs. Wyeth."

She looked up again, seeing how the hard light of a foggy sky struck across his face, the serious mouth, the blue eyes.

This sensation inside her was very disturbing, as of a well-made gelatine, firm but ready to quiver at a touch. "All right," said Georgine ungraciously. "After all, you're not sure there's been a murder, are you?"

"Not at all sure," said Nelsing briskly. "Now; we'll drop in at the Civilian Defense office for a moment."

She did not see what was written on Hollister's dossier, but as Nelsing helped her into his car he told her. "Nobody seems to know much about him; no family, as near as we can discover. He came here last August and took a lease on that house. Seemed to be retired, young as he was. After Pearl Harbor, when the Warden Service was organized, he offered his services. They were glad to get him; nobody else in Grettry Road could serve. He's been faithful and efficient, and that's what counts, mainly."

"But, skeleton keys!" Georgine said, troubled. "What on earth do those mean?"

"Maybe nothing." Nelsing shrugged. "Don't worry about that, Mrs. Wyeth. In cases of violent death, we're always running into odd little sidelines, loose ends that haven't a thing to do with the situation. Will you tell me about the boy that owned the jalopy? What does he do, go to school or just hang around?"

The car skirted the University campus and began to climb steadily through winding tree-lined streets. "Ricky?" Georgine said thoughtfully. "In vacation I suppose he does just hang around, except that he's crazy to get into the War himself, somehow, and his mother won't let him. Seems he might get into coarse company if he went fruit-picking, and he can't sign up as a warden's messenger because that'd mean being out during an air-raid—though she denies at the top of her lungs that there will ever be any. She's rather a dreadful woman, though I imagine she's really devoted to her husband and her son and doesn't know any other way of expressing it. You should have heard her telling Ricky that he was only a baby yet, and that they'd never take him as an air-raid warden unless all the available men were—Oh!"

Nelsing said nothing. He could scarcely have missed it.

"I've given you the wrong impression," said Georgine, trying to speak quietly. "He's a nice kid, and when I saw he might be in trouble through no fault of his own I wanted to help him. He looked at me so—I have a little girl myself, you see, and I'm awfully susceptible to young things."

The man set his car in low gear for the precipitous climb up Rose Street; it growled and hummed to itself. "Don't worry about forming my impressions," he said calmly. "I'll decide on my own, after I've talked to him."

Georgine did not feel much better. The higher they climbed, the lower her heart seemed to sink. The thick fringe of eucalyptus against the sky looked black and unfriendly; in a minute the car would swerve under those trees and drop down into Grettry Road.

"I'll park up here," Nelsing said, stopping near the road signs at the intersection. He looked round at her soberly. "I'll introduce myself as a city detective, but it may make things easier if the Homicide Squad isn't mentioned."

"Very well," said Georgine. "You're incog; I shan't give you away."

They rounded the turn and the slope of Grettry Road was spread before them, alive with the excited babble of sightseers. The fence at the end was completely obscured by leaning forms. At the curve of the vacant lot stood Mr. Todd McKinnon, hands in the pockets of an admirably cut tweed jacket. He seemed to be sighting carefully down the road.

"Incog, hell!" said Inspector Nelsing in an undertone.

"You know him?" Georgine looked up, surprised. "He's kind of a screwball, isn't he?"

"Acts like one," Nelsing said, walking toward him. "What's he doing here so soon?"

"He works here daytimes, I believe, but at what I don't know. He wasn't here last night, of course."

"Of course," said Nelsing, "and I bet it's eating him."

At the sound of footsteps, McKinnon looked round casually. The oddest thing happened to his face; it could scarcely be called an expression, since not a muscle moved, but his agate eyes took in Georgine and her companion with a sudden complete awareness.

With one long step he was off the edge of the lot and onto the pavement. "Great Scott," he said easily, "have I messed up any evidence?"

"What makes you think that?"

"I'm practiced," McKinnon said to Georgine, "at jumping to conclusions. Eleven feet from a standing start was my last record."

Nelsing looked him over with a wry smile; he was much more at ease with men than with women, Georgine thought. "How the vultures do gather," he observed.

"Vultures," McKinnon repeated, interested. "I've been called worse than that, by smaller men than you. Nothing ever happened to them," he added pensively. "Well, this is inter-esting, Nelse. You don't tell me—"

"I tell you nothing, as usual. Haven't you got it figured out for yourself, already?"

McKinnon looked sadly at Georgine. "I'm afraid he's making fun of me. If you must have it, Nelsing, I'd begun to tell myself a fine story. Young Devlin's jeep parked at the one spot where it would have a clear run down the road; someone who dislikes the warden, who lies in wait for him during the blackout, knocks him out in the street, gives the car a push downhill to make it look like one of our hill accidents; that's as far as I'd gone, but it has possibilities."

"There wasn't time for that," Georgine said. "Hollister was walking, right up to the minute the car hit him."

The detective glanced at her quickly. "You're sure?" he said, and at the same moment McKinnon put in, "Were you here when it happened, Mrs. Wyeth?"

"Oh, yes," said Georgine wearily. "Throwing my weight about, trying to be a little angel of mercy. Next time maybe I'll know enough to stay inside."

"Good Lord! You went out in the blackout?" McKinnon thrust a hand through his sleek hair. "I should hope you would know better. For six months the wardens have been trying to educate people, and the first time—"

Georgine interrupted him tartly, quoting the immortal utterance of a high official, "Well, no bombs fell, did they?"

"And consider this, Mac," said Nelsing quietly. "A dying statement comes in kind of handy."

"A dying—oh, God give me strength." McKinnon looked agonized, and then, in the face of this new idea, gradually appeared to forget the Warden Service. "So," he said slowly, "that's why—H'm. You think your mystery has come along at last?"

"I've told you, I think nothing. I collect facts." Nelsing had been surveying the terrain with rapid, intent glances. "Straight line across the curve of the street," he murmured, beginning to descend toward the jagged gap in the fence. Georgine and McKinnon followed as if drawn in his wake. "Where was he struck, Mrs. Wyeth? I see someone's been out with the hose and washed the street. Very thoughtful. Tramped all over the ground where it levels out, too." He clamped his lips together and shook his head quickly.

"Hullo, Mrs. Wyeth," said Ricky Devlin from the group by the fence. His eyes were dark and tired, and sometimes a muscle twitched in his smooth young face, but he was putting up a debonair front. "Hi, Mr. McKinnon." His glance traveled to their companion.

"Showing off the scene of the accident?" Nelsing asked.

Ricky shook his head. "Mourning my car."

"It's you that owned it, then. I'm doing a little investigation for the city," said Nelsing easily. His manner with Ricky was perfect. "What's your name? Frederic Devlin? Well, Fred, let's have a look. I wonder if all you people would mind coming back later?"

The sightseers straggled off, reluctant, but vaguely recognizing the voice of authority. Ricky stood tense, his head turning jerkily to watch the examination of the car. After a time Nelsing climbed back to the fence, and dusted the burrs from his trousers. "Just one spot where the man could have been hit," he said thoughtfully, squinting up the road. "Funny how it worked out. He had to be crossing the street—wonder why he wasn't keeping to the side?"

"He had to turn out a light in a vacant house," Georgine said. "The Carmichaels forgot their illuminated number."

"Forgot it?" Ricky Devlin looked at her quickly. "No, they didn't. That light was out Wednesday night, after they left. I—I was walking down here," he trailed off lamely.

Doing a warden's duty, in spite of everything, Georgine thought. She smiled at Ricky, but his face didn't change.

Nelsing said, still casually, "You happen to know, Fred, did the warden have a regular route that he followed?"

"Yeah," Ricky said. "He was awful methodical. He always went up our side of the road first, and then came down the middle and took a look at the Carmichaels' and went over to Professor Paev's, and then back to his own house."

"So that if he hadn't had to turn off that lighted number, he might not have been crossing the road?"

"Uh-huh, he'd have angled off onto the Prof's lawn. I used to kind of watch him, to see how a warden—Say, what is this?"

"Nothing," Nelsing said. "Just getting the picture."

"Listen. I told 'em and told 'em I was careful about parking the Jeep. It *couldn't* have got away."

"I hope not," Nelsing told him kindly. "You would have seen anyone meddling with it, I suppose? Did the warden happen to take a look at it during the blackout?"

"Well, gee. It was awful dark, and my room—you see, I sleep on the lower floor, they fixed up the game room for me."

"You were in bed when the siren sounded?"

Ricky glanced around, and his tongue came out to moisten his lips. "Y-Yes, sir. I—you know how it is, you're kind of scared when the noise starts, and first you think it isn't anything and decide to stay in bed, and then—after awhile I put a few clothes on and went up to the breakfast room that we've got blackout curtains in, and—well—"

Georgine's chest felt cold and tight. Not a word about hearing his mother call to him through the door?

"You went there before or after the crash came?"

"A—a few minutes after. Dad was there."

Nelsing nodded calmly. "And then, I suppose, you heard people talking and came out into the street? Look, Fred, have you salvaged anything from the car?"

"No, they said not to, last night. But," Ricky confessed, "I did take the steering wheel, it was just hanging there on a bush."

"Ah. The steering wheel."

"Thought I'd have something, you know. 'Tisn't likely I'll get another car for the duration."

Georgine kept her eyes on his face, though she was conscious of the listening stillness of McKinnon by her side, of the Inspector's subsurface awareness. She was thinking, *What have I done? I didn't mean it to be like this.* She felt the little shock that ran through the boy at Nelsing's next question, so casually, so kindly put as they started off up the road.

"Let's see the wheel, if you don't mind. What's the matter, son? You hurt your foot? No, it's your knee, isn't it?"

Ricky kept his face still, but a just-perceptible line of sweat came on his upper lip. "Fell over a chair, when I got out of bed in the dark," he said jauntily.

"Well, I'd like to talk to your mother and father, and get this thing cleared up," said the Inspector. He glanced at Ricky. "Until we do, I wouldn't talk about the matter. These questions are between us."

The boy said nothing. He followed Nelsing up the hill, and the turn of the road hid them.

The Inspector seemed to have forgotten his expressed need for Georgine. She was left behind, with Todd McKinnon. They looked at each other.

"I could *yell*," said Georgine softly and furiously. "I did this. The Inspector couldn't possibly believe that Ricky had anything deliberate to do with Hollister's death! Could he?" she finished weakly, in a whisper.

"I don't know. Indeed I don't," said McKinnon thoughtfully. "He couldn't very well have missed seeing that the kid was lying."

"Oh, dear. Did you think that too?"

"I did. And needless to say, I'll get no inside information from Nelsing until the case is closed."

"Why should you get any?"

His hard-textured face turned slowly toward her. "It's how I make my living," said Todd McKinnon. "Murder is my business."

Georgine gave a little start. "What do you—"

"S-sh. I'd like to talk it over with you later, but now—"

She glanced over her shoulder. On the Freys' front walk Claris was standing, gazing toward the Devlin house. She turned, with a swing of the hips so that her skirt swirled round bare knees, and came strolling across the narrow border of grass. "Hello there," she said, including them both in her greeting but saving an upward flick of her extravagant eyelashes for the man.

"Hello, cupcake," said Mr. McKinnon, looking down at her and faintly smiling. "I see you got downtown to buy the war bond and your sweater."

"This?" She smoothed the gray angora. "No, this's an old one, we never did get to town." The hazel eyes raked the road swiftly, but her voice continued languid. "Have all the ghouls gone away? I suppose there'll be some more after a while, but Dad wouldn't let me come out while the place was full of strange characters." And then, very offhand, "Who was the man with Rick?"

"He's investigating the accident," McKinnon told her.

"Exciting," Claris said. "Shame about poor Mr. Hollister, of course, but if it had to happen—at least it's something going on in this dead end. You should have seen Daddy when I told him. Poor thing, he slept right through of course, and never knew anything had bust loose. Honestly, he just couldn't seem to take it in."

The scarlet enamel of her mouth moved carefully, shaping the words. Georgine gazed at her, fascinated. Excitement, or something—strain, perhaps?—had matured and tightened her lovely face. She looked completely beautiful, a fact which Mr. McKinnon was not overlooking.

"Well," Claris went on, not waiting tor an answer, "I suppose I ought to be getting Dad's lunch, I just came out for a breath of air. I was wondering, Mr. McKinnon—"

She paused, and Georgine said, "Good-by for now, I'd better go into the Professor's and get some work done."

She thought, moving away, *What can you make of these young things? That child looks like something a Hollywood director would grab at, and she keeps house for her deaf father and is probably a model of virtue.* Or was she? There was something unexpectedly firm under the glamor-girl surface, anyway, no matter what it might signify.

Mrs. Blake opened the door and immediately laid a conspiratorial finger on her lips. "If you just slip upstairs quiet, Mrs. Wyeth," she said, "maybe the P'fessah won't get stirred up again. We had reportahs here this morning and they riled him worse'n I've seen fo' months."

Georgine whispered in return, "He told you what happened last night?"

"Yes, *mam*," said the African Queen. "Seemed to think Mist' Hollistah didn't get no mo' than was comin' to him."

"Really? I think he was annoyed already when he—"

"What is that whispering?" said Professor Paev furiously, from the door to the basement stairs. "Mrs. Blake, if anyone tries to make you give out infor—Oh, Mrs. Wyeth, it's you. I'm not ready for you, today's a holiday and I am revising the next section so you can have it on Monday."

Georgine wished he wouldn't make her feel sorry for him and irritated at the same time. She said meekly, "Were the lists all right, Professor Paev? You didn't have time to look them over before you left, last night."

"Lists!" the Professor barked. "Those lists are in a trash can in the Terminal Building. There was no use for them."

"The Regent didn't—"

"Bah! The Regent!" Alexis Paev strode over to her and wagged a long forefinger under her nose. "Someone was very, very funny," he said venomously. "Someone thinks, it is clever to play on an old man's hopes, perhaps one of my comical friends at the University. They'd have let me go out to Wadsworth's home, and present myself humbly at the door with my list of requirements for a new department, and be told that the Regent left yesterday morning to visit his son in camp at San Diego! They'd have laughed themselves sick, thinking of it, I've no doubt. What they did not count on was my having dinner at Solari's—to celebrate," said the Professor bitterly, "and running into Wadsworth's nephew, who used to be one of my students. I couldn't contain my enthusiasm. I told him of his uncle's offer; perhaps he laughed, too, but he spared me—kept me from going out there—"

He broke off, fiercely shaking his bald eagle's head. Georgine said, "I'm so sorry. If it was a joke, it was in very bad taste. You didn't recognize the person who gave you the message on the telephone?"

"No," the Professor said. He had recovered his composure, and his black eyes were only normally angry. "It's of no moment. It only means that now I shall keep my discoveries to myself, to be announced at the time I choose. It's better like that. I prefer it."

"So that was it," said Georgine. "I wondered how it happened that you came back so early last night."

"So *early?*" the Professor said, and his eyes narrowed.

"Yes; because the blackout began a little after ten, and you were on this side of the Bay—weren't you?" Georgine found herself stammering a little, wishing she had never made that idle remark. She backed away a foot or two, toward the door. "You said yourself that you were caught in the dark; you were sitting on someone's front porch."

"Ah. Perhaps I did."

"And—I simply thought when I saw you that you looked disappointed, and I was sorry to feel that something might have gone wrong."

"My dear Mrs. Wyeth," said Professor Paev, in a tone of ominous suavity, "when I want your pity I will ask for it. Now, please go and spend your holiday somewhere else!"

"Thank you so much," said Georgine, her eyes snapping. "If you'll allow me to work on the job that you're so anxious to see finished, I'll be here tomorrow morning. But if I hadn't already been paid, you could blasted well whistle for me!"

She went out, and would have slammed the door heartily except that the Professor had hold of it.

There was another set of eager gawkers draped over the fence, and milling about the level space in front of the Paev house. She thrust her way through them angrily. Nobody in sight but strangers; no McKinnon, no Inspector, neither of the youngsters; yet the upper end of the road, as she passed through it, gave her a troubled feeling. It was as if the atmosphere in those closed houses had become so heavy with strain that some of it had escaped outdoors. "You and your feelings," said Georgine to herself, crossly, and climbed on toward the intersection.

From an open window somewhere behind her came a terrible cry. She stopped and whirled around, recognizing the voice of Peter Frey; that curiously unresonant voice, without control in volume.

"He was murdered, you mean! Oh, God, an accident would have been bad enough. It was my fault, my fault!"

CHAPTER SIX

Hidden in the Bushes

THE HEDGE BESIDE her rustled, and Georgine started and swung around. The smooth sandy head of Todd McKinnon, making for the gap in the hedge, was just visible.

In another moment he emerged, coatless, swinging a trowel from an earth-encrusted hand. "Did you hear that?" Georgine breathed. "What did it mean?"

"That I couldn't tell you," Mr. McKinnon said. His face was impassive as ever. Only the deep-set eyes were alive, flicking from one to another of the houses across the street.

At an upstairs window of the Devlins', Mrs. Devlin was visible for a moment, her hands pressed together on her mouth. "She heard it too," said McKinnon softly, as the woman whirled and disappeared. "Murder. It's a word to stab with; goes right through the chinks of our armor."

The Devlins' door opened and Inspector Nelsing came out, unhurriedly. He spoke to Georgine, his level tones conveying a rebuke. "You're not leaving, Mrs. Wyeth?"

"What good am I around here?" Her own voice was quite as level. "If you really need my help, you know where I live."

"H'm," McKinnon murmured. "Getting rough with an officer? I'd say she was safe, Nelse. She won't run out on you. 'Dyou get anything out of the Devlins?"

"Now look," said Nelsing patiently. "If I had, do you suppose I'd sit down on the front steps and tell you all about it?"

"Well, I can dream, can't I?" Mr. McKinnon chuckled, deep within his chest. "There's one thing, though—they didn't by any chance have a guest last night?"

"Didn't mention one. Why?"

"Mrs. D. was in a hurry to change the guest-room bed. She was up there tearing at it, ten minutes after you went in to talk to her."

"The guest room? Which one is that? Oh, the one to the south." Nelsing turned to look up at it. "How did you know which—no, never mind answering... Queer," he murmured just audibly, "I thought they shared the north bedroom. She said they were together when—"

He shook his head, and walked briskly down the road to the Freys'. Georgine watched him ring the bell, and saw the door open and the tall figure vanish.

A moment later she heard Peter Frey's voice once more. He must be standing by the open kitchen window, which faced on the street. "I brought him," the voice said, loud and flat. "I brought Hollister to this place."

Still softly, Todd McKinnon said, "It seems that nobody escapes. I'd have said that Roy Hollister was nothing to these people, besides being the warden; but what'll you bet they're all bound up somehow in the matter of his death? All of 'em, every one on this street."

"Not me," said Georgine firmly. "I'm going home now."

The Devlins' door opened and Sheila Devlin came out, crossing the road with a swift stride. "Mrs. Wyeth," she said in a tone of such cold fury that Georgine took an involuntary step backward, "you brought that man here. I saw you drive up together. You encouraged him to pry into our private lives, to ask questions, to—to suspect us of being untruthful. You did that. May I ask why you interest yourself in us?"

Georgine thought, *I mustn't get mad, I absolutely must not lose my temper.* "Mrs. Devlin, I had no intention of making trouble for you; just the contrary. It was to prove that Ricky wasn't responsible."

"That was very good of you," said Mrs. Devlin coldly, "but I can defend my son if it's necessary. And it's not! Ricky has never in his life done anything wrong. He was asleep in bed last night when the siren sounded. I—I saw him. I went down to his room and looked in," she said with nervous emphasis. "He heard me, he said so."

She saw him? Georgine thought; *but she didn't say that last night! She's not trying to make us believe a lie? If so, emphasis isn't the way to do it...*

"It's unnecessary that we should be annoyed this way—questioned by a police officer! We should be allowed to forget this"—her large hand went out, gesturing down the road—"as soon as possible. You'll oblige me, Mrs. Wyeth, by not trying to help again."

Her long bony face didn't look sweet nor saintly now. It looked frightened. The dark head inclined jerkily, and Sheila Devlin turned and went back into her own house.

"Well, for heaven's *sake*," Georgine said. Her chin jutted out. "And all in such a ladylike voice, too! I wish I'd taken that trowel of yours and whacked her one!"

"Easy on," said Mr. McKinnon, with his subterranean chuckle. "Looks as if you started something, getting Nelse up here. Well, a few of us will be grateful, if Mrs. Devlin isn't."

"I'm so glad you're enjoying this," Georgine snapped. "And now I *am* going home, before somebody else slaps me in the face!"

She gardened energetically for half the afternoon, in her landlords' back yard. Get your hands in the dirt, gardening enthusiasts suggested, and go back to Mother Nature; that was how to forget your troubles and problems. Oh, indeed? How did you keep your brain from picking up phrases and irrelevant memories and churning round with them like a washing machine?

Skeleton keys, Georgine thought; *a light that was off one night and on the next; the line of sweat on Ricky Devlin's lip; Professor Paev and his lists, and the mean joke someone had played on him—if it was a joke; if someone had played it. Inspector Nelsing, tapping his forefinger on the desk: Inspector Howard Nelsing, saying, "I may need you to help me."*

Only he hadn't. He'd seemingly forgotten all about her, left her to cool her heels in the middle of the street. He seemed to he interested in the Grettry Road people, though; he might be there for two or three days.

Of course she'd have to keep on going there until she finished her typing.

It was mid-afternoon when she realized that someone was leaning on the back fence; without turning her head she knew who it was, for a lively solo on the mouth-organ had announced the presence. As she stood up, trying to brush heavy adobe soil from the knees of her slacks, Mr. Todd McKinnon lowered his instrument and remarked in a tentative voice, "Be mine, Mrs. Nickleby."

Georgine grinned. "Throw a few cucumbers at me, and I'll consider it. Come in, won't you?"

She was rather astonished to see him measured against the high fence; those lean, narrowly built men often looked taller than they actually were. He was glancing along the fence. "Must I go clear round the block, or climb over?"

"There's a gate farther along. It may stick a bit, I never use it; that back lot is too weedy and bushy."

"Very handy," said Mr. McKinnon approvingly, finding the gate-latch. "This short-cut gets me here from my apartment in no time."

H'm; did he mean to beat a little path to her door? She discovered that the prospect wasn't unpleasant; he had a gift of accepting people as they were, making them feel comfortable. "Can you find a place to sit down?" she said, kneeling again to gather up her tools.

He appeared to fold up all at once, like one of those bedtrays; when she looked up there he was, cross-legged on the grass. "Nice," he said, with a comprehensive look around the enclosed garden.

"What was that tune you were playing over the fence?" Georgine said. "Catchy, somehow; I've heard it once or twice on the radio."

"It's called *Jingle Jangle*."

"Of course. Isn't that the one about, 'Oh, ain't you glad you're single?'"

"It is, and I am." said McKinnon. "Forgive me, Mrs. Wyeth, I seem to have got settled without waiting for you. How about sitting on the ground and telling sad stories of the death of wardens?"

Georgine also sat cross-legged. "I was expecting this," she said. "You seemed to be consumed with curiosity."

"Not just the vulgar kind; more of a serious study."

"There's no way out, is there? Everyone's going to want to discuss Hollister."

The far-off twinkle came into his eyes. "What have you been thinking of all afternoon?"

"Hollister," said Georgine, laughing. "But what's your serious study? Are you—you're not connected with the police yourself?"

"Only in a friendly way, I assure you. I pursue them. I make their off hours hideous, asking questions."

"Oh. A crime reporter. No? But you said you made your living at it."

Mr. McKinnon sighed guiltily. "I write detective stories."

"I'm afraid I've never—"

"You wouldn't. They come out in the pulpwood magazines, under five or six pen names. Hack work, but I can live on it. I'm no creative artist; I can't get started without some knowledge of a real crime—the surroundings, the people, the background." He offered her a cigarette, his voice running smoothly on. She had never met anyone who could talk so much without tiring one's ears. "Given one good complicated crime, I'm off to six or seven stories. You see where the police come in; sometimes they'll describe old cases, the ones that were closed years ago, and those are nearly as good as fresh ones. Just the same, I'm getting an awful kick out of being in on the ground floor."

"No wonder Inspector Nelsing thought you'd be sick because you weren't on hand last night."

"Yes," said McKinnon, looking off into space, "It's a pity I wasn't. But you were, and I'd like to get your impressions. You make anything of it, Watson?"

"Nothing but complete confusion. You probably know as much about it as I, by now; except that Professor Paev was lured off the Road by a low impostor who pretended to be one of the University Regents."

"Was he, indeed!" said McKinnon, his agate eyes direct and intent upon her. "Would you mind telling me the whole story?"

She told it. The scattered bits of information were now arranged neatly in her mind but still meant nothing.

He listened with rigid attention. When she had finished, "But, Mrs. Wyeth!" he said. "This is interesting. It's better than I'd thought. It begins to look like premeditation, as if somebody tried to arrange that the whole end of the road should be clear of witnesses. Did anyone know you were to stay over for the evening?"

"On the contrary. I told Mrs. Gillespie I was going home."

"Would she have spread that news, do you think?"

"She wouldn't have had to," Georgine said. "We were talking about it in the garden, anyone who was around could have heard us."

"There you are. That fact alone might not mean much, but combined with the Carmichaels' light it begins to look like business. Someone turned on that light to make sure of Hollister's being in a certain place in the road; and the light could have been arranged any time after Wednesday night. Anyone could have gone into that garden without being conspicuous. We all had the excuse of picking the old ladies' flowers."

She thought, *Ralph Stort was in there, and seemed to feel he had to explain his presence. Was Hollister the person who had "tortured" him?* It almost looked that way. Horrible, how your mind ran on; and the minute you allowed a suspicion to creep in, the whole thing got too concrete.

"Do you believe all that?" she said.

"Well, not as absolute gospel," said McKinnon mildly. "Maybe the light turned itself on at some vibration. Maybe the car did get loose by accident; that flapping top might have given the illusion of a person in the driver's seat. But naturally I prefer it the other way. I can do a nice job with it. Put somebody in that car, bent on murder, thinking there was nobody at home from the Gillespies down. Then think of the shock to that person when your voice came out of the darkness, just at the moment when he was walking up the road to safety."

"If I didn't imagine those footsteps."

"For my purposes, you didn't. Then there's Hollister," he went on musingly, "tramping around with his pocket full of skeleton keys. There's a picturesque detail I'd never have thought up myself, because it doesn't seem to fit. More than likely it's irrelevant. He could have got hold of 'em somewhere and kept 'em to get into houses where people had gone away and left lights burning. It'd be like the poor guy. He took his warden job seriously."

"Didn't he, just." Georgine shook her head pityingly. "All that methodical zeal—"

"—Putting him on the spot," McKinnon caught up her sentence. "He must have looked round; think of that, too; hearing something rushing down on top of you, turning, trying to dodge instinctively, still not knowing quite what it was until you went sailing through the air—or fell, and felt that weight crushing your chest in—I'm sorry, Mrs. Wyeth, I'm *sorry*. I didn't want to upset you. Completely thoughtless of me."

"It's all right," said Georgine faintly, "only it seemed so horribly real from Hollister's point of view. It's dreadful, when you come to think of it, how hardly anyone considers the feelings of the—the one who got killed. It doesn't matter if you liked him or not, it's—"

"Please forgive me," McKinnon said gravely. He laid his hand on hers for a moment. "Did it sound as if I were gloating over the details? I can't help seeing it vividly, you know. And believe me, this isn't a Roman holiday."

She looked at him. She said slowly, "Are you sure?"

"Completely sure." Their eyes held for a minute. "If we can imagine accurately enough what goes on in people's minds and feelings, we get some indication of how they'll act. It works backwards, too. It's one of the most serious studies on earth to figure out what went on in a murderer's mind, what lay there for days, weeks, years before his crime—or sometimes only for minutes, as long as would be needed to work up a murderous impulse."

"Dear me," said Georgine, somewhat recovered, "you sound like one of those psychological detectives that the police turn to when they're completely baffled."

McKinnon laughed aloud, abruptly. "Couldn't be farther from it—if there ever was anyone like that. The force tolerates me politely, and that's about all. If they're in a good mood they may give me a little information—after it's been made public."

"And do you give *them* any?"

"Now and then." He chuckled again, ruefully. "Usually I find out they've known it all along, and they're a dam' sight better than I at digging up actual motives."

"Yes. That's a slight snag, the motive."

"Not in fiction, of course," said Mr. McKinnon with renewed hope. He pulled gently at a blade of grass until it slid out of its sheath, and nibbled at the tender end. "Easy enough to make 'em up, or magnify li'le indications that are there already. Take Harry Gillespie, for instance; he's jealous of anyone who comes within a mile of his wife, he's even glared at me when I stopped once or twice to pass the time of day on the front walk. Maybe Hollister made a practice of dropping in there, after Gillespie had gone to work at night." If he saw Georgine's twitch of recollection, he appeared to ignore it. "And there's Stort; he and Hollister were thick as thieves for a while, and then had some kind of bust-up; who knows why?"

"This is *all* fiction, isn't it?" Georgine said warily.

"Well, not entirely." He glanced up with one of his faint smiles. "It's all possible in fact."

"Ralph Stort had gone home to his ranch the night before Hollister was killed, and Harry Gillespie left for work early that night. I heard his car go up the road half an hour before the blackout began."

"If one of them," said McKinnon, still smiling, "had turned on the light and put in that call to Professor Paev, a small detail like going away wouldn't bother him. He could come back."

"Well, but who on earth knew the other conditions would be right? The blackout, I mean. Unless it was a practice one? You're a warden, were you notified to be ready?"

Mr. McKinnon raised his eyes to heaven. He spoke with careful emphasis. "There is no such thing in the Bay region as a practice blackout. They're too damned dangerous. The Army orders an alert only on real provocation. Last night's was 'unidentified aircraft, afterward found to be friendly.' That's what the papers say, and that's all we'll ever hear about it for the duration."

"All right, warden," said Georgine, "you've given your lecture and ruined your own theory."

McKinnon whistled softly. "So I have. Nothing like the lay mind—a sharp mind—to pull up a fiction plotter on his wildest flights."

"I feel about as sharp as a dishmop, but thank you."

"And now look what you've done, thrown me all off. At least four good shorts and one novelette gone up the spout," he said, shaking his head at her reproachfully.

"Don't blame it on me, it's just fate." Georgine grinned.

"I hope you'll allow me the impulse theory? Let's see if I can do anything with that. Wash out all those things that looked like premeditation. Okay; the alert sounds, catching everyone flatfooted, but the murderer quickly recovers himself. This impulse seizes him; he pops out before the sirens have done sounding, hides in the Jeep or near it, and waits his chance; it just happens that Hollister gets into the right position on the road; the impulse comes to a head, and the murderer lets the car roll and takes the chance of hitting him—"

His voice trailed off and he shook his head despairingly. The sun cast muted shadows through thin fog and low-hanging branches, across the summer-bleached grass of the garden, across the intent eyes under the sandy brows, the firm mouth. Georgine had a moment of complete incredulity. It wasn't possible that she was sitting here discussing theories of murder with this comparative stranger? And how funny that she hadn't thought of it before! There must be something about a mystery that forced acquaintances into premature bloom.

"That won't work,' said Todd McKinnon soberly, and shook his head. "The method's unsure enough without putting in all those ifs and maybes. It's got to be premeditation—and it can't be. There go all my magnificent plots."

"That's too bad," said Georgine. "I'll give you one; why don't you invent a bad man somewhere outside the Road, who'd hated Hollister for years and years and jumped at this opportunity to kill him? Why does the murderer have to live right there?"

"Sorry, an outsider won't do. Wouldn't it be asking even more of coincidence, to have this bad man—who presumably lives at least a mile away—lurking on the edge of Grettry Road on the very night the Bay region was blacked out? And if he'd been lurking there night after night, on the off chance, he'd have been seen; wouldn't he have chosen a quicker way that didn't depend on a very problematical set of circumstances? No, I won't have it. I am a seeker after artistic perfection," said

Mr. McKinnon impressively, "and I find it much neater and more likely to have the murderer live right there. It's the old desert-island gambit; narrows the field."

"Fact or fiction?"

"Both."

"Oh, dear. I dislike even thinking it could be one of the neighbors, it's impossible to imagine one of them as a deliberate killer. I *like* them; most of them, that is," she added, thinking of Mrs. Devlin's ladylike tones.

"Sure. Lots of murderers have seemed likable, until you found out what they'd been up to in secret. Why, Mrs. Wyeth, that's what makes a murder mystery. Somebody among the suspects is living a colossal lie; under a pleasant harmless surface he's another person—brooding himself into insanity over a wrong that's been done him, or being a Casanova when he looks like a solid family man, or quietly stealing his employer's funds and spending them on dope. There's a lie somewhere in everyone; a big one, a little one, it doesn't matter much. If you could see into these people's lives—"

"I don't want to," said Georgine vigorously. "What a mind you have! Isn't there anyone who's truthful?"

He looked at her slowly, with an odd expression: quizzical, personal, challenging. "Thee and me, Rachel," said McKinnon, "and thee is a li'le queer sometimes."

The gaze held for a moment longer. She thought, *What does he want of me? What is he trying to impress on me?*

"Does that include the representative of the law?" she inquired.

"Nelse? No, he's a right guy. He lives for his profession— you might say, he cares more about justice than anything else. But that's there, right on the surface as well as underneath. Anyone can see it."

"You're sure he's not a Casanova?"

"Far from it," McKinnon said, fixing her with a sharp glance. "He's a highly conservative bachelor."

Her eyes dropped. "Sounds like *Iolanthe*," she said.

He got up from the grass as suddenly as he had sat down, and with a bewildering change of manner offered to take Georgine out to tea. She refused; he refused her invitation to a cup of coffee in the house; honors were even.

"I'll take a rain check on that," McKinnon told her. "You may be seeing me around, as long as this investigation goes on. I'd better go home now and practice my music."

"You keep that as a sideline, I take it."

"No," he said solemnly, "as an inspiration. While I'm thinking out a yarn, playing the mouth-organ takes up the slack of my mind, so to speak; lets the old subconscious rage unchecked. When I strike a snag, I work on something unsuitable."

"Such as *The Trout*?"

"That's it. Makes a nice life for me, but it's hard on the neighbors, what with trout and typewriters."

Georgine said nothing. He must somehow have read her expression, for he added, "You're thinking that this idleness would come to an end if I got into the Armed Forces? True; but I have to arrange my affairs first and that'll take some time. No one but you knows this, Mrs. Wyeth, but I was brought up in the Mohammedan faith and I have five wives, all dependent on me."

"I'm sure you deserve nothing less," she told him.

"Hey," said Mr. McKinnon reproachfully, "I'm not sure that was kindly meant."

"Neither am I," said Georgine.

She thought of him more than once before the next morning, usually with an involuntary smile. Those mild little absurdities of his were really amusing, delivered in the casual voice that said, "You don't have to listen," with the expressionless face that assured you you didn't have to laugh. Yet she couldn't quite make him out; the absurdities cloaked something a great deal more serious.

She was still thinking of him at nine a.m., as, once more late and in a hurry, she went down the steep path into the canyon and began to climb the other side. She was returning to Grettry Road with a mixture of interest and cold reluctance; but Todd McKinnon, she reflected, would be in his element, strolling around and chatting with the neighbors, and doubtless picking up rather more information than they thought they were giving. She wouldn't put it past him to do a bit of detecting himself, on the side.

Halfway up the slope she turned her head suddenly. That clump of bushes to the north was quivering strangely in the windless air. *I bet I know what that is*, thought Georgine, beginning to laugh silently. *My pal Sherlock is digging for clues.*

There *was* somebody there. She stepped quietly through the tall dry grasses toward the thicket. Suppose it were the police, really finding clues? In that case, presumably, one just begged pardon and went away fast.

Very gently she pressed one of the bushes aside.

By some freak they had grown in a circle, enclosing a small bare space like a room; rather a cozy room, too, with its slippery carpet of dry wild oats, its aromatic leafy walls. Inside the circle Claris Frey was kneeling, furtively stuffing something under the lowest layer of branches.

She turned; her horrified eyes met Georgine's; she uttered a startled scream.

For a moment they were both transfixed. Then Claris's hand fell limply to her side.

"Oh, God, now it'll all have to come out," she said, and dropped her head on her knees and burst into tears.

CHAPTER SEVEN

A Secret Revealed

"WHY, MY DEAR," said Georgine, conscience-stricken, "don't cry like that. What will have to come out?"

"You would have to find me," Claris said in a low voice, choking. "You would come snooping through the canyon, just now, when I'd been waiting and waiting my chance to get down here and sneak these things out before the police started searching."

Georgine looked at the cache under the low bushes, from which trailed the end of an army blanket. "Claris," she said, troubled, "were you hiding something that was—in your house?"

"Oh, *no*. Can't you understand anything? We—we left our stuff down here, almost always we take it home with us but it was hard enough getting up the hill in the dark without carrying it—and yesterday morning those goons were looking over the fence, and yesterday afternoon after we found out about the murder Daddy was down near here every minute until the light went, painting like crazy because he was so upset, it's one of his favorite places for the easel; and after dinner he didn't let me out of his sight, I couldn't get away until just now—you can't have any privacy in this lousy place!"

Trying to follow this desperate outpouring, Georgine had scrambled through the shrubbery and bent over the slim boneless figure in the gaudy peasant dress. "Claris, dear!" she said gently, "I can't follow what you're trying to tell me... Don't *do* that, don't cringe as if I were going to hit you!"

"You'll tell," Claris choked, lifting a furious tear-stained face. "We weren't doing anyone any harm! We've got a right to—to—neither of us has any chance to live their own life! And old people make such a fuss about things, we tried to k-keep it secret—we had to!"

Georgine said crisply, "If you want any secrets kept, you'd better pipe down. Someone's coming."

Claris gasped harshly, and shot up to a kneeling position. Peering through the screen of bushes, "Oh," she said, relieved. "It's Mr. McKinnon. That's okay, he's zoot."

"He's *what?*"

"He's all reet," said Claris impatiently. Mr. McKinnon was now strolling past the thicket. "I thought I heard a scream," he remarked to nobody in particular, evidently willing to go away again if not needed.

"C-come in here," Claris whispered, holding aside a prickly branch of manzanita. "Make her not tell on me! Oh; make her keep still, *you'll* understand!" And as McKinnon forced his way into the enclosure, she flung herself upon him and once more burst into tears.

"Now, take it easy,'" the man said soothingly. He got out a handkerchief, raised the streaming face and mopped its tears in a manner so expert that Georgine's eyebrows went up. "Point out, please," she said in an offhand tone, "that I had no intention of telling on anyone, and that if I did I shouldn't know what to say."

"You might as well know now," said Claris dully. "I would have to fly apart and give it away, of course. We—we were down here Friday night, when the blackout began."

"Who were?" said McKinnon, frowning.

"Ricky and me."

"When the blackout began?" McKinnon said in a steady tone that did not conceal deep interest. "How long were you—"

At the same moment Georgine exclaimed, "Ricky! Then he couldn't have had anything to do with—"

"Wouldn't it just have to be last night?" said Claris. Her voice stayed low and rough, and she wadded the big handkerchief nervously in her clasped hands. "We—we hadn't been able to meet for a week or so, and I thought how lucky it was still light when I saw Ricky's signal, and I hurried up to my room and fixed the curtain so he'd know I was coming—"

"You signaled to each other regularly?" McKinnon said. "D'you mind telling me how?"

"Oh, if Daddy was going to bed early I'd pin up my bedroom curtains on one side, and then if Rick thought he could get out he'd fix the garden hose in a place I could see it, coiled up the way he's supposed to leave it instead of lying around the way he usually does; or it worked the other way round. And last night seemed a good chance. We'd go to our rooms just before dark, usually, and then duck out. Rick sleeps on the ground floor, and of course it's easy for me to get out of the house if I'm careful not to shake the stairs so Daddy'd not feel them." Claris reddened a little, as if aware that she had taken unfair advantage.

"I—I don't even know if he'd care, he always lets me do everything I want. And if that old bag wasn't so mean we could just have had dates like anybody else!" She took refuge in self-justification. "When we left my grandma's in the City last summer, and came up here to live, I said I'd do all the work if Dad'd realize that I was old enough to live the way I want to, and there was Rick next door, he got awfully tall and good-looking all at once, and I thought what fun—we're *young*, we ought to have a good time!—and that old bi—"

"Easy," said McKinnon again. "You're not referring to your grandmother?"

"No, Grandma was just ghastly strict, but at least she was fair. It's Mrs. Devlin. She'd die if she knew I ever spoke a word to Ricky when we weren't right under her eye. Well, it was her fault!"

McKinnon exchanged a glance with Georgine. "Let's get this straight, about Friday. You met down here after dark?"

"Yes, and we'd hardly got settled before the blackout started, and we didn't know what to do. I'd have been all right, but Rick didn't know if his family might look for him; but we were scared to move because we might have made a noise, stumbling through these bushes in the dark, and old Hollister might have heard us. We thought we heard him in the canyon, there was somebody on the path with a light. So we stayed put for awhile, and then it got longer and longer, and we were scared," Claris said with a childish quiver of her mouth, "so we started up the hill, and Rick fell down and took all the skin off his knee."

Georgine drew a quick breath.

"And he'd hardly left me before that awful noise came. I guess he got in without anybody finding out." She looked from one to the other of the adults, as if still afraid they were in league against her. "So now you know. And you promised you wouldn't tell."

"But, my dear," Georgine said soberly, "*you* must tell."

"No! We said, Rick and I, that we'd stick to our story, that we were home in bed. I'd be okay, but his mother—"

"Claris, don't you know what you're up against? This may be a murder case. Hasn't it occurred to you that Ricky might be in serious trouble if he lied about being in bed, and then wouldn't tell where he was?"

The hazel eyes burned suddenly hard. "He'd rather go to jail for murder than let his mother know. He doesn't think he's perfect, but she does."

"Isn't it time," said McKinnon, "that she found out?"

"You try telling her," said Claris, breathing hard. "I'm not supposed to know this, but one time an old lawyer who used to take care of her money tried to make her believe that Mr. Devlin didn't know enough about investing and things, and she oughtn't to let him keep all her money. She thinks Mr. Devlin is just perfect, too, and she—she jumped at that lawyer and nearly killed him. And you ought to have seen her at high school the time Ricky got a bad report card!"

"It didn't occur to her," said McKinnon impassively, "that Ricky himself hadn't earned a good report?"

The soft, lovely young face took on a look of unexpected shrewdness. "She knew," said Claris in a scornful voice, "but she wouldn't believe it, ever." She grasped McKinnon's shoulder with a shaking hand. "Don't you see? He does what he wants, and it's all right so long as she can pretend not to know. But if you make her realize, all hell busts loose!"

"I see." Once more the man glanced at Georgine.

"And if we told, she'd be sure to get hold of it. So—"

"Let's put it like this," McKinnon said. "If Ricky should get into any serious mess, you'll have to go to Inspector Nelsing and let him know where you were during the blackout. If the whole thing blows over—"

"Then you needn't tell," Claris said eagerly. "I'll promise, I'll promise anything."

"So that's settled," said McKinnon briskly. "I still don't know why you were revisiting the scene of the crime."

"Oh, to hide this stuff, or get it away somehow." She gestured at the blanket, the battered cigarette tin and match-box.

"You mean, carry 'em away in broad daylight?"

"Well, it was the first chance I had."

"Wouldn't it be a bit less conspicuous if I took them?"

Claris, with a melting upward look, said it would be. She added further that Mr. McKinnon was a doll, which seemed a strange description; and slipped away between the bushes, to the head of the canyon.

Georgine had been gazing at her soberly. The child was always fluent, but she'd gone into such detail this time...well, maybe she was glad to get it off her chest. Yet—was it possible that Georgine had been meant to find her, and to hear the story?

If so, that might mean that Claris was trying to manufacture an alibi for Ricky—or for herself. No, that couldn't be. Somehow, the story had sounded like the truth.

"That would explain," she said aloud, following her train of thought, "why Mrs. Devlin tried to convince herself Ricky was in bed all the time. By now, she probably believes she saw him."

Todd McKinnon finished picking up the burned matches, and stood up, giving her one of his inscrutable looks. "Possibly," he said. "I thought you looked troubled. Was that all?"

It wasn't; she had followed the thought a bit further, and discovered that if the children hadn't been at home, none of the three parents had an alibi for the moments just before the crash. Not that they really needed it, of course, she told herself, and then scowled.

"This is a mess, all of it," she said distastefully.

"Oh, come," the man objected in his casual voice, "surely you aren't suspecting the worst of those kids?"

"Never mind what I'm suspecting." She started to climb the hill; he walked beside her for a few yards.

"Not to hand myself any bouquets," he continued mildly, "but I can usually tell a nice gal when I see one. Most men can, you know. And just because young Claris has a talent for duplicity, you mustn't jump to the—"

"Stop putting words into my mouth," Georgine snapped. "How do you know what I'm thinking?" She left him, with the echoes of his remote chuckle in her ears. She didn't really know why she should be so irritated, nor why, as she passed the Freys' back gate, she should have an infantile impulse to kick it. This, however, she managed to control.

The newspapers had contented themselves with one printing of the accident story, on the morning after the blackout. It was submerged next day in the vast tidal wave of the Sunday papers, and no mention was made of Inspector Nelsing's investigations. The war went on, and the life of the city settled once more into its normal grooves; but in Grettry Road that steel-sharp word *Murder* flashed in every conversation.

You heard or sensed it whenever the residents met in the street, when two or three of them stood talking on someone's patch of front lawn. It was a curious fact that nobody, except Sheila Devlin, had any doubt as to the manner of Hollister's death. Their minds had bridged the shock and the horror, and gone to awed speculation.

Nobody said, "I'm glad." Nobody was sorry. Nobody seemed either to suspect his neighbor or to be apprehensive for himself—not, at any rate, in public.

It was all questions, whispered or murmured, and after each a silent pause for speculation. "Did you know Mrs. Gillespie has been in bed with a nervous collapse?... Did they ask you not to leave town or go anywhere without notifying the police? You know Mr. Devlin wasn't allowed to go out on his trip this week?...Why d'you suppose they've had Hollister's place sealed up? Did you see those cops in there, going over his things?..."

Presently bits of irrelevant gossip began to salt the questions. Georgine heard them; she couldn't help it, for she too had been caught in the centripetal force that held these five households in forced communion.

She didn't believe much of the gossip, nor find it particularly interesting, until on Tuesday noon she met Mr. Peter Frey. She had come out into uncertain sunlight and a chilly breeze, and was walking up and down the road, at once exercising and keeping warm. As she passed the Carmichaels' high hedge, Frey came through the gap that led to the front walk, carrying an armload of weeds.

He nodded and smiled jerkily at sight of her. Georgine said, "Not a very nice day for gardening, is it?" She never remembered that he could not hear her.

"Did you?" Peter Frey said politely, in his insentient voice. Then his glance followed hers. "Oh, these; the ladies were so kind about asking us to pick their flowers, I felt it wouldn't come amiss if I cleaned up their garden once or twice, and put out some poison for the gophers. More like paying for what one gets, you know."

His tone had become more and more breathy, until at the end it was almost inaudible. Georgine smiled again, embarrassed. "There's Mr. Gillespie, I wonder how his wife is?" she said, carefully mouthing her words.

"Oh, better, I think," Mr. Frey muttered. "I believe she was out this morning." Georgine looked at his tired face, and the red-eyed sleepless expression of Harry Gillespie, who came strolling across the road to join them. Nobody was feeling very well these days, she thought.

Mr. Gillespie wasted no time in agitating his lips, he held out a hand and Frey produced a small pad and pencil. "Have you heard any more about Hollister, what's going to happen?" he wrote in an unsteady sprawling hand.

"Or have you, Mrs. Wyeth?" Harry said aloud, showing her the note and passing it to Frey. Neither of them, it seemed, had heard.

He wrote: "That dick was asking qu. about where we were when crash came. Told him I was caught somewhere nr. Richmond in dark, how in hell going to prove it? Don't like this." He was doing all the work so far; Georgine and Frey had only to shake their heads.

Again he wrote. "You knew H., didn't you? Mimi was sure you did, moving in here at same time. We hrd. you said you brought him here. ?????"

Peter Frey spoke, his voice loud and harsh. "I did know him, slightly." He saw Georgine wince, and flushed. "Too loud again?" he murmured. His eyelids, drooping toward the outer corners with a melancholy effect, were lowered now; he began to jerk dried pods off the bundle of weeds he was holding, his long hands moving nervously among the slippery stalks. "There's no reason why you shouldn't know. It was painful to me for awhile, but it isn't now. I met him over—over the matter of my wife's divorce. She wished to leave me while Claris was quite small, and I didn't think she was—fit to bring up the child. I might have been certain of it," he said, his face settling into deeper lines, "from the day when I was foolish enough to marry her. But one always hopes, you know. So I was—forced to have her movements investigated, so I could ask for Claris's custody. Hollister and I didn't become intimate, one doesn't become fond of a private investigator who's been hired to—"

It had been slipped in so casually that neither listener grasped it for a moment. Then—"He was a private detective?" Georgine cried out. "Hollister was?"

Frey went right on, obliviously, "—spy on one's wife. He seemed not a bad fellow, though, and once or twice afterward we exchanged letters, even after we moved to the Bay region, Claris and I. Then he wrote to say that he was retiring from the Chicago agency, going into some other kind of business, and asked me to look for a place where he could live, in Grettry Road. It happened that one of these houses was to be vacated in a month or so, everybody was moving around last summer—"

"Wait a minute!" Georgine shouted as he went on. She seized the pad and scribbled: "Do you mean Hollister asked *specifically* to live in Grettry Road?"

Frey read it. He seemed unconscious of the sensation he had caused, perhaps because he was looking at the ground as he talked. "Why, yes," he said gently. "He may have supposed it was one of our main thoroughfares, perhaps through hearing it mentioned. It was only by chance that his house fell vacant, and the one we're in, too. I liked the look of the place, and decided to—"

"But where did he hear about it? Why here especially? Did you wonder if he was looking for something?"

Peter Frey looked up from the pad, his sad eyes puzzled. "No; he said he'd retired, and he asked me not to mention his profession, because people got curious."

Hadn't he ever been curious himself, as to Hollister's oddly specific request? Hadn't it ever entered his head...

"Did you know that, Mr. Gillespie?" Georgine said, turning to Harry. He was moving away slowly, his strained eyes gazing fixedly into space. "No," said Harry Gillespie absently, as if he were following some important and private train of thought. "I didn't know. No. You'll excuse me?" He began to climb, fast, up the road to his own home.

"And I must get back to work," said Georgine. "You've certainly given us something to think about."

"Have I?" Frey said mildly.

She was still holding the pad. She poised the pencil above it for a long moment, wondering how to word the thought that had sprung full-grown into her mind. Finally she wrote, very lightly as if she were whispering, "Did H. ever say what form his 'retirement' took? He couldn't possibly have been hired by govt. bureau?"

Frey took it in at a glance. At last, it seemed, something had roused his curiosity; his eyes, suddenly feverish in their intensity, met hers and then slid off toward the house across the street, from which Ralph Stort had departed.

He started to speak, and Georgine put her finger to her lips. He wrote on the pad, "FBI? I don't know." And then he tore off the sheet, and took a match from his pocket and held the paper to its flame.

She had not seen Todd McKinnon since Sunday morning, and as usual had forgotten having parted from him in irritation. On Tuesday night, as she climbed to the top of the road on her way home, Mr. McKinnon materialized at the gate of his borrowed house and asked if he might walk down the hill with her, following this with an invitation to dinner.

Georgine accepted after only a slight hesitation. She had never been to Trader Vic's, and, although not a drinking woman, she was curious to taste a Zombie. Also, McKinnon's voice and manner had exercised their usual soothing spell. She laughed comfortably at one of his deadpan absurdities, with only the smallest prick of uneasiness at realizing that somehow he knew everything that went on in Grettry Road, including her own movements.

Halfway down Rose Street a car stopped beside them. Georgine looked up and met the blue eyes of Howard Nelsing. Her heart gave an agreeable little flop.

"Hullo, Nelse," said McKinnon smoothly. "Looking for us, or just offering a ride?"

"Both," said Nelsing, opening the door. "I wanted a talk with you, Mrs. Wyeth," he said over his shoulder.

"I've just asked her to dinner. Will you join us?"

Georgine thought with a kind of exasperation that McKinnon's face never gave a hint of his true feelings. It was impossible to tell whether he was politely disappointed, or pleased at the idea of sitting in on a discussion. "Will you both come in while I freshen up?" she said, leading the way through her front gate.

"Speed it up if you can," said McKinnon. "If we don't get there early we may have to stand."

"That'll be all right," said Nelsing smoothly. "I know the Trader."

When she came out after a remarkably quick change into a printed silk jersey, the two men had taken possession of her living-room in a manner entirely characteristic of each. Nelsing was patiently waiting on the window-seat, not smoking, not looking at anything, though she was sure he'd surveyed every detail of the room the minute he stepped inside. McKinnon was prowling lightly up and down, reading the titles of her books, stopping impassively before the framed photograph of Jim Wyeth. *He wants to know about me, my own life*, Georgine thought. He turned to her and indicated another picture, a snapshot of Barby. "Is that your li'le girl?"

Georgine nodded. He looked inquiringly about the house, and she said, "Barby's away for a few days, at the Russian River. It's her first vacation away from home."

"I bet you miss her," McKinnon said. He smiled at the small face in the picture, plain and radiant.

"You want me to cry?" said Georgine tartly.

Nelsing stretched out his hand for the picture. "This isn't your daughter?" he said. "I thought of her as being about three, at most."

"I was a child bride," Georgine said. "My parents took me to India on purpose."

Both men glanced at her. Mr. McKinnon looked amused and reproachful. Inspector Nelsing looked completely nonplussed.

Trader Vic's had bamboo walls, and inside it were illuminated tanks of tropical fish, and woven grass mats for paneling, and a hanging veil of cigarette smoke that could easily be thought of as a kind of South Sea haze. "It's like something out of Somerset Maugham," said Georgine, thoughtfully tasting her Zombie. There were supposed to be four kinds of rum in it, but it was deceptively smooth.

McKinnon pointed out three items on the menu. "Those make us a balanced meal, Charlie?" he said. The Chinese waiter nodded and departed. Georgine, who was hungry, felt slightly dashed.

Later, when the food arrived, each of the three items proved to be a Chinese dish generous enough for one person's whole dinner, which could thus be divided three ways. She was further surprised to find that she had never tasted anything so marvelous.

Being by now halfway through the Zombie, she was permeated by a warm feeling of courage. "Inspector," she demanded boldly, "are you getting anywhere? Are you still sure this is a murder case?"

His indulgent look and his silence didn't seem to daunt her at all. Rum was a wonderful discovery. "I think we ought to know," said Georgine firmly. "If you could just say it wasn't, people's nerves might calm down. I'm way behind in my typing again, because everyone wants to talk over the situation."

"It beats all," said Nelsing, absently playing with his food, "how things get around, up there in Grettry Road. I hadn't much hope of the Devlin kid's keeping the secret forever, but he didn't waste a minute spilling it on Saturday morning. The little Frey girl was telling her father all about it before I was half through at the Devlins'. And I suppose Frey told you all about Hollister's past?"

"Probably saw no reason to keep it a secret," McKinnon put in mildly, "but it's thrown the neighbors into a frenzy."

Georgine said, "I wish people wouldn't pour out confidences, but when they do, you can't help listening, and—thinking." She glanced around her cautiously. "Do you always know it, Inspector Nelsing, if there's a—a Federal investigation going on in town?"

"Not always. Sometimes the FBI men ask for our help; more often not." His mouth went into a straight line.

"If, uh, one of them should get killed in the line of duty, what would you look for?"

Todd McKinnon began to chuckle quietly. "Nelse," he remarked, "let's put all our cards on the table; Mrs. Wyeth's and mine, that is, I don't expect much from you. The whole Road knows that Ralph Stort disappeared into thin air after he left the Gillespies' on Thursday, and that his sister can't reach him, so it's presumed you can't either. The place is buzzing. Talk about my imagination! John Devlin painted a word-picture that left any of my works in the shade, of Stort coming back on Friday evening and lurking in the canyon until after dark. Great Scott, Devlin didn't miss a thing, the thrill of hope in Stort's breast when he heard the sirens go off, the stealthy clamber along the hillside until he came to Ricky's car, the wait—"

"Vivid," said Nelsing shortly. "The point being, of course, that no warden could have patrolled the canyon during the blackout so that anyone could barge about all over the place?"

"That was the point. Most of the people up there know that canyon path like the backs of their hands."

And, Georgine thought uncomfortably, *Ricky and Claris heard someone there.*

"Devlin told you this, you say?"

"Uh-huh."

"When?"

"This afternoon, after Frey had broadcast the detective story. I think he knew I'd be likely to pass it on to you, if you hadn't already heard it."

"You heard that theory too, Mrs. Wyeth?"

Georgine nodded. "It's no sillier than the others," she murmured, pouring tea into her handleless cup.

"Just which others?"

"She's too kind-hearted to repeat 'em," said McKinnon, "but I'm afraid I am not. There's also the story that Mrs. Gillespie was a li'le too fond of Hollister at the beginning, and that their affection cooled, and she behaved in the manner of a woman scorned; or, on the other hand, that Hollister had threatened to tell her husband how far things had gone—reason for that yet unknown—and she felt he must be silenced."

"*You* don't need to invent any motives, for your stories," Georgine murmured. "Everybody else does it for you. Nobody believes these things."

"But it's instructive to hear them," said Nelsing. "Go on, Mac. What else has gone the rounds?"

McKinnon hesitated for a moment, and glanced at Georgine. "The Devlin theory. The only thing we're not sure of is whether it was in Reno or Las Vegas."

"I heard Reno," Georgine said. "But the person who told me didn't know whether the union was bigamous or simply adulterous."

Nelsing was looking at her with peculiar intentness when she glanced up at him. "It's horrible, really it is," she went on. "I was ashamed of myself for listening, and I'm ashamed now for having repeated any of this, even if you both knew it already. Yes, I know, when there's a murder investigation nobody can have secrets from the police—but to have them become public property, to have all the neighbors' ears prick up if you get upset and say something in a loud voice when the windows are open, and then have them run as fast as they can to spread the news—that makes me sick. It's not our business to suspect and accuse and gather evidence; that's *your* business, and I don't envy you."

Nelsing nodded. "But," he said, "you forget how interesting it is to me, to hear just who has been dishing out the accusations. Some of these stories, most of them in fact, may be either untrue or simply the sort of irrelevant dirt you always dig up when an investigation's going on. All right; nobody likes to have his private scandals dragged into the light; but if those scandals are true—more, if they're dangerous—what's the subject going to do? He'll say, why pay so much attention to me, when there's Joe Doakes up the road, a confirmed hophead?—or something like that. I'll bet good money that it was Mrs. Gillespie who spread the story about the Devlins. Wasn't it?"

Georgine said nothing.

"It sounds like her. Takes a woman to dig up something with a flavor of sex, and jabber it to the neighbors in a whisper." His tone was cool, disdainful.

"If she did," Georgine said with a flash of annoyance, "it wasn't out of malice. It was more like what you said, trying to turn our attention to somebody else's household. She's been nearly crazy with nerves ever since we found Hollister."

"As to that," said Todd McKinnon in his most casual voice, "we all sound nervous. Here I sit, elaborating valuable theories which Nelse would certainly pre-empt if he hadn't thought of 'em himself, first. Maybe I'm nervous too. It's a wonder that nobody in the Road has thought up the Case Against McKinnon." His tone burlesqued the words; then he caught Nelsing's eye, and his laughter cracked sharply in the crowded room, so that one or two of the other diners glanced at him. "Someone has? Not so slow. McKinnon is queer to begin with, and to make it worse he writes about crime. Suppose he's using some first-hand knowledge, and Hollister found out about it in his detective capacity and pursued him to the wilds of Berkeley, and was waiting to pounce; and McKinnon got in his licks first. Who's to know where a warden is during a blackout? Presumably he's making his rounds; actually he's not easy to place, unless there's an incident in his block and he has to report it. What if McKinnon hadn't gone home on Friday night? Did anyone think to search the Clifton house?"

"That one's strictly from hunger," Georgine said.

McKinnon considered. "Artistically," he said, "it wouldn't be bad. The old gimmick of having the most unlikely person turn out to be guilty is still going strong. I'll think of a better one, though. Suppose Roy Hollister was to be murdered, and his enemy wanted to have a perfect alibi. He imports someone completely innocent-looking, and uses that person—who has no connection with Hollister and so is never suspected—as an accomplice. There are all sorts of possibilities in that."

Georgine reached for the teapot. "Who's the accomplice?" she asked suspiciously.

"You, of course."

"Good. I'd hate to be left out." She grinned, and tipped the pot over her cup.

Then she looked up at Nelsing.

He was not smiling at all; his eyes were invisible behind dropped lids, and his forefinger was slowly tapping on the table.

She felt a warm drip on her knee, and looked down with dazed eyes, to see that she had poured the cup full and that the tea was running over its edge, over the surface of the table; and still the teapot hung suspended.

CHAPTER EIGHT

Trust Not Unlimited

FROM BESIDE HER, McKinnon's hand came out and gently took away the pot, and then went to work with a napkin, mopping. Across the table Howard Nelsing looked up, his blue eyes focused on a point beyond her. "Excuse me a minute, will you?" he said, and rose.

"H'm," Georgine said, trying to laugh. "We could have made an omelet with that last joke."

"Nothing's funny to Nelse when he's on a case," McKinnon said, also gazing intently after the detective.

"He wouldn't believe any of those stories were true? They were all fiction, weren't they?"

"Sure. He must know that. But he thought of something, all at once; something that was said gave him an idea, maybe."

"But what?"

He gave her one of his sidelong looks. "Couldn't tell you. I hope your life is an open book?"

"Well, certainly; but that doesn't mean I want it investigated. I didn't want to be *in* this."

"You can't always choose," said Todd McKinnon.

Nelsing extricated himself from the telephone booth and returned. "Sorry I can't stay to drive you home," he said remotely. "Here, Mac, let me have that check."

"I'll be damned if I will," said McKinnon cheerfully, keeping a tight hold on it. After Nelsing had gone he added, "Bad enough for him to horn in on the dinner, and get us a table.—Now what do you suppose struck him?"

"You're the one who ought to know, he's your friend."

"Acquaintance. Shall we go? Can you get us a cab, Charlie?"

Georgine got up thankfully. Somehow, in the last few minutes, the bamboo walls had seemed to be closing in on her, and the South Sea haze had become thick.

They walked up and down in the chilly air outside, waiting for the taxi. "What struck Nelsing?" the man repeated, musingly. "Great Scott, you don't suppose one of those stories could have hit close to the truth?"

"No," said Georgine uncompromisingly. "There are times when I think Hollister must have died by an Act of God. Look here, can you imagine any of these Grettry Road people being *bad* enough to commit murder?"

"It doesn't always take badness," said McKinnon. He gazed straight ahead of him, and for a moment there was no sound but that of their feet regularly striking the sidewalk. "It may be weakness," he said at last. "Somebody who's afraid of consequences, and can't stop to figure out the worse ones that come from murder. There are plenty of minds like that. It's an immature reaction, of course."

He stopped walking, and stood still on the pavement. Georgine also stopped. "Not those children! You can't be thinking of them again!"

"I could make you out a case against them," he said slowly, beginning once more to pace, "or against anyone in Grettry Road. And I wouldn't know which of 'em was possible and which impossible until the pattern begins to show up. Look; start at the top of the Road. Let's give John Devlin a real mistress in Las Vegas, and at the same time a sense of obligation to his wife.

He handles her money, he may have lost some of it or spent it on the mistress, but we'll put it on a higher plane and say that he recognizes Sheila's devotion and when he's at home stays faithful in his fashion." His eyes narrowed; the lights that spelled out "Trader Vic" shone fleetingly on the hard bony structures of his face and then they went on into the darker stretches of the walk and Georgine could no longer see him. "You know what kind of man Devlin is?" he said. "I'm guessing, from one thing I saw of him, but I think he's the victim of a conscience. He signed up for the sugar ration last May, and swore his family had no more than ten pounds. They had a hundred pound sack in the basement. All right, plenty of people had done the same thing. But Devlin couldn't do it and *forget* it. After he'd falsified that report it kept weighing on him; he told half a dozen persons about it. But he didn't give up the sugar."

"Well, what's that got to do with—"

"Not much, except that I think he'd be the last man on earth to face a blackmailer. The only way to get rid of 'em is to say, publish and be damned. But that means giving up one side or the other of your double life, and it's possible Devlin wants to keep both of 'em."

"You're thinking of Hollister as a detective? But he was supposed to have retired."

"That's something else," McKinnon said. "Maybe he had, but nobody believed it. Maybe Frey told that story before Hollister's death, and someone heard about it and got nervous. Devlin might have jumped to conclusions, and begun fighting with his guilty conscience, and compromised by getting rid of the only threat to his way of life—at least, that's how he'd see Hollister.

"Or," he went on, "what if Sheila Devlin had got wind of some of the double-life story through Hollister?"

"She wouldn't believe it, true or not. You have to say for her that she's loyal."

"Is she?" said McKinnon thoughtfully. "I'd say she was loyal to just one thing—her illusions. And you heard Claris say what she does to anyone who tries to shatter them!"

"Both the children have perfect alibis," Georgine said.

"Have they? You know, Ricky's at a very touchy point of his development. Hollister's made one or two nasty cracks at him, not only about his youth, but about what he does of nights. I can imagine him—"

"Well, don't," Georgine said. "I went to a lot of trouble to get Ricky out of a mess."

"So you did," he agreed equably. "Just what you might have done if you'd killed Hollister yourself and saw some kid being falsely accused."

"Don't start that again, joke or no joke."

"Very well. Take Frey. Hollister might have had some hold over him, maybe they worked some shenanigan over the divorce all those years ago. He lured Hollister out here, and lay in wait for six or eight months—"

"Good heavens," said Georgine, "if you put that in a story, could you get anyone to believe it?"

"If I worked hard at it," he said chuckling, "and ignored physical impossibilities. Here's the taxi."

They were halfway to her home before either of them spoke again. Then McKinnon, gazing at her through the darkness of the cab's interior, inquired abruptly, "Mrs. Wyeth, would you mind telling me what you're thinking of, with that soulful look on your profile?"

"About going to testify at the inquest tomorrow."

"Ah, yes. Does it worry you, or do you like thinking of yourself as the handmaiden of justice?"

"Neither. But I was thinking," said Georgine, "that I can't possibly go in cotton stockings."

Astonishingly, Todd McKinnon burst into subdued laughter that sounded almost affectionate.

The inquest was long and dull, and filled with words like "rupture of the mesentery" and "luxation of vertebrae."

Georgine looked round carefully, and, seeing no sign of Mr. McKinnon, determined that nothing exciting was likely to happen, or he would not have missed it. She was able to relax, to answer the few questions that were put to her with fair brevity and presence of mind, and nearly to go to sleep afterward—to be roused by the verdict.

Deceased came to his death as a result of being struck and run over by an automobile. No mention of blame, no mention of a possible driver. So that was all.

She had just finished her solitary supper at home when Inspector Nelsing telephoned.

"Mrs. Wyeth? I'm sorry to disturb your evening, but it would be a great help to me if you could come up to Grettry Road."

"Tonight?" Georgine said doubtfully. "And alone?"

"I'll—" he cleared his throat and seemed to hesitate. "I'll see that you get there. Someone will come for you. I'd like you to be present at an interview, and there are a few questions that must be asked on the ground."

He couldn't have sounded more impersonal, like the voice of Justice itself. She balanced the telephone in her hand, gazing absently out her front window. It showed her the long path that had been a driveway, and the artistic gate under the landlords' balcony. "That's quite all right, Inspector Nelsing. I'll do anything I can to help."

Framed in the aperture of the gate, like a picture within a picture, appeared the passing forms of Georgine's landlords, moving in a stately manner along the sidewalk outside. Their heads and shoulders seemed to swim along the top of the wall, and then to vanish. She thought, *What night is this?—Of course, Wednesday; Bank Night at the neighborhood theatre.* That meant they'd be gone until midnight.

Well, it was only seven now, and the light usually lasted until nine or after. You could hardly ask for more stalwart protectors than the police. Nevertheless, she put down the telephone slowly, almost reluctantly.

Nelsing himself drove up only a few minutes after she had gone out to the curb to wait for him. He wasn't in a conversational mood.

He took his car down into Grettry Road and parked it against the fence at the end. Another young man in plain clothes was awaiting him; they conferred in low voices for a moment. Then he helped Georgine out of the car, and, still uncommunicative, led her up the road to the spot where Hollister's body had lain. Nobody was about, but Georgine had an uneasy sense of faces at windows.

"While it's light, Mrs. Wyeth," he said, "I'd like to try an experiment. We may be some time at the Professor's."

Georgine stood still in the road. "Some time? I hoped we'd not be too late, my landlords have gone out and I'm afr—I don't like going into my house alone after dark."

"We'll arrange an escort," said Nelsing stiffly. "Now, where were you standing when you heard the sound you thought was footsteps?"

"On the Professor's front porch."

"Go back there, please, and listen. Slater"—this must be the other plain-clothes man—"will you walk as lightly as you can up the pavement, from that point, until Mrs. Wyeth tells you to stop?"

With a queer tightening of her midriff, Georgine thought, *Reproducing the crime. What on earth does he expect to prove?* She gazed straight before her, at the curve of cliff rough and gray in the dull evening light, and her nostrils widened to the aromatic scent from the canyon. Pretend it was pitch dark, pretend that once more the night pressed on her like a muffling curtain, and that the wind was damp and stinging on her face...

"Those sound like the footsteps, Mrs. Wyeth?"

"Not quite. Mr. Slater's are heavier than the sound I heard."

"Come back," Nelsing said to the silent young man, "and try it again, more quietly."

"That's more like it," Georgine called across to Nelsing. "How far did the steps go?"

"Try it again, please." She closed her eyes. Those sounds, up to the moment when she stepped out into the street, seemed burned into her mind. "Stop."

As if in a game of Ten-Steps, the silent young man froze in his tracks. Georgine looked up the road. Hollister's path had led him diagonally across the street, from the Carmichaels' toward Professor Paev's. He had been struck down midway in that diagonal, and Slater, moving away from the imaginary mark of X, had come opposite Hollister's own house.

She walked up toward the two men. "That's about right; but I called out, you know, and I didn't hear a sound after that. If there was someone walking away, he didn't move after he heard my voice."

Nelsing's eyes went to the grass and fallen leaves on the verge of the road. "He may have been making for the edge, where he wouldn't be heard," he pointed out. "He could even have taken off his shoes where he stood, and gone clear to the top of the road in his stocking feet. Damn it, if only there were servants, we could ask 'em about the washing."

"Could—the person have gone into Hollister's house? Did you find any signs of a burglar, or anything—or shouldn't I ask that?"

"No secret," said Nelsing. "We found nothing but finger-prints, all over the place; I guess Hollister didn't do much polishing of woodwork. Some of the prints might have been months old. But, the trouble was, everyone in the road was represented."

"Oh. How'd you get their prints to compare?"

"Various ways." He gave her a level look. "You left a beautiful set on the telephone in the hall. Other people had theirs on file already, in the civilian records. The point is, it doesn't help us. He'd had everyone in the place in there at those meetings. And his valuables didn't seem to have been touched, so it probably wasn't a burglar."

She remembered something else, and frowned. "When I went in to telephone, Hollister's door was closed but not locked. If the—the person had gone in that way, wouldn't I have heard the door open and close again?—Or no, maybe not, because by the time I'd felt that—the body by my foot, I wasn't in any state to hear small things."

"You're sure you didn't hear the door open?"

"Sure. And yet—you know, it seems to me that there was some other noise. I couldn't tell you what. It didn't seem— important, so maybe it wasn't unnatural; might simply have been the wind, or something like that." She put a palm to her forehead, pressing hard. "It can't mean much, but I wish I could think of it."

"Maybe it'll come to you," said Nelsing hopefully. "And tell me one more thing. Two persons came down, through the dark, to help you when you called. Did the footsteps of either one sound like the ones that stopped when you called out?"

She closed her eyes again. "I can't think," she said presently. "How could one tell, if the first ones had been on tiptoe? I couldn't be sure. I could never—"

She stopped, and her eyes went past Nelsing, up the road to the curve of the eucalyptus lot. Someone was standing there— surely too far away to have heard this low-voiced colloquy? As she watched, the figure moved away from behind a tree. It was John Devlin. Without another look he went toward his own house. A moment later the sound of a car's engine, starting in a garage, came down the hill.

Georgine looked at Nelsing. He stood with the level light full in his face, casting his shadow on the thick greenery of the Carmichaels' garden hedge. She thought, I suppose I'll always remember him this way, those eyes under the soft gray hat looking out at me with no more expression than a judge's eyes… He can't think I'm lying? Suppose I were guilty, how easy it would have been to lie about the footsteps, the dying words, everything.

"Let's go in and talk to Professor Paev," said Nelsing abruptly, "You too, Slater, if you please."

The young man said, "I'm right with you, Inspector," in a rumbling basso that surprised Georgine into a foolish impulse to giggle. She had almost expected him to go on, "So be-ware; so beee-ware."

The door of Professor Paev's house opened, and in the gloom of the blacked-out hallway stood the Professor.

"You are late, gentlemen," he said testily. "Was your conversation in the street so important?"

Nelsing said, "May we all sit down, Professor?" He waited in the hall until Alexis Paev, his high naked head moving like a dull moon in the twilight, had grudgingly flung open the door to the living-room.

"You want light, I presume?" the old man said harshly, and pushed a button. The overhead globe sprang into brilliance, its inverted shade reflecting coldly white against the ceiling; and all the colorless, expensive discomfort of the room was illuminated. Georgine sat down in the corner of a carved settee, and at once regretted her choice.

"It was good of you to receive us, Professor," said Nelsing formally. "There are a few points to be followed up in connection with the death of your neighbor last Friday."

"I know nothing about it. I told you on Saturday afternoon that I could contribute nothing."

"We understand that at the time of the accident you were in San Francisco, and didn't reach home until after the blackout."

"That is quite correct."

"You weren't caught on the train? Which one did you catch from the Terminal?"

"The, uh, nine thirty-four."

"That got you to Berkeley station about five minutes before the siren sounded. Did you take a cab home?"

"Young man," said Professor Paev with deliberation, "if it is any business of yours, I did not. The Euclid Avenue streetcar connected with the train, for once, and I rode past the campus on that. I debarked when the blackout began, hoping I'd be allowed to walk the rest of the way home. I am accustomed to the dark, and I carry a pocket torch. Do you think those officious sons of—I beg your pardon Mrs. Wyeth, those officious gentlemen in the white tin hats would let me proceed? They insisted that I must seek shelter. I sat on a stranger's porch, which was as near cover as I wished to get, for an interminable time."

"Thank you," said Nelsing. "That's very clear. And you walked home across the canyon after the all-clear sounded."

"I did."

"Now, Mrs. Wyeth; how long have you been acting as Professor Paev's secretary?"

"About ten days. I hoped to be through with the work before this, but what with murders, and having to stop work to go to inquests, I don't know when I can finish."

This was a sore subject with Georgine, and she saw no harm in letting Nelsing know it.

"What were your qualifications? Or rather, of what does your work consist?"

Georgine looked doubtfully at her employer. He had one long thin hand clasped about his chin, and over it his black eyes regarded her unwinkingly.

"I'm copying a—a sort of manuscript. It seems to have been worked up from notes about some sort of scientific process."

"What is the process?"

"Not you too, Inspector Nelsing! Everyone's asked me that, and I can't answer it. I don't know the first thing about science, only how to copy words."

"The Professor hired you in spite of this ignorance?"

"Because of it," Georgine said, and saw his eyes narrow.

"Why was that?" Nelsing asked the old man.

"Obvious, don't you think?" Professor Paev seemed almost to be enjoying himself.

"That's very interesting," said Nelsing. "Perhaps you felt it might be dangerous for your secretary to know too much?"

"Dangerous?" The black eyes snapped. "God help me, Inspector, you hadn't heard that story about the Death Ray?"

"I heard that," said Nelsing calmly, "but I also heard a much more arresting story. One of your neighbors, Professor, suggested that we find out what you were concocting in your laboratory that would be important enough to cause a man's death."

For a moment nobody said anything. Slater, in the background, bent his head over a notebook. Georgine found herself pressed back against the hard stuffing of the settee. From the ceiling, white light poured down on the glistening bald head, the smooth dark one.

Then Alexis Paev began slowly to lean forward, his eyes on Nelsing's face. "Hollister?" he said in a low voice. "You have found—some connection between Hollister and my laboratory?"

Nelsing smiled, with his lips alone, and the Professor sat back abruptly. "We don't often guess, Professor Paev," he said, "but we guessed at this. There was no other household in Grettry Road that was as tightly locked as yours. That laboratory is probably the only place to which Hollister, as a warden, wouldn't have had natural access. Did you ever show him through it?"

"Never," Alex Paev barked. "Though not for lack of asking."

"And you heard about the keys Hollister was carrying—an unusually heavy collection for a man to have with him."

"I heard nothing about them. I do not join in the gossip of this community."

"He had skeleton keys on his ring, Professor."

Before anyone could say anything to soothe him, the Professor was up out of his chair like a jack-in-the-box. He was raising his fists toward heaven and yelling, "Spies! I knew it! I am surrounded by spies! And this man, this Hollister, I trusted because he was recommended by the city. Everyone, the city officials, the University—spying on—"

"Easy, Professor," said Nelsing, his calm voice cutting into the old man's incoherent shouts. "The CD office isn't responsible for the private lives of wardens. The officials try to be careful, but they're not infallible. They've made some mistakes in appointments. But suppose they hadn't, in this case? Suppose Hollister had been an official investigator?" He leaned back comfortably, his forefinger gently tapping the chair-arm. "Some of the neighborhood gossip is reasonably well founded. I've heard it suggested that your research is secret, because when you've finished work you mean to sell the result to the highest bidder—whether he comes from the United Nations or the Axis! If it were a new and deadly gas, for example..."

"Ga-ah," said Professor Paev contemptuously. He had lowered himself slowly into his chair, and was watching Nelsing with unwinking eyes. "Gas, indeed! And as for selling, sir, I would die before I'd allow my discovery to be commercialized."

"What is it, Professor Paev? Can't you see this must be cleared up before we can go on?"

The Professor clamped his mouth shut.

"What is it, Mrs. Wyeth?"

Georgine jumped. "I don't know, I tell you."

"The Professor keeps it a dead secret, I can see. I wonder how he would feel if he thought someone was trying to find out what he was keeping so private. You suspected Hollister of that, didn't you, Professor?"

"I suspect everyone."

"Are you sure you didn't take an earlier train from the City? Your whole trip over there was on false pretenses. You never saw Mr. Wadsworth. Perhaps you never intended to see him. Who answered the telephone? Who took the call that purported to be from the Regent?"

"I did," said the Professor in a sulphurous voice.

"Was there ever such a call? Did you go to San Francisco at all?"

"God help me," said the Professor with a mighty effort at control. "Did I go—did I go! *She* knows!" He swiveled round and pointed at Georgine.

"Mrs. Wyeth?"

"I—I saw him start off in a taxi, but of course I don't know about the rest. And he told me there'd been a telephone call, he was elated about the news. But—Professor Paev, didn't you come back early?"

"What makes you think he did?" Nelsing asked.

"I said something about it," Georgine began, "and he looked terribly angry. Of course I don't mean to accuse—"

"Accuse?" The Professor was out of his chair again, thrusting a shaking hand toward her. "*You* accuse anyone? You've played your part well, I'll grant you, from the first minute; pretending ignorance of science, coming here by chance—by *chance!* ha!—to take this job. I see it now. You were in league with Hollister."

Georgine's voice came out in an outraged squeak. "*I* was? Are you crazy? I never spoke three sentences to him in my life!"

"Sure you didn't know him, Mrs. Wyeth?" Nelsing asked.

"Of course I'm sure. He asked me what the Professor was working on, and I told him I didn't know."

Nelsing's head turned, and the cold blue eyes rested full on her. She had never seen him look so remote and formidable.

"What did you talk about," Nelsing inquired, "when he called on you at your home?"

CHAPTER NINE

Spade Work at Sundown

HER FIRST COHERENT thought was, *He expected me to be good and flustered by that remark. Well, I won't be.*

"What makes you think he was there?" she said evenly.

"I went to talk to your landlords this afternoon. It was a routine check-up; I scarcely expected to hear anything interesting, but that's where we get our information—in the course of routine. The landlords looked at photographs, and picked out one of them. It was Hollister's. They identified him as the man who'd gone up the walk to your cottage, one evening last week while it was still light."

"What night?"

"Thursday, they thought."

"Did they happen to say I wasn't home?"

"They weren't sure but they mentioned the fact that he didn't come out again before they went to the movies, so they took it for granted you were there."

"I was up here Thursday, working. You know that, Professor Paev."

"Do I?" said the Professor, smiling. "I was in the laboratory, and you let yourself out."

Georgine realized she'd had that coming. "Inspector Nelsing," she said, "it was last Thursday when my house was searched. I found out about it when I went home, late. Harry Gillespie drove me to the door, so I can prove I didn't meet Hollister."

"Your house was searched," said Nelsing, meditating. "It's the first I've heard of that."

"It happened before the murder, so I didn't think to tell you about it. The desk sergeant convinced me it didn't mean anything, because nothing was taken. He's probably got the report filed under 'Hysterical Women.'"

Professor Paev walked across to her, exactly as he'd done on the first day she saw him, and bent threateningly over her chair. "That won't do," he said harshly. "It's a thin story you trumped up, when you knew you were caught. You were spies together, and you were the one to work from the inside. How many copies of my notes did you make? I should have had you searched every night. The whole thing is plain. He told you, foolishly, trusting to your look of innocence, that my secret was valuable. And you planned to have it all to yourself, you led him on until the last minute, and then—"

"You old coot," said Georgine furiously, "take your face out of mine. Get back, there. You—you dare to think up a ridiculous story like that about me, and say it out loud! Trying to turn attention away from yourself, that's what you're doing. You're afraid to have anyone get into that lab of yours, or look in the file cabinet. You'd be even more afraid to have the police look into that grave under your bathroom window!"

"That what?" Nelsing said incredulously. And then, seeing the look on the old man's face, he got slowly to his feet and moved forward with an ominous quietness.

Georgine turned to him. "He's got something buried there. Ask him what happened to the secretary he tried for one day, two weeks ago! He didn't keep her because she couldn't spell his name—he *said*. Did anyone ever see her again?"

She looked round defiantly. Alexis Paev was smiling again, with that odd lifting of the lips that had so little mirth in it. "*I* did not, I'll admit," he said, "after she had gone away by the canyon path. Doubtless her friends have seen her. Inspector, has the Acme Typing Agency reported the disappearance of any of its employees?"

"I'm bound to say it hasn't," Nelsing said. He looked at the old man with peculiar directness. "Is there a grave under one of your windows, Professor?"

"A flower-bed," said Professor Paev.

"Surrounded by shrubs?" Georgine inquired, breathing fast. "And placed so it can't be seen except from one room—his own?"

"If it's only a flower-bed," said Nelsing, "surely you won't object, sir, if we investigate it."

The Professor's eyelids lowered, very deliberately. He said in a curious flat voice, not quite steady, "You—you have no right. The woman is hysterical. I can't allow—"

His voice trailed off into nothing, and his head trembled.

"Slater," the Inspector said, "will you see if there's a spade on the premises?"

The sun had gone down, but enough afterglow lingered, reflected from the high fog above the Golden Gate, to cast a leaden light over the back gardens of Grettry Road. The high flowering shrubs quivered in the sunset wind, tapping and scraping against the rough stucco of the house.

It was chilly, but Georgine was still hot with wrath. She led the way around the house, standing back only where the bushes grew so thick that the men had to force their way through. "That's what I saw," she said grimly, pointing out the open space beside the blank wall. "Nobody was supposed to know about it. After the first time, Mrs. Blake told me that the Professor had a fit if anyone used his bathroom."

The Professor had joined the group, but stood apart from it. His black eyes were fixed, with a queer expression, on the shovel-blades that were scraping aside the covering of leaves, biting into the loose soil underneath, turning, lifting, turning. His long head moved, bobbing, a little at each thrust of the spades.

"This is preposterous," he said once, roughly.

Nelsing himself was taking a hand at digging. It seemed to require no effort, his speech was not even jerky, though punctuated with violent exercise. "Why didn't you mention this before, Mrs. Wyeth?" he inquired over his shoulder, tossing aside a shovelful of earth.

"It was here when I came, so I didn't think of that, either, in connection with Hollister's death. And I was working for the Professor—*then.*"

"You're not now?" Nelsing stepped down into the rapidly growing hole.

"Indeed I am not. I'll get that money back somehow, I hate to ask the doctor to lend it to me again, but I'll do it. I'll pay back every cent of it, and never come near this place again."

Professor Paev said nothing. He jammed his hands into the pockets of his shapeless coat, and his hot black eyes followed the spades; lift, toss, thrust, lift, toss. Georgine also watched the excavation, with a growing feeling of hotness at the back of her neck. What if they found nothing, wouldn't she look a fool? It wasn't possible that the whole thing was a gigantic leg-pull? The old man wasn't without humor of a malicious type. But he'd certainly put on a good act, if so; she'd have sworn that he was startled, reluctant to let the men dig...

Nelsing said, over his shoulder, "Did he ever try to do anything to you?"

"No. You think I'd have stayed if he had? I hardly ever saw him. That was what fooled me into thinking the job was all right."

Slater gave a muffled grunt, like a plucked string on the bass fiddle. "Spade hit something, Inspector," his asleep-in-the-deep voice came out of the twilight.

Nelsing had heard the little clink; he straightened up, balancing on the loose earth. Georgine leaned over the edge of the pit. Her heart thudded rapidly.

The young assistant bent down and found something long and thin, and knocked the soil from it. He rose with it, holding up his arm so that the fading light struck a gleam of dull white from the object.

In the background, Professor Paev did not move, but he gave out something between a sigh and a groan.

Howard Nelsing spoke, his voice shaken out of its usual calm into something like stupefaction.

"So help me," he said, "it's a thigh bone."

Shocks always went to Georgine's knees. She found herself sitting down weakly on the edge of the excavation, gazing with horror at Professor Paev. The darkness was drawing in fast, so that his bent-over bald head seemed to shine with its own faint luminosity. He did not move.

He looks caught in a trap, she thought. *Of course it wouldn't be any use running, trying to escape... I brought him to this, I gave him away.*

She wished she did not feel so obscurely sorry for him.

An electric torch shed its glaring circle on the earth, and the bony cage of ribs that projected from it. "Looks big,' Slater murmured deeply, as if to himself. His shovel stirred the earth again. "Here's another substance, Inspector; body wrapped in leather, d'you suppose?"

"Here," said Nelsing in a queer voice, "find the skull, will you?" The spades clanged fast, dragging away the loose soil. He grabbed at the rounded thing that was half uncovered, and lifted it...

Then he turned, with great deliberation, and climbed out of the hole, dangling the skull from his hand like a careless Hamlet. "I believe, Professor Paev," he said with awful courtesy, "that we have just dug up the skeleton of a calf and some portions of its skin."

"I believe," said Alexis Paev, "that you have."

"And what—what in the hell, Professor," said Nelsing, still politely, "were you doing with a calf? And why were you so reluctant to have us see it?"

The old man gave a long sigh, and turned away his head before he answered. "I had every right to it," he said dully. "It may have been on University property, but it—it was dead when I found it."

"Indeed?" said Nelsing. "I suppose you knew that the University doesn't care to have its livestock stolen. What was this, a sort of revenge because a cow got loose and trampled your garden?"

"No," said the Professor. A little of the old fire returned to his tone. "Anything I can get from the University is no more than due. They refused me—"

"Yes, I know," Nelsing cut in. "They wouldn't take all the endowment away from their other departments and give it to you for research." He sounded gentle, almost plaintive. "But why in the back yard, Professor? Just so you could gloat?"

"Let us go into the house," said Professor Paev, abruptly turning to lead the way. Mr. Slater lingered to pick up the shovels, and to help Georgine to her feet. He seemed to be suppressing some powerful emotion. She felt that her face might burst into flames at any minute.

"It is not so humorous as you think," the old man said absently, in the living-room. He turned to face the other three under the hard glare of the ceiling light. "I can make a general statement about my work, if"—he avoided Georgine's eyes— "you will promise to keep it a secret."

Georgine murmured something, and retreated to a corner.

"I needed animal protein as a soil amendment," said Alexis Paev. "It was necessary, to build some new strains of fungi. And gophers were not enough, nor a dog that had been put out of the way at the pound. I—I had to have that large fresh supply."

Inspector Nelsing looked at him sharply. "Professor. Your research isn't, by any chance, on gramicidin?"

The bald head nodded. "In that field, but I am preparing a germicide that will be equally effective on Gram-positive and Gram-negative bacteria."

"Well, for the good Lord's sake," said Nelsing mildly. "You might have got a hint of that from the notes, Mrs. Wyeth."

"I still don't know what it is," Georgine snapped.

"Yes, you do. It's been in the papers, and magazine articles."

"I don't take a paper. I read headlines off the newsstands. And that manuscript was nothing to me but a pack of scientific words."

The Professor began to talk, wearily, still not looking at her. A powerful antiseptic, one that would heal wounds in record time, made from the fungi that grew in earth around decayed animal matter... No cost, or almost none...healing of open wounds...others had been working on similar research for years, but they hadn't yet discovered how to make the germicide reactive on all types of bacteria... He had worked on it for five years, independently, and by certain additions and changes had evolved a new technique; that of anesthetizing the wound as well as destroying the germs...

"In a way," said Professor Paev, his black eyes turned toward the carpet, "it might be called a Death Ray, on infection and pain. It will be almost as sure. The University might have shared in the credit of my discovery, but it chose otherwise. It was then that I determined no one else should know."

"I should think, Professor," said Nelsing thoughtfully, "that it would be of incalculable value."

"It is. The treatment of war wounds can be speeded by sixty percent."

"The sort of thing a Foreign Power would try to steal, do you think?"

"Nonsense," said the Professor.

"I'm inclined to agree. A new gas, a bomb-sight, an explosive, yes; but not an antiseptic, unless they could get it with very little trouble. They'd scarcely have bothered to send a spy into your neighborhood and have him live there for six months, biding his time."

"Certainly not."

Georgine broke in. "You're not talking about Hollister?"

"Yes, I am. Now I think we may have a better picture," said Nelsing smoothly. Without a change of voice he let off his dynamite. "Professor, you've heard of the Fenella Corporation. In fact, you worked for them as research chemist, the first year you came back from Vienna."

Professor Paev seemed to have gone very still.

"A third-rate firm of chemists, and not too ethical. I imagine you found that out, and that's why you left them so suddenly. Would you have considered letting them handle your discovery, Professor?"

"Inspector Nelsing!" The black eyes darted light. "I have told you that I'd rather die than let my discoveries be commercialized. My antiseptic, sir, is to be a gift to humanity!"

"How would you feel toward someone who was planning to steal or copy your notes, so that Fenella Corporation could announce that one of its own research chemists, working independently, had arrived at the same conclusion as you? That happens all the time in science, doesn't it? You could scarcely prove that someone else hadn't had the same inspiration. Fenella Corporation could make a great deal of money from the sale of such an antiseptic as you describe. It would be well worth one man's salary and maintenance, over a period of months, living near you, trying to find out what you were doing, trying to get into the laboratory."

"Hollister," said the Professor thoughtfully, "posing as a warden."

"Not posing; being one. Who'd have a better excuse for investigating, knowing how your household was arranged, possibly getting in during your absence with the excuse that he'd thought a light was burning, or that he'd seen a prowler and was protecting your property?"

"You're sure that he was employed by Fenella?" The Professor wet his lips.

"A letter from them was in his mail, Monday morning," Nelsing said. "He must have destroyed all the other correspondence. There was nothing in his desk, in the house."

"I see," said Alexis Paev, still looking at the carpet. His long hands lay relaxed along the arms of the chair, but he gave a queer impression of holding himself wanly still.

"You're not surprised, Professor. You suspected him?"

"No."

"You didn't arrange your trip to the City last Friday with the express intention of fixing an alibi?"

The Professor twitched impatiently. "Alibi?" he barked. "When I told you frankly that I never reached the Wadsworth home?"

"We could have checked up on that, easily. You're too shrewd not to realize that, Professor. Much better to make it seem you were the victim of a false summons."

Professor Paev lifted his eyes, and again that incongruous smile appeared on his face. He was in full command of himself now, almost as if he had led his questioners by devious routes to the point where he could, with one blow, demolish their case. "You forget," he said suavely, "that in order to arrange this alibi, presumably for the murder of Roy Hollister, or whatever his name was, I had to invent a telephone call to myself at four o'clock in the afternoon; and this fanciful deception must be coincident upon the calling of an alert that very night. I had to know, six hours beforehand, that there would be a blackout—*which nobody knew*, including the police, the warden service of which Hollister himself was a part, and the Western Defense Command!"

He leaned easily back in his chair, and folded his bony hands. "A stalemate, I think, Inspector."

"Is it?" said Nelsing pleasantly. "At all events, you admit you were in this section of the city when the blackout started."

"In this general section, near the campus."

"If you had taken the train twenty minutes earlier, you might have been in the canyon, where no warden could see you, by the time the sirens were sounded."

"Do you think so?"

"And if you'd come home forty minutes earlier, you could have been in Grettry Road during the whole affair. Perhaps we could check on that with the train and streetcar employees."

"It is good of you, Inspector," said Alexis Paev formally, getting to his feet, "to keep this in the realm of hypothesis. In return, I will give you a bit of information that might interest you. As I approached the other side of the canyon, on my way home after the All Clear, I saw one of my neighbors turning the corner onto Buena Vista, in a car. He was leaving Grettry Road in a hurry. You might also check with the timekeepers at the Richmond shipyards!"

"Why, thank you very much, Professor," said Howard Nelsing, also rising. His courteous smile did not illumine his eyes. "I think that will be all for tonight."

He turned to Slater. "You brought your car? You live up on Grizzly Peak Boulevard, isn't that right? Then it'd be out of your way to drive Mrs. Wyeth home." His eyes touched her. "May I offer you a lift?"

"You may, thanks," she said, walking past the Professor with her head turned away and her chin firmly set. She got into the car, still smoldering. When Nelsing was beside her, "That old so-and-so!" she said wrathfully. "When I think of all the dirt I've taken for a hundred dollars!"

"Why did you do it?" he inquired.

"I needed the hundred dollars," said Georgine shortly.

"You got some of your own back tonight, anyway."

"Yes, as a part of your campaign to make people tattle on each other. If I'd known I was to be high-pressured, I'd never have come up here."

"See here, Mrs. Wyeth," said Nelsing quietly, "there's something you ought to understand. The police don't solve cases by inspiration. Ninety percent of the time we have to depend on information received."

"Stool pigeons, you mean." Her tone lashed at him.

He was unperturbed. "In the criminal classes, yes. In these rare cases in the upper middle class, hardly anybody wants to tell tales on his neighbors; and in this situation, where the murdered man was unpopular, nobody's willing to give us so much as a hint, unless we put on a bit of pressure."

She maintained an annoyed silence. "Take the deaf man, Frey, for instance," he went on. "He was eager to get that story about the detective agency off his chest. Then, for fear we'd lay too much emphasis on the fact that he'd known Hollister years ago, he mentioned—almost casually—that Mrs. Gillespie had more than once entertained Hollister at night. Mrs. Gillespie bursts into tears, threatens to faint"—there was a wry note of disgust in his voice—"and tells us that Mr. Devlin never talked to Hollister if he could help it, and acted nervous when he did. We do a little investigation on Devlin, and the pressure can be put on him, too."

Before she could stop herself, Georgine burst out, "That Las Vegas story wasn't *true?*"

Nelsing ignored the question. He went on, his hands expertly twisting and straightening the steering-wheel for the dark curves of the streets. "Devlin brought out the FBI story. Hollister was watching someone in the Road, he suggested; perhaps, Professor Paev. Paev to Wyeth, Wyeth to Paev, Paev to Gillespie. Most of 'em took a little side-swipe at McKinnon, too, but we didn't need to put any pressure on him. He fairly spouts information."

"Oh, dear," Georgine said. "Oh, dear *me*. Isn't anyone completely free from suspicion?"

"Yes," Nelsing said. "Mrs. Blake."

"That's right. She told me she was home, on the night Hollister died, with 'her husban', her daughtah, her two grand-sons, and her no-'count nephew.' I remember thinking that ought to have stopped you in your tracks!"

"We checked it," he said seriously, "as we did everything else."

"Including my mysterious visitor," she said acidly.

"Certainly. That was a shot in the dark, but it got something out of you, didn't it? When on earth," said Nelsing irritably, "will people learn that an investigator wants to know everything, no matter how irrelevant it may seem? If we'd heard about that grave earlier, we'd have had a clear line to Hollister's real purpose in Grettry Road."

"Well, you know everything now. And—I'm sorry to seem dumb, but what *was* Hollister? Not an FBI man, I take it, but—oh, please, not an international spy?"

"Hollister," said Nelsing grimly, "was a hired thief."

Georgine thought this over for a moment, and sighed. "What a fine street I chose to work in. That sort of coincidence isn't like me, either; I mean, I'm the type who always gets to the fire after it's all out and the engines have left. Just bad luck this time, I guess."

"Don't you see, Mrs. Wyeth," said Nelsing quietly, "that all these things started happening *because* you went to work for the Professor?"

She looked round, startled. "You can't think—"

"Hollister'd been hanging around there for months, watching his chance. Maybe he'd managed to get access to the Professor's files before, and had found that the experiment wasn't finished. Naturally, this Fenella Corporation would want its information as complete as possible, so he waited. Then, a secretary turned up—you, as it happened—and Hollister knew the notes were to be typed into a workable form, which meant the research was almost done. He had to work fast, now, and copy those notes before you'd finished typing, and rush them to his employers so they could beat the professor to the draw. It was your arrival that gave the signal, that set the whole thing off."

"Oh, no. But that's uncanny, because the first day I went there Mrs. Blake met me at the door and said, 'We been waitin' fo' you.' It gave me a horrible shiver, just for a minute; and then I thought it meant something quite different. But it was true," Georgine finished in a low tone, and drew her coat closer around her shoulders.

"Someone was waiting for you, certainly. Hollister."

She frowned into the darkness. There was something that had been troubling her all evening, ever since she'd learned his true mission. "Wasn't that blackout convenient for him, though? I never heard of anything that came so pat, just when it was needed."

"It was handy, all right," said Nelsing, suddenly ferocious. "But believe me that lad knew how to take advantage of it when it came." He added a string of lurid adjectives to qualify the lad's name, and did not apologize. "When I think of the way he deliberately fooled the Warden Service! They wouldn't let in an habitual criminal, they take all the precautions they can, fingerprinting and investigating, but how in the hell can they spot a man who joins for the express purpose of committing his first crime? All that zeal, all that patriotism—the whole thing was a fake."

"No, it wasn't," said Georgine surprisingly. "He meant it."

"Nuts." Sometimes Nelsing relaxed his official formality, and the moments frankly gladdened her heart. She thought, *I'm doing all right; if I have the nerve to contradict him now and then, it's more like a conversation!*

"Nuts nothing. I heard him talk. He came to Berkeley last August, and I really don't believe he got the United States into the war in December, on purpose to make his job easier! If any bombs had really fallen last Friday, he'd have been in there pitching, saving lives, doing his job. It's perfectly possible to be a real patriot and still do something that—that may be wrong but that may seem all right to you. You know—if you could see all Hollister's letters from that corporation, maybe you'd find that *they'd* fooled *him*; told him, maybe, that Professor Paev meant never to release his germicide and that the corporation would be doing something for humanity if they could manage to get hold of it."

"You're very charitable, Mrs. Wyeth. You're not by any chance including yourself in those excuses?" Nelsing made the suggestion so gently that for a minute she didn't catch his meaning.

"Now, look, Inspector Nelsing," she said, "You can't really think I had anything to do with this. I started you on the investigation myself, by telling you about the dying words and the footsteps. You think I haven't any sense?"

"Well," said Nelsing simply, "you're a woman."

Georgine flounced fiercely in her seat. "According to you, women are all cowards and liars, and spiteful and senseless! I suppose a policeman does get the seamy side, and not much else, but you—you ought to know better."

"I'm very sorry," said Nelsing in his politest tone. He stopped the car in front of her house.

I didn't mean, she thought, *to carry it to the length of fighting with him!* She swung round to get out, wishing she could stalk away by herself, with dignity; but there was the dark path behind the gate, and the dark house, and the shuddering moment before her hand found the light switch.

"Would you mind coming in with me?" she murmured ungraciously.

"Not at all." He was as maddeningly calm as ever.

She stopped on the sidewalk. "Listen," she said incredulously. "Am I hearing things?"

From the gloom of the rear garden came a thin rippling strain of music. "*In einem Bächlein helle, da schoss in froher Eil'…*"

The tune was clear and simple as running water; it was incongruous enough to be funny, heard like this from the darkness; and for some reason it rasped on Georgine's nerves.

"That can't be our friend Mac?" Nelsing said. "What's he doing, sitting on the doorstep waiting for you to come home so he can pump you?"

"Crudely put, but probably far from wrong." She started up the short walk to the gate. "You'll come in anyway, won't you?"

"Certainly." He sounded indulgent, patronizing, moving beside her. "You afraid something'll jump at you out of the yard? It'll be darker yet next month, when the dimout starts."

Georgine was conscious of lingering, trying to prolong even this impersonal moment with him. "Do they have to do that?"

"Afraid so. The city lights make too much skyglow."

Both of them looked up at the sky. "I suppose they do," said Georgine, sighing, and putting her hand on the gate.

Against the fog the pots of petunias on the landlords' balcony, directly above, loomed like huge round heads peering over the edge. "Only good thing about it is, the stars will show up better." She pushed hard at the gate, which seemed to be stuck. "You ought to see them in Colorado, on cold—*Look!* Is there someone up there—?"

On the balcony above, one of the huge heads seemed to be leaning gently forward, as if to get a closer view of her, its bulk curved and black against the sky-glow. She stood with her face tipped up, one hand still outstretched to the gate. It seemed queer that she couldn't move...

Dreadfully inexorable, the head leaned farther; faster, faster.

CHAPTER TEN

Murderers One to Seven

THE EARTH SWUNG UP on edge and struck her, hard and searingly rough on arms and chest and knees. Beside her a dark form skimmed horizontally as if sliding for base. Behind, and terribly near, sounded a great shattering explosion.

Too stunned, too breathless to scream, Georgine lay gasping with her face buried in grass and leaves. Howard Nelsing had scarcely touched the ground before he was up again, with an acrobatic leap to his feet, and away—toward the corner of the landlords' house. Someone else was coming, running fast down the dark pathway. Or was it running away?

Outside the whirling ache in her skull the sounds came, clear but far away. A deep voice shouted, "Here, Mac! Hurry up, head him off at the corner." There was a sudden thunder of feet on the balcony's outside staircase. Those running steps had been Todd McKinnon's. He was bending over her, calling into her ear, "Georgine. Georgine, are you hurt?"

With an immense effort she raised her head, got up somehow to a half-sitting position. McKinnon's arm was behind her shoulders. "Are you hurt?" he repeated quietly.

"I—I don't think so. S-Skinned a little. What *was* it?"

"One of the big flowerpots fell," said McKinnon grimly, "just where you were standing. Lucky you saw it!"

"I couldn't move," Georgine said, her teeth chattering. "I saw it tipping over, and I c-couldn't get—get away. He must have p-pushed me, or thrown, or something—"

The light casual voice soothed her. "Take it easy. Do you feel any pain? Ankles all right?"

"I'm—I'm fine. Where—what happened to—"

"He's having a look around," McKinnon said. "Feeling better? Sit quiet for a minute."

In the neighboring houses lights were going on, windows were raised. "What happened?" voices called. "Did you hear that? Where was it?"

Nelsing came back, breathing hard. "Got away," he said gruffly, "if there was anyone there. Damn it, McKinnon, you might have given me a hand."

"I'm a first-aider," said McKinnon mildly, "not a cop."

The detective's torch flashed briefly on the gate; then he stepped closer, examining something. "So that was it. There wasn't anyone here to chase. It was a booby-trap; string tied to the gate, to make that pot overbalance when the pull came." His foot stirred among the scattered earth, the limp petunias and jagged fragments of pottery. "Must have weighed fifty pounds."

He stepped suddenly to the walk, intercepting the first of an excited group of neighbors. "Just an accident, ladies and gentlemen," he said smoothly. "This lady and I managed to jump out of the way in time. Yes, a big flowerpot; you can see for yourselves.—Get her into the house, Mac," he flung over his shoulder. "Carry her if you have to. No, I forgot. I'll do it."

"I can walk," said Georgine crossly. "I'm all right."

There was a blank interval, and she found herself miraculously on her feet, going up her own front steps. "That could have killed us," she said earnestly to McKinnon. "That could have killed both of us. That could have—"

"Yes, I know. Sit down a minute, and let's see what that fall did to you."

The sight brought back her senses with a rush. "My stockings!" Georgine wailed. "My last good ones, in *rags!*"

McKinnon materialized from the bathroom with a bowl and a washrag. He passed the cloth gently and expertly over her face, brushed leaves and twigs from her hair, and then turned his attention to her knees. "You took most of the skin off your legs, too," he remarked mildly. "Bleeding in one or two places."

"Skin grows in again," Georgine snapped. "Nylon doesn't. Oh, *dear.* And not another pair to be h-had for love or money." Her voice was perfectly all right, except for an annoying tendency to break in the middle of words.

"She hurt?" Nelsing said, coming in and closing the door behind him. "Sorry I had to throw you around, Mrs. Wyeth."

"D-don't mention it." She gave a little gasp of laughter. "You—you—just in time…"

His small gesture silenced her. "Mac," he said deliberately, "how long have you been here? Where were you?"

McKinnon did not look up from his task of applying iodine and gauze. "About twenty minutes. Sitting on the steps."

"You were"—Georgine began faintly—"you were playing—"

"I heard you coming, and I was afraid I'd startle you if you happened on me suddenly. I knew you were out, Mrs. Wyeth; you and Nelse passed me on your way up to the Road."

Nelsing stood looking down at him, his blue eyes cold and remote. "How did you get into the garden without pulling that thing down on *your* head?"

"Came in the back way," said Mr. McKinnon casually. "I've made a habit of it, luckily."

"A habit?"

"Yes. I've called on Mrs. Wyeth once or twice." He finished the bandaging and rose, meeting Nelsing's eyes for the first time. "Want to make something of it?"

"No. A call's innocent enough. That contraption, out

there"—Nelsing gestured over his shoulder—"that was malice. Somebody figured on a ten-to-one chance of killing *her*."

"Not I, I assure you," said McKinnon. "Somebody else. Take that suspicious look off your face, Nelse. Don't you get the similarity? Somebody who hasn't quite the guts to use a gun or knife, somebody who takes these chancey methods— running a man down with an automobile, setting a trap that may or may not work—leaving a loophole for the victim to escape through, to soothe his conscience—" He looked round at Georgine, his straight sandy brows drawn together. "But why you?"

She sat upright, an incoherent jumble of words forcing their way out. "How should I—I won't be classed with Hollister, that's a lot of—you know I've had nothing to do with this in any way, b-both of you know that!"

"But you were there when Hollister died," McKinnon said, looking at her intently. "If you were a witness, perhaps someone wants to put you out of the way." His eyes glinted suddenly. "By God, Nelse," he said in a hushed voice, "it's the Nervous Murderer. Old Number Four."

"What are you holding back, Mrs. Wyeth?" said Nelsing.

"Nothing!" Georgine got to her feet, found they wouldn't support her, and fell back on the couch. The room began to tilt oddly across her blurred vision.

"Here," said McKinnon quickly, "lie down. Put your feet on this pillow."

"I'm all right. D-Don't fuss."

"You look mighty pale for a well woman," said the quiet voice.

"Well, I feel pale. But don't fuss over me, please! Just g-go on talking for a few minutes."

She let her eyelids fall. She could hear the two men moving about the small brown room; plenty of noise they made, too, their feet clumped so in those big shoes... Funny sound in this house of women; no men in your life for seven years, and then suddenly two at once.

She heard McKinnon's voice, running on without cessation, without hurry. "I thought for a while this one might be a standpatter. Thought it with hope, I'll admit, because I've never seen one yet. It would have been a good set-up, come to think of it: a murder committed on impulse, or almost so, and then—just nothing. No panic, no give-away, no evidence. You haven't got any material evidence, have you, Nelse? I thought not. Someone was smart enough not to leave fingerprints."

His voice faded away and resumed from another point in the house. What was he doing in the kitchen, opening and shutting cupboards? "But this attack comes along, and Number One is out. A standpatter would hardly take a chance like this. Number Two wouldn't either; the Perfect Murderer. He makes his plans in advance, and arranges to leave no evidence, or to frame someone else. And it isn't often he repeats. Repeaters choose simpler methods."

He was back beside her. "Come on, Mrs. Wyeth, turn your head and take a sip of this."

She smelled alcohol. "Where'd you find that sherry?" she murmured dizzily. "There wasn't much left..."

"Drink it," Nelsing's deep voice commanded her. "It'll do you good. Too bad you haven't any brandy."

"Go on talking," Georgine said, managing to rise on her elbow and drink a little of the sherry. It wasn't much good, but it warmed that icy place in her chest. "What were you j-jabbering about, number one and number two?"

"The types of murderer-character," McKinnon said.

"He's got theories," Nelsing observed.

"No sneering for the duration, if you please," McKinnon requested as lightly as ever. Then his voice took on once more the tone of a lecturer fascinated with his subject. "As every murder investigation develops, it reveals a pattern; and that pattern is caused by the character of the murderer. There are approximately seven types. Number One, the Standpatter; Number Two, the Perfect Murderer—you can spot him," McKinnon interrupted himself with a ghostly chuckle, "because he's thought it out so cleverly that he usually forgets some simple li'le point and trips himself up. Number Three, the Repeater. Repeaters come under two heads: the sort who kill for money, over and over, get themselves made beneficiaries of insurance and then get to work with the poison or what not; and the sort who kill for ritual or with a kind of sadistic pleasure. Most of them want to be on the spot to see the victims die, and all of them, peculiarly enough, choose victims who are alike, who belong to the same, uh, ancient profession, for example. But in this case," the pacing feet came to a stop, "I don't believe we've got a Repeater, because there's no connection between you and Hollister in anybody's wildest moments of imagination, including mine."

"He thinks there is," said Georgine vengefully, opening her eyes to look at Nelsing. His expression did not change. Todd McKinnon lifted her upright and put a pillow behind her. "There," he said. "Feeling better? Want me to go on while you finish your drink? Well, there's Number Four, the Nervous Murderer. We'll come to him in a minute. Number Five, the Damn Fool. He leaves a trail a yard wide, all the evidence pointing to himself, but just the same he'll deny his guilt up and down. Once in a long while you'll find one like that who just happens to be innocent."

He strolled up and down, his hands in the pockets of his tweed jacket. He seemed completely immersed in his own theories, but he was watching Georgine narrowly if covertly. "Number Six you might call Policeman's Li'le Helper. He's frank and cheerful and comes round to the police with theories and evidence that'll point to somebody else, or mix 'em up. They're supposed to overlook him, because he's so coöperative. Of course," continued Mr. McKinnon smoothly, "I don't count political assassins, nor hopheads. The homicidal maniac is out too."

"Huh," Nelsing said, almost snorting. He was sitting quietly, patiently, on the hard seat beside the fireplace, his arms tightly folded across his chest. His grave eyes watched McKinnon, occasionally shifting to Georgine.

"Out for fiction purposes, I mean," said Mr. McKinnon, gently reproachful. "There's only one type of maniac I can recognize, and that's Number Seven; the sort of person who's not mad on the surface, but hides a twisted mind under a perfectly normal appearance. With that type again, there's usually some sort of plan or obsession, traceable through the pattern; and again, I'll be damned if I can think of any similarity between a virtuous young housewife who's doing a li'le typing on the side, and a retired detective."

"A hired thief," said Georgine bluntly, without thinking. Nelsing opened his mouth as if to stop her, but McKinnon was in ahead of him. "Thief?" he said, struck with a kind of holy joy. "Whose house was he going to burgle? No, wait; I think I know. The Professor's, because the old boy was lured away for the evening. Right?"

"Near enough," Nelsing grunted.

"Okay, so there's even less connection." He swept on. "But the Nervous Murderer, Number Four; there's my pal. He leaves his mark as plain as an oily fingerprint; as soon as he begins to act in character, the pattern shows it. He's the standpatter gone wrong. He can't let well enough alone, he tries to escape or to go back and clean up evidence—*or* he's so nervous that he takes a crack at a possible witness. And damn it if this bird doesn't look like that type. You agree with me, Nelsing?"

"Maybe,'" Nelsing said. "Well, are you through with your little bedtime story? Then—if you're feeling quite recovered, Mrs. Wyeth, may we discuss the solid evidence?"

"I guess so," Georgine said. She had been considerably revived by the sherry and the even, impersonal flow of McKinnon's voice had given her mind a chance at adjustment. He said now, "I haven't a cigarette on me. Will you give her one, Nelse?"

"All right, Uncle," said the Inspector a trifle grimly, lighting the cigarette for Georgine. McKinnon, having seemingly arranged things to his liking, retired to a corner and sat down with his knees crossed. Absently he took his mouth-organ from his pocket and tapped it silently on the palm of his hand.

Howard Nelsing pulled up a straight chair and sat facing Georgine. "Is there something else you know, Mrs. Wyeth, that you haven't told me?"

Georgine opened her mouth, and found she wasn't quite ready for the inquisition. The blue eyes were looking right through her again, and the rugged face was implacable. "Must we go on," she said irrelevantly, "using Mr. and Mrs.? Or Inspector? After all, you gentlemen have been throwing me around the front yard and taking my stockings off. Can't we use something less formal?"

"Any way you like. Now, tell me, please. Is there any suspicion, any evidence, that you've been holding back?"

She took a deep breath. "On my word, there isn't."

"Something you forgot?"

"Not anything I can remember now! Except—" She shot a glance toward the corner.

"Claris told him about the rendezvous, after I'd talked to her a bit more," McKinnon said.

"Oh. Well, then, that's all. N-Nelse, you remember I came to you that first day, with everything—not only the evidence about Hollister, but all the stuff I'd imagined or suspected, too. The business about the house-searching and the grave—well, you know why I didn't mention those. Otherwise I didn't hold out on a thing. That'd be foolish, wouldn't it, when all I wanted was to help? I don't suppose you've thought of me as—what did he call it?—the Policeman's Little Helper who's a murderer on the side."

Nelsing said, "Let's go over this from the beginning. I telephoned you at seven-thirty. When I got here you were waiting on the sidewalk. Presumably nobody knew you were going out, until that moment. You told no one? Right. We got up to Grettry Road, and as I remember, you said something about your landlords being at the movies until midnight. You said it aloud, in the open street."

"There wasn't anyone in sight. Well, yes; Mr. Devlin at the top of the road—but he couldn't have heard what we said, do you think?"

"I don't know. He was there, listening, was he? Throughout our conversation?"

Georgine nodded.

"It's a possibility. There's another, though; and I was a crashing fool not to think of it and investigate. There might have been someone behind that thick hedge."

"All the neighbors," Georgine said slowly, "have been in there picking flowers, at one time or another."

"So," Nelsing said. "Well, I should have looked; but it was all innocent stuff, we'd been over it before, and I had no idea the talk would be dangerous. Whoever was there had plenty of time to get down here in the dusk, and go up the outside stair to that balcony, and rig up a trap. It needn't have been a man, any more than it had to be a man driving the car that ran down Hollister; but I'll say *he* for convenience. He heard something, in that conversation of ours, that made him feel you had dangerous potentialities as a witness. That's one idea. Let's work on it."

"Go ahead," said Georgine. "But I can't think—"

"You figured out for us how far those footsteps had gone. I asked you if you'd recognized them."

"And I said I couldn't."

"Think again, uh, Georgine. Was there anything peculiar about them? The tempo, the length of a stride? A limp or hesitation?"

"I couldn't tell you to save me."

From his corner, Todd McKinnon spoke. "That's nothing to kill a witness for. Even if she'd identified them, that wouldn't mean anything in a court of law."

"Shut up, Mac, I know that. But suppose the murderer didn't?"

"You mean somebody's going to throw flowerpots at me because I very firmly said I did *not* recognize footsteps? I don't believe it."

"Very well, we'll leave it. We'll go on. We talked about fingerprints; nothing there to alarm anyone. Then you said you thought there was another sound, after the footsteps. You couldn't remember what it was at the moment. Have you remembered since?"

"No."

"Will you try to think of it now?"

She tried, while the room held itself still, while the two men looked at her; Nelsing as if to hypnotize her into recollection, McKinnon with an air of rigid suspense. Finally she spread her hands helplessly. "If it was anything, it won't come back to me. It couldn't have been important, Nelse; it must have been something like a barking dog, or an owl. It didn't make any impression of—unnaturalness."

"Well," Nelsing said heavily, "that wouldn't be cause for trying to kill you."

"Are you sure," McKinnon observed, "that the flowerpot business was meant for Georgine?"

"Who else?" Nelsing said.

"I just wondered—are you holding out yourself, Nelse? Have you dug up something that you didn't recognize as important? Go back over your own conversation."

"That won't do," said Georgine, entering into the spirit of research, "because nobody knew he'd be bringing me home. I didn't know it myself."

"Yes, you did," said Howard Nelsing almost under his breath.

"Why, no. All you said was, someone would pick me up."

"You knew, just the same." It might have been wrenched from him. For a minute their eyes held; then Georgine sank back, looking beyond him, her lower lip softly folding over the upper.

"All right. Skip it." His teeth shut together with a click. "It boils down to this, that you know something that's dangerous, somebody feels you must be put out of the way before you betray him. What is it you know?"

"Shall we go round again?" said Georgine testily.

"Will you promise me something?" He leaned forward until their knees were almost touching. "Will you try to remember what it was you heard? It's important. I've a feeling that it's what I need. Will you try?"

"No, I won't," said Georgine.

Nelsing pushed back his chair and got up, slowly. "What do you mean?"

She looked up at him, towering almost to the ceiling of the small room, his gray-clad shoulders outlined against the brown and cream of the walls, his face angry. Her heart began a dull thumping rhythm; but this had to be said. "I mean I won't help you if it means making a target of myself. It was bad enough tonight, having the Professor accuse me of that nonsense; and he didn't try to kill me, he couldn't have rigged up that flowerpot because we were with him every minute. But if there's a murderer listening to everything I say, and possibly planning to take another crack at me, I want him to know that I'm no menace to his safety!"

"You'd—deliberately conceal evidence?"

"Oh, no. I've given you all I had, and if I could remember now what I heard I'd tell you like a shot. But. I won't spend a week trying to remember."

"Just how are the various suspects to know that?" Nelsing's eyes had turned bleak.

"Todd's going to tell them," said Georgine, glancing at the motionless figure in the corner. "Everyone talks to him. He's going to let drop the fact that I've—as the detectives say, I've withdrawn from the case."

"I can't let you,' said Nelsing harshly. "You hold the key, can't you see that?"

"I don't care if I hold a whole bunch of keys. I'm through."

"That flowerpot business," said McKinnon's voice languidly, "was a long shot. Ten to one, I'd put it. Anyone who pushed at the gate was almost sure to hear the thing scraping, and look up, and jump out of the way. May have been meant just to scare you out, Georgine."

"If it was, it worked perfectly. I'm good and scared!"

There was a silence. Nelsing gazed incredulously down at

her, and McKinnon raised the mouth-organ to his lips and blew through it. One faint chord sounded.

Howard Nelsing spoke, at last. "Scared out," he said bitterly. "Rather let justice go to pot than take a nickel's worth of risk!"

"Is that how you rate it?" Once more Georgine looked up at him, "Now you listen to me for a minute. Have you thought about Barby? She's seven years old. Her father died five months before she was born, and for two years I fought for every minute of her life. She's just begun to get well since we came down here to a low altitude. If I take risks, and go round making myself into fine material for a second murder, and if I do get killed, who's going to take care of her? She hasn't anyone in the world but me, except some second cousins of my father; and where do you think they were the last I heard of 'em? *In Java.*"

Her eyes had gathered light and intensity until they seemed to give out sapphire sparks. She got to her feet and stood facing Nelsing. "I can't help what you think of me. This attack tonight has changed everything. I don't give a hoot for justice! You can catch your murderer or let him loose, I don't care. It won't be through me. Todd, isn't it safer this way?"

"Can't help agreeing with you," said McKinnon.

Nelsing's dark brows drew together. He looked from one to the other, and made a contemptuous sound in his throat. "Sounds like the way the isolationists talked, before the war," he said, "Save your own skin and let everyone else's go. Lock yourself in your own tight little house and never come out!"

"That's just what I intend to do," said Georgine.

"And," he went on as if she hadn't spoken, "plenty of those characters turned out to be fifth columnists." He took a step that brought him close to Georgine and looked down into her face. "You did know I'd be here tonight. I picked you up from the sidewalk: you didn't touch that gate until we came home; you begged me to come in with you..."

With a wrenching effort she controlled herself. "You'd

better go home. Haven't you forgotten some of those grand police manners?"

Without another word he snatched up his hat and stalked out the door. She flung a sentence after him. "Thanks for saving my life!"

Nelsing looked over his shoulder, and the corner of his mouth twitched up. It said as plainly as words, "I doubt you were worth the trouble." Then he was gone, and the front door closed with ominous gentleness.

Georgine spun on her heel. Only Todd McKinnon was left, and on him she directed the full blaze of her fury.

"That fool, that idiot! And you're just as bad, you babble those crazy theories and act like a harmless screwball, and in the middle of it you slip in a suggestion that someone was trying to kill Nelsing! He'd never have thought of it without you! What does either of you mean, accusing me of—of—"

"Steady on," said Mr. McKinnon, rising in a leisurely manner. "Nobody's accusing you. That was a slip of the tongue on my part. I meant Mr. X, not you."

"All right, all right! Fine time to say so! And he's gone away thinking—thinking I don't know what! You act as if I'd wanted to be in this affair. All I want is to do my job and earn what I've been paid for it and get out!"

The hard-textured face remained completely unmoved. Todd McKinnon stood looking at her without expression, and after a moment she stopped and drew her palms vigorously across her face. "I'm sorry," she said more quietly. "Temper's my besetting sin, and you've been treated to too many displays since we met."

"I don't mind," McKinnon said. "Easy to see why you get mad; it's your substitute for whining, or collapsing in tears. Besides," he added with a faint smile, "it makes your eyes bluer. Very becoming."

Georgine glared at him. "There are times when I detest men. Always thinking up the worst motives—I knew Howard Nelsing despised women, but to have you—"

"I like 'em," said McKinnon peaceably. "I'm very, very fond of women."

"So I've noticed," said Georgine, lashing out in all directions. "Claris Frey seems to think of you as a great beau, and I've no doubt that Mrs. Gillespie—"

"I like them," he continued unperturbed, "because I've had 'em around me a lot. No, not the five wives; my four sisters. Why shouldn't I like them?"

"Go home," Georgine said. "Do for heaven's sake go home."

"I don't want to leave you here alone," he said bluntly.

"I'll be considerably better off that way!"

He was standing half turned away from her. He said something under his breath; it sounded like "Damnation." Then Todd McKinnon swung round, took Georgine in a hard embrace and kissed her soundly.

For a moment sheer surprise held her quiet in his arms. There was time for her senses to register what had once been familiar and sweet, and had almost been forgotten since young Jim Wyeth died; warmth, and the scent and texture of male skin, and the sharp prickle of close-clipped hair; nothing more.

Nothing more. She stood back, breathless and half laughing, and he let her go at once. "Well!" Georgine said, and let her hand slide to his and pat it, briefly, gratefully. "That's a new way to cure hysteria, but it worked. Did they teach you that in the Warden Service?"

The agate eyes looked out at her from their deep caverns. "No," he said thoughtfully, "no, they didn't. I picked it up by myself." He went back to the chair in the corner and got the mouth-organ which he had laid down there.

"I'll really be all right now," she went on cheerfully. "It was only my getting worked up, but you'll admit it was nat—"

The rest of the word never came out. She sat down rather suddenly on the couch.

So there had been something more, after all, and it had just got to her. She looked at his averted head with astonished respect. Well, for heaven's sake. And he looked so cool and controlled!

Incredibly, she found herself hoping he'd do it again.

There, he was turning; he was crossing the room, bending toward her...

McKinnon's hand descended on her shoulder, in a gentle pat. "You're a nice woman, Georgine," he said casually. "You're one of the nicest women I ever met. Don't take anything second-rate; you can have the best, you know."

He turned at the door. "If there's any disturbance in the night, you might call me. I left my number near the telephone." Then, with perfect aplomb, he gave her a slight wave of the hand and was gone.

Georgine began to laugh, helplessly, without much mirth. *Rags to riches; riches to rags,* she thought... *Handed right back to me... I'm so tired I could die, and I can't even fling myself across the bed as I am; I have to wash my face and put up my hair in curlers, and empty the pan under the icebox or there'll be a mess in the morning... I wish Barby were home! I want Barby, just to look at her, to know we're both safe...*

And then the thing she'd almost forgotten came flooding back into her mind: the picture of the huge thing like a head, leaning slowly over her, falling... "There was malice behind that..." She hadn't wanted to be in this!

She could do only one thing to save herself. She must sit very still, crouching, not moving, like a field creature frozen to escape the eye of the hawk.

CHAPTER ELEVEN

The Lady Who Vanished

THE KNOCKING WOKE HER; knuckles tapping, diffidently but with persistence, on her front door. In the moment between sleep and waking Georgine found herself burrowing under the covers; trying to fling off that recurrent panic. She'd never feel safe again, not anywhere.

Then, as she reluctantly pulled herself upright and reached for her housecoat, another memory came swimming to her mind's surface: a rugged face and a pair of angry, hostile blue eyes. With a shock of relief she knew that anger or no anger, that was where safety lay. It might be elsewhere too, but she was sure only of Nelsing.

It wasn't he who was knocking. There would never be any diffidence about his touch. She peered cautiously through a crack of the door, and saw the last person on earth whom she'd have expected.

Professor Paev was speaking before she could get the door shut. "I apologize," he said fiercely, and cleared his throat like a sea-lion demanding fish. "I have come especially to apologize, Mrs. Wyeth."

Oh dear, she thought, *I wish he didn't look so old and broken even when he's fiercest. I wish I didn't owe him anything.*

"Come in," she said grudgingly.

The Professor sat down on the edge of her big chair, looking at the floor and crushing his hat into a shapeless mass. "My assumptions about you were quite unwarranted," he said. "You have never shown any open disloyalty, and last night you—though you might have been more helpful, you did not deviate from the canons of scientific truth." He paused. That part had been prepared; the next sentences came out in a broken rush. "I—I can't get anyone else, there's no one who can—it's got to be done, Mrs. Wyeth, it's the work of six years, and if it's not announced soon there will be—Could you over-look my rudeness," said Alexis Paev, almost humbly, "and come back to finish the paper?"

Georgine said nothing. She sat gazing into space, her lower lip pushed up. She didn't feel safe in her own home, in broad daylight; she would be scarcely more uneasy in the Professor's house, guarded by the stalwart Mrs. Blake; and the humiliation of going to Barby's doctor and asking to borrow back the money that had paid her debt would be almost too much...

No, that wasn't it. She looked at herself with bleak honesty and thought, *Howard Nelsing hasn't finished his investigation. He'll be there, at Grettry Road, some of the time anyway; and he'll never be here again.*

The Professor spoke once more. "If you have any doubts about your own safety," he said pleadingly, "they can be laid at rest. The police are there for most of every day. I myself will escort you home if you like—and if I am not too absorbed in the laboratory," he added very seriously.

Georgine could not restrain a grin. "That would hardly be necessary, Professor Paev," she said, and knew she was lost. *The police are there.* H'm. Had the old galoot read her mind?

"Very well. I'll be up as soon as I can make it."

"I brought my car," the Professor said. "I thought if I could persuade you to come back, it might save some time." She glanced out the window. Sure enough, there at the curb stood the vintage coupé.

"You'd have to wait while I got dressed and ate."

"Food, food, food," the Professor snarled.

"Yes, food. It'd do you good if you thought more about it," said Georgine severely, reflecting that she'd better keep the whip hand while possible.

The Professor drank two cups of coffee and ate four pieces of toast, in an absent manner which indicated he didn't know what he was doing. He drove his car, she discovered later, in much the same manner. "I'll never be nearer to death again," she told herself, clutching the door-handle of the coupé and uttering mental prayers as stone walls, trees and blind curves loomed at great speed over the car's hood, and were miraculously avoided.

As the car stopped in Grettry Road she drew a great sigh. This was partly relief that she was still alive, and partly the return of that oppression she had felt, increasing every day, as the Road closed around her.

The Professor let her out, looking grim. As they passed the upper end of the road, a muffled but unmistakably derisive "Moo-oo" had floated from an open window. Somehow, the story about the calf was already current. She suspected Mr. Slater.

The car moved toward the basement garage, and she saw, climbing up from the canyon path, the tall figure of Howard Nelsing. He caught sight of her, and stood still.

Georgine walked toward him. He didn't look angry any more. "You came back, then?" he said.

"I came back."

"Does that mean…"

"It means I'm going to finish my job."

"You haven't—remembered anything?"

She met his eyes. "I still don't care about justice."

And that was all; except that during the morning, the African Queen brought up a note: *I told them. You'll be safe enough now. Chin up. T. McK.*

Safe enough, Georgine thought. Only two more days of work, and she'd be finished—if there were no more interruptions.

But when she went out at noon, there was no sign of a policeman, and the road lay quiet under a gray sky. This sunless weather gave an oddly changeless quality to the hills and the houses. The light looked exactly the same when she emerged again at mid-afternoon, and now the street seemed not only asleep but half dying.

There was someone awake and alive; Georgine started as the urgent whisper reached her. "Mrs. Wyeth! Oh, please, Mrs. Wyeth, come in here for just a minute."

Georgine stopped in the street, looking toward the door from which the call had come. She didn't want to talk to Mimi Gillespie, she was busy, she'd come out only for a minute...

But Mrs. Gillespie had been crying, her blond prettiness was blurred and swollen; and she hadn't dressed; she was hanging pathetically against the edge of the door, wrapped in the familiar white chenille housecoat and wearing white fur slippers like two small muffs. She was in trouble.

Reluctantly, Georgine moved up the front walk. "I can't come in, I'm afraid," she said gently.

"Oh, you must! *Please.* I was so afraid I'd miss you, I've been watching for two hours, I was going to watch till you started home. I tell you," said Mimi, "I damned near *prayed.*"

She laid her hand on Georgine's arm, almost forcing her into the house. "I've got to talk to you."

"But why me?" Georgine inquired, somewhat dryly.

"I need someone so badly. And you're nice, you're not like these old cats up here that wouldn't—wouldn't believe anything I said. You know what trouble is," said Mimi, her brown eyes filling, "and you'll help me. I know you will."

"Well—what is it?"

"Come on out here." Mimi pushed her into the kitchen, whose windows overlooked the street. "Have a drink, won't you?"

The bottle of Black and White was almost half gone, but it had been opened recently; the tinfoil seal still lay on the kitchen table. "No thanks," Georgine said.

"Well, I will. God knows I need it." Mimi poured a generous four fingers. "Look here, Mrs. Wyeth, maybe you don't know what's happened."

Her brother, Georgine thought swiftly. *They've decided he was the murderer, they're on his trail...it isn't possible she's got him hidden here?* She took an instinctive step toward the door.

Mimi put out a hand. "They've got Harry down at the police station."

"Oh. Not—under arrest?"

"They said for questioning, but he's been—he didn't come home at all, they got him from work—he hasn't been home all day and I don't know when they'll let him go."

Georgine sat down slowly. "That may not mean so much."

The golden head turned from side to side, as if in pain. "He was here the night Hollister died," Mrs. Gillespie said drearily. "They made him admit it. He just let on to go to work, his night off had been changed to Friday and he never told me. He let me think he'd be gone, so he could c-come back here and maybe catch me. And all because he heard me telephoning to Roy that morning about something else—oh, I don't know what to do."

"I'm terribly sorry, but I don't see how I can help you."

"You've got the inside track with that cop, what's his name? Nelsing. You know what he's thinking, you can tell me what I—"

"I'm afraid you're mistaken, Mrs. Gillespie. The last thing I have is an inside track!"

"Go on," Mimi said roughly, "he's in love with you."

Georgine gave her an incredulous look, and glanced at the bottle.

"No, I'm not tight. I wish to God I was." Mrs. Gillespie sloshed another generous portion into her glass. "Anyone could see how he feels. I was looking out the window this morning when you were talking to him, and..."

"My dear," Georgine said, "far from being in love with me, Inspector Nelsing half believes I'm a murderer."

"Ba—I mean baloney. If he's made you think that, he's trying to fool himself 'cause it makes him mad to fall for a woman. I know that much," said Mimi, swallowing, and turning her flushed face toward Georgine. "He despises me; I know that too, and he'll think the worst of me if he can. And so I don't know what to do. You've got to help."

She began to cry again, her lips loose and quivering, but after a minute she rubbed the tears away with the sleeve of her robe. "He thinks Harry was jealous because Roy used to come here nights after he was gone. Well, he was jealous, but there wasn't any reason. There wasn't! What if I did take Roy pies and things when he first moved up here? He was all alone, and a bachelor, and I didn't do it for very long. By that time he'd started to pal up with Ralph, with my brother, and it was Ralph he came to see."

"You could tell the Inspector that yourself, Mrs. Gillespie, if that's all. I'm not sure how much it would help."

"No, I can't!" Mimi whispered. "I can't let anyone know he came to see Ralph."

"Why not?" There was a cold feeling at the pit of Georgine's stomach. "You—you don't know anything about Hollister's death that you haven't told? You don't think it was— your brother that killed him?"

"No—oh, no!'" Mimi laughed, forlornly. "He couldn't have done it, Ralphie couldn't. He's the one person on earth who couldn't!"

"You mean you have real proof of that? He has an unshakable alibi?"

Mimi swayed a little, recovered herself, and looked at Georgine. "You bet he has." Her hand came up, rather unsteadily, and the white sleeve fell away from the arm as her wavering forefinger pointed at the sky. "He was—up there!"

Georgine found herself standing. "Up where?"

"Sidd—sit down, won't you? Up there flying around, that's what I mean. It was Ralph that made the blackout, in his plane."

Georgine sat down again, very slowly, her eyes fixed on the disheveled silhouette of Mimi's head against the gray window. Outside sounded the majestic steps of Mrs. Blake, going homeward. They died away. Now her vision and hearing narrowed again, to take in the homely setting of this kitchen, and to echo the fantastic words that had just been spoken.

"He wasn't!" she said at last, incredulously.

Mrs. Gillespie's head went up and down in a portentous nod. "Oh, God,'" she said then, faintly. "Maybe I shouldn't have told you that. I'm—I've been half crazy, I tell you. I go to the police and say Harry's innocent, they say how do you know, and I have to tell 'em, and get my brother into the worst jam—I don't know what they'll do to him if they catch him, or if they know what he did; and suppose that he got away after all, they could go after him!"

"But—but, my dear—you can't have this straight. He had his own plane, did he, before the war? But don't you know that those planes were immobilized the day after Pearl Harbor? I think they had to take out the engines and turn them in to the authorities, at least in the defense area."

"Sure," said Mimi wearily. She sat down and rested an elbow on the enamel table, her hand supporting her rumpled head. "And in about a week they told people to put their engines back in again. The ships had to be kept under guard or somep'n, there was an old deputy sheriff they had watching Ralphie's plane. There aren't any public hangars out there in the sticks, I guess his was the only ship for miles around. And he—I don't know how he fixed it in the end, but he was going to get the sheriff away or give him a Mickey, so's he could get the plane out."

"You knew about this beforehand?" The head nodded again. "But *why*, Mrs. Gillespie?" Georgine felt her preconceived ideas spinning into confusion. "Your brother had quarreled with Hollister, I know, but he couldn't possibly have—provoked the blackout on purpose, knowing that someone was planning to—to kill—"

"He did it on purpose, all right." The heavy eyes came up and dwelt somberly on Georgine's. *"Hollister made him do it."*

The spinning ideas flew together, all at once, and fused into their inevitable whole.

"So that was it," Georgine breathed.

That said it all. The incredible coincidences were there no longer: Professor Paev's absence from home, Ralph's disappearance, the blackout coming on that very night. She remembered Hollister's terrifying word-pictures of what would happen if you didn't shut yourself into your refuge room, his threats of penalties.

Hollister had engineered the events of that night—up to a point. With a clear field, he could have gone completely unobserved and at his leisure to Professor Paev's laboratory. He'd have had time to inspect the almost-completed notes, perhaps copying the ones he needed, or abstracting some of the carbons—whose absence afterward could be blamed on the typist's carelessness.

A clear field. What would Hollister have done if he'd found her, Georgine, unexpectedly in the house? Well, that wouldn't have been ruinous. As the warden, he was the one person who might have a legitimate errand there. He could have got rid of her somehow, told some story...

An accidental blackout wouldn't have been the same thing. There'd be no way to gauge its length, nor the time when it would begin. But with Ralph's plane up there above the fog, Hollister would know that it would take some time to chase and identify it. Weren't the patrols up over the Bay all the time, in foggy weather? But perhaps they were all flying half blind in that thick mist. He could have counted on at least forty minutes of darkness. The plan must have seemed perfect.

And before he could begin it someone had killed him. Someone had thought, perhaps mistakenly, that he knew Hollister's errand in Grettry Road, and had feared for his own precious secrets; someone had baited his trap with a tiny spark of light, so that person must have known, too, that there would be a blackout that night.

Mimi knew it.

The long, stunned silence was broken by the clink of bottle against glass. "I wish I could get tight," Mrs. Gillespie said dully. "I might get up the nerve to do something about Harry."

Georgine said, "You're sure you haven't—worried yourself into imagining this? How on earth could Hollister have made your brother do anything so dangerous, to himself and everyone else?"

"Ralphie had to. He *had* to. Didn't you guess Roy was— after him? He was a Fed, Roy was."

"Did he tell you so?" Georgine exclaimed. How had he dared? Weren't there penalties for impersonation?

"Why, no." Mimi gazed at her wild-eyed. "We—just knew. At first he talked to us just like anybody, and then he got Ralphie to talkin' about the gover'ment, Ralphie always hated it no matter who was in, he always felt he didn't get a fair deal in life, him or nobody else who grew up between wars. And it used to be all right to say so, nobody cared how you felt before—before we got into this. He shut up after that, he was afraid. But Roy knew already. And then when we got in the war, he—he changed. And then Ralphie and I were both afraid," Mimi said, taking another drink and gasping, "We didn't know what they'd do to him for handing round those pamp'lets in L.A., and there was what happened to Pelley, and all."

Poor Mimi's little veneer of correct speech had worn away, and the true self was coming through, common, not too brilliant, pitiably devoted to her husband and her worthless brother. Georgine felt a pang of sympathy. The little creature must have been living in a hell of terror.

"And Roy—about a couple weeks ago, he told Ralphie maybe he wouldn't have to turn him in to the gover'ment if he'd do something to prove he was loyal after all. It was to—to carry some secret papers to Mexico, somep'n the army or navy fliers couldn't do, because it was secret service. If he did it, Roy said, the gover'ment would forget about him being a Silvershirt."

"Your brother didn't believe all that!" Georgine said in spite of herself. The minute after, she thought: *Of course he did. Someone "told him what to do," and he was frightened enough to think he must obey.*

"I dunno," Mimi said despairingly, "He was scared to and scared not to. He thought he might get killed, shot at or somep'n, but when Roy said what they'd do to him if he didn't try to go on this business, he thought he might's well die. He was—he hated Roy, but he couldn't keep away from him. He'd go see him, nights, or beg him to come over here after Harry left."

Georgine could hear Hollister saying, "You can quit doggin' my footsteps." For a while, his monster had turned on him, watching his every move. He had to get Ralphie away, so that he might make sure of being completely unobserved. It would be doubly secure if he knew where Ralph was—and with the same stroke perfected his own plan.

She said slowly, "Your husband didn't know about this?"

"Oh, God, no. We'd never dare tell him. He hated Ralphie, he only had him here because I begged, and Ralphie swore he'd forget all his old ideas. Harry would've—jumped at the chance to—" Mimi dropped her head in her hands.

She had had to stand by, credulous and terrified, and watch her brother being mentally tortured, and never say a word. *How she must have hated Roy Hollister,* Georgine thought.

And thought again, with a dreadful shock, *I shouldn't be listening to all this! I shouldn't know anything about it.*

"Have you told this to anyone else?" she said. "To—Mr. McKinnon, for instance?"

"No!" Mimi said. "Not him! I wouldn't—" There was a little silence. "I was nearly crazy," she added, her voice going dull again. "Ralphie didn't have near enough money, and I couldn't get any more out of Harry without him guessing. I thought I might have to borrow. Then Roy said he could maybe get a little bit, and he come in with thirty-seven-fifty, and that about did it."

"He gave your brother some of his own money?" Georgine breathed. Surely, when that happened, they must have seen that it was all false...

"Sure. He was trying to help, Roy was. He said he'd back Ralphie up"—Mrs. Gillespie poured it all out, her words tumbling fast—"if he got caught. He'd keep still about the reason why Ralphie had to steal back his plane and get out of the country. He'd say it was all his fault, Roy's I mean, because he worried so about the way people didn't take the war hard enough and thought there wouldn't be any more blackouts, and if there was one it'd teach 'em a lesson. He was going to say that. Or maybe he wouldn't," she added tonelessly. "Maybe he'd of let Ralphie down. So Ralphie told me all about it before he went away on Thursday. He was s'posed to go up to the ranch and stay there till Roy phoned him, when there was a fog and it'd be safer. And then he had to circle round over here, once or twice, so Roy'd know it was him, and be sure he was doing like he was s'posed to. And then he was going to make for the border. He had an extra gas-tank in his ship, and it'd ought to 'a' been about enough to get him there.

"I don't know where he is, or what's happened," she cried out suddenly, in a dreadful voice, and got to her feet, swaying. "I never saw him nor heard from him again, after Thursday. And I tried, I called up Roy that morning after, and begged him and begged him not to make Ralphie do that, only I couldn't say it right out. I guess he didn't mind me knowing," her voice dropped again, miserably. "He had me where he wanted. He knew I'd never give Ralphie away. But Harry heard me phoning and that's why he come back here that night, and—have I got to tell? Have I got to?"

Georgine thought it over. "I don't know if it would help. Don't you see, if Harry only *thought* he had a reason for jealousy, that'd be plenty of motive? But, Mimi, listen to me. The police ought to know this about your brother. You just have to tell them everything you know."

Mimi looked at her. The brown eyes were not focusing well, now, and Georgine wondered, *Can she still think clearly?*

But it seemed she could, up to a point. "They'll think I—" she whispered, and could not go on for a moment. "They'll think—they asked me how I felt about Ralphie. That dick, he says, 'You're very devoted to your brother, ain't you, Miss Gillespie.' That's how he says. He'll hear about this, and know I knew there was gonna be a blackout, and he'll think I—"

"That's a chance you'll have to take," said Georgine.

"I'm scared," Mimi said. "I'm scared. You didn't think it'd help if I told, and so I'm not gonna. And don't you tell!"

"I'll go down to the police station with you, if you want. I'll back you up as much as I can."

"And s'pose they haven't caught Ralphie?" Mimi said with a kind of sodden shrewdness. "I'd be giving him away for nothing. I don't know what they'd do to him! They might think I made up that story about Roy makin' him do it, nobody couldn't've heard Ralphie telling me about it. If they had, they could anyway say that was what he believed; but there wasn't a soul around who could've heard us."

"Not your husband? He couldn't have—pretended to be asleep, and crept downstairs to listen?"

"No," said Mimi Gillespie. She got up, not too steady on her feet, but not actually staggering. It was remarkable that her speech had not thickened. "No. We was—we went down there," her arm described a sweep toward the canyon, "behind that little round clump o' bushes that makes a sort o' room. I wish there'd been somebody who'd—Oh, I wish I could get tight and not be scared."

"Don't you take another drink," said Georgine firmly, snatching the bottle before it could be tipped up. "You're going to put on your clothes this minute, before you lose as much nerve as you've got, and go down to the police with me. You must, Mimi! This might not get Harry free, but it'd give the detectives something new to think about. If you don't—I'm awfully afraid I'll have to tell them."

"No! Oh, for God's sake, don't you. I—I guess I'll tell 'em," poor Mimi said on a groan. She began to move toward the hall door, her tousled golden head hanging, her furry slippers padding with a touching childishness. "You let me tell, please. You just back me up." She passed into the hall, her hand lingering on the doorpost. "If there was just somebody—but *nobody* could've heard us."

Her feet, still remarkably steady, padded on down the hall. The door that closed off the staircase opened; the footsteps paused. Then, "*Oh*, my God," said Mimi Gillespie in a stifled voice; the door slammed behind her, and Georgine heard her feet thudding on the stairs. Somewhere another door closed.

"Sick," Georgine said half-aloud, with a wry smile. She had never been one to rush in and hold people's heads; Mimi might better be left alone, to become more sober.

She thought: *If I can just stay impersonal, if I can only get that poor creature to tell her story and be done with it!* Nelsing wouldn't allow any miscarriage of justice.

But what if Mimi, her tongue loosened by whisky, had told the truth only up to a point, and then been afraid to go on? She had pointed out her own strong motive for hating Hollister, but she hadn't said "I didn't kill him."

Well, in that case, thought Georgine, moving into the living-room in search of cigarettes, *in that case, she's the one who has to tell about it. I couldn't give her away by myself, going up to Nelsing's office, all virtuous.* "I think you ought to know, Mrs. Gillespie is a murderer." *I couldn't*, Georgine thought with a shudder.

She had never been in this house before. She glanced around the L-shaped living-room, exactly like the corresponding room in Roy Hollister's house. Looking at Mimi, you'd expect to see an ultra-feminine room; but this was furnished for the comfort of men. The sofa and chairs were of colored leather, they were big and roomy and equipped with footstools. The place had been exquisitely neat, but a thin one-day film of dust now lay over every surface.

The gray afternoon light came hard and merciless between the slats of the Venetian blinds. The house was very still, except for the dry wind that now and then slid past to rattle a window.

Georgine smoked her cigarette, and stubbed it out, and waited. She began to wonder how much time had passed; five minutes, ten, a quarter of an hour? She hadn't looked at the small electric clock when she entered the room. And how long was it since she had heard Mimi's feet softly thudding on the staircase? There had not been a sound since then, she realized; she had never heard those steps moving above her.

"Oh, *dear*," said Georgine aloud, exasperated. She was rather startled at the way her voice came back from the empty room. "Oh dear, I bet she passed out cold."

She ought to go and see, she supposed. The hall, a dim, chilly passageway, stretched from the front door to the mid-portion of the house. Its end was closed off by two doors; she pulled open the right-hand one.

Yes these stairs led to the upper story. She began to climb steadily, for some reason acutely aware of the thudding of her own feet on the carpet. It was rather like that first day, when she had come down so innocently into Grettry Road, and no one had seemed to hear her, and her footsteps had echoed so queerly in the afternoon silence. There was only one bedroom up here, and a dressing-room and bath. Their doors all stood open, and through those doors she could see perfect order; and the day-old film of dust, again; and not a soul in any of the rooms.

A curious little chill went racing over her skin. It was so *still*, so still she could hear the faint drone of the electric clock on the bedside table, and a tiny thwack on the roof that might be a falling seed from the eucalyptus; and—something else, like music.

It was a tune clear as running water, and it was being played very smoothly now. It might have been going on for an hour, but she hadn't listened consciously until now, until she had begun to grow cold with this eerie feeling of something gone wrong. "*In einem Bächlein hel-le...*" every time she heard it before, it had presaged terror or danger; McKinnon's mouth-organ, playing *The Trout*.

"Mrs. Gillespie," Georgine said aloud, hoarsely. "Mrs. Gillespie, where are you?"

She made herself move to the closet doors, fling them wide. Nothing there. Nobody behind the shower curtain, nor on the high-railed sun deck built over the living-room ceiling. Nobody here at all.

"Mimi!" Georgine heard herself almost screaming.

She was downstairs again, standing in the hall, her cold hands clasped tightly together. Mimi couldn't have come unseen down the stairs, past the living-room door.

She looked at her own face in the circular mirror above the hall console, and for a moment scarcely recognized it. A drop of water trickled suddenly in the sink, and made her start painfully.

It couldn't happen. It was like the *Mary Celeste*, no sign of violence, no sign of life. It *couldn't* happen; but Mimi Gillespie had run up those stairs, and at the top had vanished into thin air.

And, all at once more frightened than she had ever been in all her life, Georgine Wyeth snatched open the door and almost tumbled through it. The door banged to behind her, and the clap of sound echoed in the stillness of Grettry Road.

CHAPTER TWELVE

Rimmed with Steel

THERE WAS NO ONE in sight. *I've got to get out*, she thought, and went up the steep slope at a half run. Lucky that she hadn't taken off her coat, that her keys and purse were in its pockets. She climbed frantically, like a miner who hears the walls of the shaft crumbling behind him. If she could only pass the top of the street unmolested, it seemed as if she would be safe.

"Hi, Georgine," said a familiar voice. The hedge rustled, and there were footsteps coming after her. Georgine turned away her head, and almost ran. "Hi, wait up for uncle!"

McKinnon came up beside her, easily matching his stride to her hurrying feet. The echoes of that damnable little tune were still teasing her ears. She thought, *He's always there, announcing terror like those messengers in the Greek plays... that first day, when the Road felt so scary and I was uneasy without knowing why, the afternoon before Hollister died, last night...now.*

"My word, you're in a hurry," he said. "More sensitive guys might take this as a brush-off."

"Oh, no," Georgine assured him, with no idea of what she was saying. "Not at all. It's perfectly all right."

"Surely you're not going to be embarrassed about last night?"

"Oh, no, not at all. It's perfectly all right."

"Handy set of phrases, those," said Mr. McKinnon, chasing along beside her. "Seem to fit any situation. If you're sure it's perfectly all right, how about conceding the race?"

She looked sidewise at him, and saw the hard planes of his face, and the quizzical eyes under their jutting brows. She thought, *Am I off my head, tearing around the Berkeley hills in broad daylight as if someone were after me? This is only Todd, walking home with me after a day's work, trying to put me at my ease.*

Her pace slackened. "I don't know why I was in such a hurry."

"You were looking for Mrs. Gillespie, I take it," McKinnon said casually. "I heard you calling her. Wasn't she home? Seemed to me I saw her early in the afternoon."

"Yes. No." Some instinct stronger than thought kept her from telling him, from telling anyone.

Anyone except Howard Nelsing.

So that was where she was going; hurrying to the only place of safety. Then, with a reviving spurt of inner laughter, she thought: *A fine thing when I can't feel safe anywhere except at the police station; and haven't I walked myself into a steam, though?*

She jerked her handkerchief from her coat pocket, and her compact came with it, shooting halfway across the road and scattering powder, puff and mirror. The mishap restored her to sanity. "Oh, dear!" Georgine said furiously, stopping short. "Oh, *dear!*"

McKinnon was laughing as he retrieved the battered objects. "Such profanity," he said, restoring them. "You must have been very well brought up."

"As a matter of fact, no," said Georgine, walking onward.

"Is that all you ever say, Oh dear?"

"When I'm deeply moved I say Oh, dear *me*."

"You don't, uh, know any other words?"

"Plenty. My father dragged us around every mining camp in the southwest, when I was little. I've had to forget the vocabulary, though, because of Barby. I don't want her to be like the kid next door, telling the kindergarten teacher that he would be damned if he'd make any more of those lousy paper mats... Laugh away if you want to, but it doesn't sound funny when it's your own child."

"I'm overcome with respect," McKinnon assured her. "When I meet Barby, I'll curb my own language. Do you smoke in front of her?"

"Oh, yes. She urged me to. It seems that most of the other mothers smoke, and Barby's anxious to have me conform."

She looked at him again, and added with ominous sweetness, "I amuse you?"

"Not you, Georgine. Just femininity. And I'm with you all the way on the—Well, well; there's the good Inspector. Going up to Grettry Road, d'you suppose?"

"Nelse!" Georgine cried out, in a tone that made McKinnon glance at her sharply. Nelsing stopped his car beside the curb.

"I was going," he said, and cleared his throat, "I was going up there to get you."

"I trust," said Mr. McKinnon smoothly, scrambling uninvited into the car, "that you're offering me a lift home, too."

"I seem to be," said Nelsing, a trifle grimly. He backed the car around and headed south. "You left early, Georgine. Did the atmosphere get you down after all?"

"M-More or less," she said, relaxing in exquisite relief. Todd's inconsequential chatter had begun the process, but this was needed to finish it. Now she could put her terror into words. "Is Harry Gillespie still being questioned?"

"We let him go about an hour ago," Nelsing said.

"Then he's probably home by now. And if she was hiding, she'd come out when she heard him."

"If who was hiding?"

"Mimi."

"God's sake," McKinnon said, over her shoulder. "What were you doing, playing hide-and-seek? Way you were calling her name, it sounded as if you were begging her to come back from the dead."

"What's this about?" Nelsing said peremptorily.

"She—we were talking," Georgine said, gripping her hands together, "and I'd talked her into—I mean, she wanted to go down to the station and see you, Nelse; something about her husband. She was pretty tight, but she was able to talk. And then she went upstairs to get dressed, and—disappeared into nothing."

No sound came from the back seat. Nelsing, looking straight ahead, pulled the car to the curb and stopped. "Disappeared in her own house?" he said slowly.

"Yes." The blessed relief of saying it was tempered by an uneasy caution; Mimi had meant to tell the story herself, it would not be fair to give it away. "I went up after her, and there wasn't anybody there. Not anyone at all."

Nelsing squared his shoulders around to face her. "Do you know what you're saying? You looked for her?"

"Oh, everywhere. It scared the daylights out of me."

"Did you *see* her go up?"

She shook her head. "Heard her. And then—nothing. She couldn't have come down again without passing me."

"You're sure of that? H'm. What shape was she in?"

She wet her lips. "Upset; about—about Harry, mostly."

"Suicide frame of mind?" said Nelsing.

"Good heavens! I never thought of that. But what could she have done to herself?"

"Jumped out a window."

Georgine shut her eyes, visualizing those empty rooms. "The windows were all closed, except for one open a crack in the bedroom."

"Off the sun-deck, then."

"That's over the living room, isn't it? I'd have heard her walking; and I never heard a sound after her feet on the stairs."

Nelsing seemed to relax. "On what stairs, going up or down?"

Her eyes opened and she looked at him, startled. "I don't know."

"Look," he said kindly, "didn't you happen to think how those houses are built? There's a short flight of steps going up to the bedrooms, and another that goes down to the game room.

"*Oh,*" Georgine said on a long note. "I forgot. The poor thing probably passed out down there. Somebody ought to be told about it, she might lie there for hours."

"We'll call up Gillespie," Nelsing said, stepping on the starter. "Your house is nearest."

"So," McKinnon's mild voice said from behind her, "that's why you were in such a dither when you came out."

"Had me going for a minute," said Nelsing. "Here, where's your door key? Let me have it." In her cottage, he went straight to the telephone. "Gillespie. When'd you get in?...Oh, I see. Is your wife at home? Look on the lower floor, will you?...Yes, in the hall or your brother-in-law's bedroom." He turned, leaning against the table, and said to his companions, "Dear Ralphie slept down there. Gillespie'll be back in a minute."

Ralphie's bedroom, Georgine thought; *Mimi remembered something he'd left behind.*

"What?" Nelsing said into the telephone. "She's not there? Oh, the garden door was unlatched. Well, she probably went out that way, and Mrs. Wyeth didn't see her go. She was planning to see me at the Hall of Justice, it seems. Good-by."

She'd scarcely have gone to the police by herself, Georgine thought uneasily; *it was too much trouble to convince her at all.* And yet, there was a chance that Mimi would prefer a voluntary-seeming visit. She could have had a dress and shoes downstairs, somewhere, and slipped out by herself—maybe forgetting that anyone was waiting.

It was just possible, but a stronger possibility was that Mimi hadn't been able to go through with it; that, with guilt as a spur, she'd run away.

I don't want to believe it, Georgine told herself. *I liked her; I liked her better when she was common and pathetic, and half seas over. I can't tell anyone I suspected her, not till I'm sure.*

"Not at the Hall of Justice, either," said Howard Nelsing, turning away from the telephone.

"Give her time," said Georgine. She sat down, not looking at either of the men. She braced herself for the inevitable question.

"You and she were talking," said Nelsing meditatively. "What was she coming to tell me?"

"I can't tell you that. Let her do it."

"Evidence?"

"Not—not direct evidence."

"A confession?"

"Nothing of the sort."

"Did she know who killed Hollister?"

"Oh, don't look so menacing!" Georgine snapped. "If she'd said anything of the kind, don't you suppose I'd have let you know long ago?"

"I'm not so sure. Why won't you tell me what you talked about?"

"Because I told her I wouldn't," said Georgine defiantly. "If it had been anything of immediate value, I'd have telephoned you at once. You'll have to take my word for that."

"You told her you wouldn't," Nelsing repeated scornfully. "Why, you meant that about not caring for justice! I thought it was only a figure of speech, I was ready to believe you hadn't any more information about Hollister's death; but now you admit—"

"Hey, Nelse," said Todd McKinnon from his obscure corner, "leave her a few human virtues. In some circles, people who keep their words are highly thought of."

"Damnation, I'd forgotten you were there. Keep out of this, Mac. I'll question a witness in my own way, and if you don't like it you can get the hell out."

"I do not like it," said McKinnon deliberately. It was the first time Georgine had seen him when he wasn't casual. He sat relaxed as ever, but his voice rang like a coin flung down on marble. "We private citizens can't be expected to share this passion of yours for abstract justice and the hell with good faith and kindness and everything else. We've got to live with ourselves afterward."

Nelsing turned slowly. For half a minute something flickered almost visibly between the two men. "Very pretty," he said. "And just what's your interest in helping Georgine keep information from the police? Anything personal?"

"Only what I said." McKinnon's voice was quiet again, his face immobile. He shrugged and got up. "I'm on her side, that's all. I'll be going now. No, it's all right, Georgine, he's not going to torture you. I know him better than that."

"Just as soon have him gone," Nelsing murmured, closing the door behind the erect figure. "Would you mind, after this, saving your revelations until we are alone?"

Georgine looked at him, startled. "I will if you think I should."

Todd was a writer, he was interested in every detail of the crime whose scene and actors he was studying. It was natural that he should be omnipresent. Nelsing couldn't suspect him.

Although, she reflected ruefully, he'd never tell *me* whom he suspects. Well, he won't shake my story about Mimi.

She sat up, preparing for battle; but unaccountably, Nelsing's severity had abated and he didn't try many more questions. He said, finally, "Please don't think I doubt your word." He called up his office again, and was told that Mimi Gillespie had not appeared.

"If she's run away she won't get very far," he said, his handsome mouth set in a straight line. "The boys will be on the lookout for her. I'd better get up to her home and have a look around before the light goes." And stalked out.

Georgine locked the door tightly behind him. She sat down again, trying not to think of Mimi's hand reluctantly detaching itself from the door-frame, of Mimi's piteous voice breaking as she said her brother's name.

But of course. She was still afraid of getting Ralph into trouble for his part in the blackout. "Maybe," Georgine told herself uneasily, "I should have given away that part so they could catch him"—and at once found arguments in her own support. How could it help now? The blackout was nearly a week ago and by now Ralph Stort must either have been caught or got away.

Been caught—or got away. She drew herself together, uncomfortably. She didn't know what they would do to anyone they caught.

"There's no very serious penalty," the army officer said in a cautious murmur to the doctor. "He'd be grounded for life, of course. The ship would be confiscated, if there were anything left of it." He paused, his eyes narrowed, seeing again the barren stretch of desert, and the grotesque crumpled shape of the Cub cruiser. "What I want to know is *why* he did it?"

"If you don't find out now, sir," the doctor said, "maybe you never will. Yes, he's conscious, able to talk a little. No more than fifteen minutes, please."

The window gave on a stretch of desert, and on the formidable wall of the Tehachapi mountains. A bulky dark shape cut diagonally across it; a leg, held high in the harness of a fracture bed. The man in the bed was almost invisible under swathed bandages.

The officer sat down and began his inquisition in a quiet voice. He spoke for several minutes. Now and then the man in the bed muttered a word of affirmation or denial.

"Why was it, Stort?" the officer said. "Why was it necessary?"

"...Teach whom a lesson?"

"...You can't mean that. They weren't doing so badly; not enough for you to concern yourself about them."

Fishy, he thought disgustedly; and thought of the stoppage of work at the shipyards, of the four deaths from heart attack, of the dubious citizens able to slip about unnoticed in the sudden darkness.

"Who made you?"

"...Yes, we should be interested in confirmation of the story."

"...*Who?*"

The officer sat back, his brows drawing together. "I'm afraid that will be impossible." He looked narrowly, curiously at the swollen eyes peering from under the bandage. "That man is dead. He died during the blackout."

"...I'm telling the truth, of course, Stort, Hollister was killed in a freak accident; a driverless car plunged downhill and struck him as he was going on his rounds."

"...What's the trouble? What did his death mean to you, besides this matter?"

The battered mouth under the bandages stayed tightly shut, and the tortured dark eyes turned to the window and would not meet the officer's.

The officer repeated his questions, gently enough. He asked others. There was still no answer.

He could bring no pressure to bear. There was nothing more that could terrify Ralph Stort, who was dying; nothing except the possibility of saying too much. He did not speak again before he died.

Georgine Wyeth wondered if she had slept at all, if the miserable dreams from which she had so often started up had been the product of sleep or of the waking mind. And there was the rap of knuckles on her door, again; for a blurred moment she thought this was yesterday morning, and it was the Professor knocking, and it was all to be done over again. "I won't go into Mimi's this time," she told herself dizzily, struggling out of bed.

"Just a minute," she said, startled wide awake by the sight of Nelsing on the doorstep; and rushed back into the bedroom to tie up her hair in a neat bandanna—he would catch her in curlers!—and put on some clothes.

"She hasn't turned up?" Georgine asked anxiously.

"Who, Mimi? No," said Nelsing soberly. He sat down, his eyes fixed on her so that no evasion was possible. "You asked me to wait till this morning, Georgine. I've done it. Now, will you help me, please?"

She nodded, for some obscure reason unable to speak.

"I'll tell you what we've done. We've made inquiries of every person who was at home in Grettry Road yesterday after-noon, and got nothing. Peter Frey is the only one who might conceivably have seen Mimi go out the garden door, and as it happens he didn't. He was in his basement studio, and all the south and west windows have been covered; something about the light. He wasn't watching, anyway. Sheila Devlin was at home, but she's very uncommunicative, beyond saying she saw no signs of Mimi. McKinnon was on the other side of the street, around the curve. He couldn't have seen anything, either. Professor Paev—didn't seem inclined to help us."

Georgine smiled faintly, for the first time that morning.

"So it's up to you, to give me some idea of why Mimi Gillespie was upset yesterday; so upset that she rushed down-stairs and into the garden and disappeared."

She felt tired and defeated. "All right, I'll tell you," she said dully. "She knew there was to be a blackout last Friday night. Her brother knew it too. He caused it." She stopped, and looked at Nelsing. "You're not surprised."

"We had some kind of an idea," said Nelsing smoothly, "when we investigated at Stort's ranch and heard the deputy

186 LENORE GLEN OFFORD

sheriff's story. His sister had claimed she knew nothing about what he did after he left on Thursday."

"She did, I'm afraid," said Georgine. "And if that wasn't a mystery to you, I didn't do any harm by holding it back. That's all there was to her story."

"Oh, no, it isn't. The fact that she knew is plenty impor-tant. Oh, you saw that too, did you? I want the story in full, please."

"You knew that Hollister made him do it?"

"I know it now. Pretty much to have been expected, don't you think? Could have been guessed when we found out why Hollister was in Grettry Road. What more?"

"Nothing much." Georgine told him, though, looking with a sort of painful wonder at his face as she talked.

All that fuss last night had been for nothing, if he knew the story already.

Then why was he listening so carefully, relaxed yet intent? Because he was checking up on how truthful she was? Well, she was doing her best. "And so I asked her," she concluded wearily, "if anyone else knew about this; and she said no, that nobody could possibly have heard her and Ralph talking. And then she—went."

"Just like that, quietly?"

"No. She stopped a minute by the stairs, and said, 'Oh, my God,' as if she'd just thought of something, and ran."

Nelsing nodded. "She was fairly tight, you said? Probably just dawned on her what kind of spot *she* was in."

"Nelse, do you really think she has the stuff of a murderer in her?"

"You'd be surprised what real devotion can do," he said.

"Would you blame her?"

"Now, Georgine, you know better than to put it that way. No matter how unselfish the motives are, you can't condone the taking of human life. Isn't that so?"

She said nothing. "It's plain enough," he went on, "what Mrs. Gillespie did. She took a powder. If you'd been willing to tell me last night what was worrying her, we'd have had a better chance of catching her."

"Then I'm glad I didn't," Georgine muttered stubbornly. "And haven't you considered that she could be innocent, and might simply have wandered away and passed out somewhere in the brush?"

"We'll take everything under consideration," said Nelsing, all at once bored and impatient. He got up. "Are you going to work up there today?"

"I suppose so. I've only about twenty more pages to do, but I don't get a chance to finish them!"

"Very well. But please don't talk, don't spread this story about the blackout. Among other things, it's a military secret."

Going down into Grettry Road seemed to get harder every day. Georgine paused at the top, late in the morning, and braced herself as if she were about to plunge into icy black water. Yet the street was as placid as ever under the gray light; a sprinkler whirred on the Devlins' lawn, and Claris Frey looked out the Frey kitchen window, where she seemed to be washing dishes, and smiled. Georgine found herself looking around, just why she did not know, for a lean graceful figure with sandy hair. No sign of him this morning.

But when she came out, after a completely uneventful day, at five o'clock, he was sitting on the broken white fence at the foot of the road. He had taken his mouth-organ from his pocket, and was breathing into it.

"Don't play that!" Georgine cried out at the second bar.

"You don't care for it after all?" The agate eyes turned to her, and McKinnon gave a mock sigh.

"It's bad luck," Georgine said with a little shiver, and saw his eyes go blank and narrow. She added hurriedly, "Maybe I'm getting superstitious, but I can't ever hear *The Trout* again without thinking something's going to happen."

"Then I've played it for the last time," McKinnon said. "But surely things haven't been happening for twelve hours out of every day, since I've known you?"

"You haven't been playing it that often!"

"Just about. Maybe," he suggested gently, "you've listened only when you were sort of sharpened up by apprehension."

"Maybe," Georgine said, again shivering. "The other day, when I was waiting for Mimi, it—it seemed as if your music had lured her away, and she'd followed it and disappeared. They haven't had any word of her?"

As they passed the three white houses, she looked nervously at each one. The first two already looked empty and desolate, with accumulations of dead leaves drifting across their shallow porches. "They haven't had any word," the quiet voice beside her repeated.

"Just to go off like that, into thin air!" Georgine said apprehensively. "It isn't right, she can't have gone far. I wish I could get hold of her again, it seems as if I blundered horribly somewhere." She looked back over her shoulder, and stopped in her tracks.

"Todd," she said, keeping her voice level with some difficulty, "I seem to have left my—my keys behind, at the Professor's. Don't walk all the way back with me, you go on slowly and I'll catch up with you. Oh, no, no, I know just where I left them, thanks."

This was something that must be done alone. If Mimi were afraid of anyone else's knowing her secret, she would hide again if anyone but Georgine spoke to her, or entered her house; and it must have been Mimi whose hand had lifted that curtain, upstairs in the Gillespie house, and so hastily, furtively, let it drop again. She *had* been hiding somewhere, and managed to elude Nelsing's search; and when the search was dropped, she had crept home again.

There, Todd had rounded the corner, and was out of sight. Georgine turned swiftly and ran uphill. She rattled cautiously at the Gillespies' door, and found it unlocked, and stepped in.

If that hadn't been Mimi? The only other person it could be was Harry, and there was no reason for him to be furtive. If it should be, she could just inquire if there was anything new...

"Mrs. Gillespie," Georgine called softly. Surely there had been a footfall above her; the hall was chilly, close and dark; the blinds all over the house had been closed. "Mrs. Gilles-pie!"

That was a perfectly good name, but it took on a silly sound when you were constantly shouting it upstairs, and getting no answer. "Mimi," she said, more loudly. "Come on, it's safe enough, I only want to help you." No answer.

Georgine, conquering a slight uneasiness, started up the staircase. She rounded the turn of the stairs.

On the top landing a huge figure stood motionless.

For one startled moment she thought it was a suit of armor, so broad and dark was its silhouette against the eastern window, so round the shape of its head.

Then the figure stirred, and she saw that the round crown was a shipyard worker's helmet, and the wide shoulders were those of Harry Gillespie.

"Oh!" Georgine said on a gasp of relief. "You scared me. I—I hoped I'd find Mimi."

He spoke in a voice so flat, so drained of expression that it sounded like that of a man under torture.

"She's not here," said Harry Gillespie. "What have you done with her?"

"Why, nothing, Mr. Gillespie!" Georgine retreated a step or two, and he began to descend steadily, his weight making each tread groan a little. "Nothing! What could I have done with her? I haven't seen her since yesterday."

"You know where she is." His feet thudded on step after step. "You're going to tell me."

"I'd be glad to if I could, but I don't know." Georgine was feeling her way backward, down and down; the turn of the stairs hid his face from her momentarily, and she thought: *There's something about his voice...I'd better run for the door.*

Then his feet were on the landing, and he stood looking down at her. He was still dressed in his working clothes, with the stiff windbreaker and the greenish helmet making him look more than ever like something not quite alive. In the dimness of the hall his face was half shadowed, but its outlines looked like a grotesque mask of tragedy.

"You're going to tell me," said Harry Gillespie, in his flat far-away voice, "or I'll kill you."

She found herself looking into a round black hole rimmed with steel.

CHAPTER THIRTEEN

Where Mimi Was

HER FIRST IMPULSE WAS to nervous laughter. Why, she knew this man, better than any of the other neighbors in Grettry Road! A simple, obnoxious, candidly patriotic soul, who loved his wife and was proud of his new prosperity. She had ridden with him, chatting about movies and the war and the graveyard shift.

"Oh, go on, Harry," said Georgine cheerfully. "Don't wave that gun. How should I know where Mimi is?"

"You saw her last. Then she disappeared. That cop said so. What did you do with her?"

He was on the lowest step now, and the pistol was held unwaveringly trained on her. She put out a hand to push it aside, and saw his hand go taut.

Why, he meant that.

Her gesture died in mid-air, and she looked at his eyes. He could not have slept for two days. He had come home from a long bout of questioning at the police station, and found his wife was gone. Had he gone back to the shipyards for his night's work, thinking she would reappear, and returned to discover that she was really lost? There was only one emotion behind those burned-out eyes.

He was determined and dangerous as a half wild animal intent on the kill. "Go on in there," he said, with a motion of his free hand toward the living room. "We'll sit down. I'm tired, I've been huntin' her in every vacant house up and down the road." The words fell heavily, one by one, as he backed Georgine into a chair at the far end of the room.

He sat down a few feet away, neither his eyes nor the gun hand wavering. "She's not at the Carmichaels' and she's not at Hollister's and she's not at the Cliftons'. She's been at the Cliftons' but she's not there now. All night, I looked. Then I came back here and sat and thought."

She could see him, hunched on the edge of a chair, unshaven and unfed, his tired mind plodding round and round a despairing circle. "Harry, I'm so sorry. I've worried about her, too. But I can't—"

"I was going to get you alone, and make you tell me somehow. And then you walked in here." The dry lips stretched without amusement. "Funny, ain't it? You know where she is now. If she wasn't hid somewhere she'd come back to me." He waited. "I'll give you ten minutes."

"Now look, Harry," said Georgine in an unsteady low voice, "that doesn't make sense. Why on earth should I hide—"

His eyes flickered and rested momentarily on the door to the hall. "Come in and sit down," said Harry Gillespie in his dead voice. "Over there, not too near her, not too near me. Don't make any noise, either of you, or I'll shoot you both."

Todd McKinnon must have been caught unaware, full in the open door. Georgine had not heard him approaching, but now she heard his light step on the carpet as he slowly, warily obeyed.

"What's it all about, Gillespie?" said the casual voice.

"She knows where Mimi is. I'm going to kill her if she

doesn't tell me. Keep your hands out of your pockets. Put 'em on the chair-arms where I can see 'em."

"I haven't a thing in my pockets," McKinnon said agreeably. "Well; this is interesting. Just as well I'm curious, and spied on you, Georgine, when you came back up the road."

She tore her eyes from the hypnotizing sight of the gun, and looked round at him. There he sat in one of the deep leather chairs, his legs in their admirable flannel slacks negligently crossed. He looked cool as a diplomat at an afternoon tea. Only his eyes were brilliantly alive.

McKinnon caught her glance and screwed up one eye in a burlesque wink. "That's no way to get information, Gillespie," he said. "You can't scare it out of a woman, you know; you have to coax it. Look, Georgine do you really know where Mimi is?"

"No!"

"I'll do the askin'," Harry said deliberately. "You were the last person to see Mimi. She told you where she was goin', or else you hid her. Maybe she knew something you didn't want told. You'll tell me now."

His obsession swept away logic, and was the more dangerous for that. She knew it with a cold thrill at the pit of her stomach.

"Five minutes to make up your mind," said the dead voice.

She looked incredulously around her. Her gaze rested on the mantel, and the clock that stood there. Twenty-eight minutes past five, and the hands moving onward in silence, the thin spike of the second-hand sweeping round and round the dial… She looked at Todd McKinnon. He wasn't just going to sit there and let her—

"Go on, why don't you?" he advised, as if encouraging her to repeat an amusing story. "He's her husband, he's got a right to know."

"I can't," Georgine said in a whisper.

"She told you something," said McKinnon quietly, and his eyes slid toward Gillespie with an effect of warning. "Better come out with it now."

She could almost have laughed. If only Mimi *had* told her something of importance, how quickly she'd have come out with it! Her brain wasn't working very well, or she'd think of some plausible lie—something, anything to convince this madman of her innocence. Think. *Think.*

Her eyes seemed to have got fastened to the clock. Five-thirty, and that long glistening finger gliding unceasingly round.

McKinnon's voice cracked like a lash. "*Georgine.* Snap out of it." She looked round at him, startled. "That's better," he said, relaxing. "Tell him what you talked about, you and Mimi. That's all he wants to know."

"But it was nothing to do with me. What she told me was—a military secret."

"That doesn't matter now. You couldn't tell anyone safer than Harry, anyway. He's working for his country."

"All right," Georgine said. She hesitated for another moment, wetting her lips, glancing at the stiff mask of Harry Gillespie's face under the helmet. Why, if he could be driven half mad like this, at such a moment, it might have happened before. Creeping back to Grettry Road during the blackout, getting into the little jeep, those big hard hands sure and ruthless on the wheel...fastening a cord to that heavy pot so that it would tip over on her head...

She began to speak, slowly, watching his face. "Your brother-in-law was afraid of Hollister." He'd known that; not a muscle moved. "Hollister forced him to go home and get his plane and fly over the Bay last Friday night. That blackout was intentional."

But that had surprised him: his head jerked slightly; and, although she was not looking at Todd McKinnon, she knew that it surprised him also.

"Mimi called me in," she said, feeling her way with breathless caution, "and told me about it. You were at the police station and she was terribly worried. She wanted to know if it would help you if she told them the story. I—I didn't believe it would, and of course she wasn't willing to give away her brother if she could help it; but I tried to convince her she ought to let them know anyway."

"That's your story," said Harry Gillespie, still with that deadly slowness. "That's where they got that stuff about her maybe goin' down to the police station. Go on."

"I wondered if anyone had heard her and Ralph talking about the planned blackout. She said nobody could have known, not possibly," said Georgine with emphasis; watching him. "And then she started off to get dressed, and she must have run out the garden door, downstairs; at least that's what they figured. I never saw her again. That's all."

It was not what he had wanted. It was not enough. She saw it before the last words had died away.

"Now I'll tell you what happened." His voice came harsh and difficult, as if his throat were dry. "You stopped her before she got downstairs, or upstairs, or wherever she went. You told her she—" The lack of logic seemed to penetrate even his mind, for he paused and licked his lips, looking bewildered. "You hid her, anyhow. You frightened her, so she ran over to the Cliftons' and hid until people quit lookin' for her."

"What makes you think that?" McKinnon inquired.

Harry Gillespie put his left hand deliberately inside the stiff jacket, and as slowly brought it out. It grasped something white and furry.

"Her slipper," he said harshly. "Inside their house, dropped off her in the breakfast-room."

For a long moment McKinnon said nothing. Georgine's eyes slid round to search his face. In the yellow light that filtered through the half-closed slats of the blinds, it looked as if it had been carved from blond wood.

"In the breakfast room," he repeated. "Under that window that was left open from the top?"

"She wouldn't have gone farther by herself. I know that." Harry Gillespie said, "Not Mimi, that liked clothes, that always had to be dressed up just right. She had on her wrapper and those slippers. She got that far, and then this Wyeth woman took her some place else. I want to know where."

"I tell you I don't know," Georgine whispered.

"Or I'll kill you," said Harry, as if she had not spoken.

The gun came up slowly. Georgine felt herself pressing back in the chair until its padded leather sighed.

Then Todd McKinnon began to laugh, softly and cruelly. "My God, but you're blind, Gillespie," he said. "Thinking your wife went off with another woman!"

"What else happened to her?"

"You know. You know!" The voice jeered quietly. "You had a li'le suspicion once, didn't you, when the neighbors began talking about the man that used to call on Mimi after you'd gone to work!"

"Sure I knew that," Harry said. His face twitched painfully once. "I knew Hollister was here too much, but she told me—"

"She told you a good story, and you swallowed it because you were crazy about her. Did she ever mention the fact that her brother went to Hollister's as often as he entertained him at home, and then she was alone, and Hollister was accounted for?"

"I knew all about what she did."

McKinnon laughed again. "That's what you think. Hollister made a good stalking-horse—maybe too good; maybe he tried to muscle in on the other fellow's territory, and got bumped off for his pains. But why should he have been the only one to call on her late at night? H'm?"

The bleak mask of Harry's face was changing; a dusky flush rose slowly from neck to forehead. "Why, you—" he said harshly.

"And you think that pretty li'le blonde, that drove every man who saw her crazy, was taken away by force? Or that another woman got her to go? Oh, brother, do you rate with yourself! Thought she'd never leave you, did you?"

"What do you know about it?" The voice grated.

"Nothing, except what I heard," Todd said quickly; too

quickly, nervously. "How should I know who the other guy was? I just work up here." He gave a careless chuckle. "Yeah. At the Clifton house. I should 'a' remembered that."

Slowly, slowly Harry Gillespie swung his body in a quarter-circle, and the gun moved too. Georgine felt its going like the removal of a heavy weight. It was not pointed at her, now; it was trained on Todd McKinnon.

Her muscles jerked in reflex; get out of the chair, run...

The gun faced her again, momentarily. "Sit there," Harry said, and his eyes blazed with animal fury. "You're not goin' to run for help. It wouldn't do any good; you and him could both be dead and buried before they could ever catch me." He leaned forward deliberately. Georgine, transfixed, was turned sideways now so that she saw Todd McKinnon, sitting rigid and quiet.

"So that's it," Harry Gillespie said. "I might 'a' wondered about that. Why, you—" He took a deep breath and loosed a stream of deadly epithets. "You gave yourself away that time, braggin', bein' so afraid somebody'd get the credit for your tom-cattin' that you had to show off to me!"

"Who, me?" McKinnon said. "What are you talking about? I just said there might be somebody else. Whoa there, careful with that Roscoe!"

"I can be careful, all right." The mask was dissolved now, and Harry Gillespie's face was black with fury. He was sweating; Georgine saw a great drop trickle down his cheek; and he shifted his grip slightly on the pistol-butt. "I'll kill you. Not nice and quick and easy, but where a bullet'll hurt the most. What do I care what they do with me?"

"Listen, buddy," McKinnon said with a thin attempt at nonchalance. "Listen, you've got it all wrong."

"I saw you once or twice talkin' to my wife. I saw you lookin' at each other. I told myself she was just—just friendly. You were right, chum," said Harry deliberately. "I was blind, but I'm not now!"

"Listen, Gillespie. Wait. No, don't—Why, you can't mean

any of this; you're just fooling, trying to scare me. Well, you did. Drop it. Gillespie, for God's sake. A joke's a joke!"

The laugh jarred false on Georgine's ears. She dared not move, she could only turn her eyes from the furious man to the terrified one. The leather chair-arm was hot and slippery under her hand.

"Of course you don't mean it," McKinnon said. He was chattering fast now, as if to convince himself. "You haven't even got the safety-catch off. Hell, you sure had me fooled."

Without shifting his glance, Gillespie fumbled for the catch. His right thumb seemed to have lost its power; he brought up the other hand and steadied the gun.

"You couldn't hit me even if you did shoot," McKinnon told him, again with that chuckle that seemed to catch in the middle and go off into breathlessness. "Man, look at the way your hand's wobbling. You'd send a bullet through the window if you shot. You couldn't hit a barn door from there! Come off it, bud. Let the whole thing slide."

"I couldn't hit you?" said Harry Gillespie, and got to his feet. "Well, I can fix that, too. I can't miss from two feet away."

There were ten feet between him and the slight figure in the big chair. Georgine watched his slowly advancing feet cover the distance, step by careful step. She forgot to breathe. It wasn't possible, he wasn't going to shoot a man in cold blood, right in front of—She ought to do something, run, scream, throw herself against that massive figure and clutch at its arm; but she had no breath in her lungs.

"You don't mean it! For God's sake, you don't mean—" Todd McKinnon watched the approaching doom, his eyes growing fixed, his hands clutching painfully at the chair-arms. "Get away from me!" He shrank back in the chair, slipping lower and lower on the small of his back. "Don't—don't come any closer, Gillespie. I swear I was only fooling. Be careful, that thing could blow me to pieces!"

"It will," said Harry Gillespie in measured tones.

"You—you can't do that—don't point it like that—*Get it, Georgine!*"

The knee that had been crossed over the other straightened with lightning speed, the foot shot up and caught Harry Gillespie's elbow, and the gun flew from the sweating hand of the big man. The sharp shout of command lifted Georgine from her chair and launched her across the floor, her hands groping for the dark metal of the gun, trying to push away the larger hand that snatched for it before she could reach it. Her shoulder thudded hard against the rug, and a dark weight descended on her.

With a detonation that seemed to burst in her very skull, the gun went off. The heavy weight slumped sideways.

She got to her knees, by a violent effort. Her eyes would not focus for a moment; the floor was nothing but a dark blur. Then it resolved itself into a patterned rug, and the heavy stiffness of a windbreaker, and a big blond head from which the helmet had slipped. From a deep groove above the ear blood trickled slowly, sliding along the hair and falling in shining drops.

Harry Gillespie's face had relaxed into its normal lines. He looked like the man she had first seen at the block meeting: simple, sane, candid.

"He's dead," Georgine said in sharp whisper. "We killed him."

She looked up. McKinnon was also sitting on the floor, leaning against the chair from which he had launched his attack. He looked rather pale, and his eyes were closed.

"No," he said, opening them. "I don't think so." With an effort he got himself to Harry's side, and felt the pulse. "He's just creased a li'le, and he did that himself."

The pistol was still in the big flaccid hand. McKinnon did not touch it. He felt for the pressure point beside Harry's ear and held his finger on it firmly. "See if you can find a first-aid kit anywhere, will you, Georgine?" he said.

She could not have dragged herself up the stairs if it had not been for the memory of those slow drops of blood.

Coming down, after a brief search, with the neat tin box, she told herself weakly: *I'm always thinking that I've never been nearer death, but this time it was true. The poor devil was clean off his head.*

McKinnon's breathing was back to normal; he was still kneeling quietly by the still form. He stretched out a hand without looking up, and Georgine found a gauze compress for him to lay against the shallow wound in Harry's head. Only when the bandage was in place did he look up.

"I think," she murmured, "you saved me from a very sticky death."

He shrugged. "Maybe, maybe not. Only thing I could think of, to make sure, was to draw him off. Bleating of the kid excites the tiger."

"That wasn't—true, what you made him think?"

The hard-textured face did not change but she saw a flicker of mockery behind his eyes. "You believed it? I didn't know my fiction was so convincing."

"Of course I didn't believe it." Georgine's tone was a little too indignant, and she moderated it. "But good heavens, you made it up like a flash! He—he was right." She sat down suddenly on the rug, and put both hands over her face. "We might both have been dead and buried by the time help could have got here. Todd—he wasn't the murderer, then? I thought for a minute—he might have gone into one of those rages against Hollister, too, but surely, surely, Mimi's disappearance has something to do with this—and he couldn't have known where she is."

"I don't know," McKinnon, said drawing out the words. He looked past her, as if he were thinking of something else, a long way off. "Dead and buried," he said under his breath; and then recollected his thoughts. "I don't know, Georgine. Suppose he seized the opportunity to take another crack at you, and put on this act to justify himself. He could plead insanity—"

"You don't believe that!"

"I never know what I believe," he said, and gave her one

of his quizzical looks. "I can talk myself into almost anything. Look, I've got to report this to Nelse, and talk to him. Could you stay in here with him for a few minutes?"

"Certainly."

"You won't be too frightened? Sure?"

"Oh, get on with it," Georgine snapped. "I'm afraid of lots of things, but an unconscious man isn't one of them."

"That's better," Todd said, moving toward the telephone in the hall. "Always relieves my mind when you get mad."

He hesitated a moment and then came back, leaning over to grip her shoulder firmly.

"Georgine. Do you want to prefer charges against Gillespie?"

She looked at the unconscious face, like an overgrown boy's in sleep. "No, I don't think so. He was crazy with anxiety."

"Then look here. How about telling everyone that he'd worn himself out looking for Mimi, and got despondent and threatened to shoot himself? You grabbed his arm and the bullet was deflected. That's near enough to the truth, and we shan't have to mention anything else—his suspicion of you, or any of it."

Georgine glanced up at him. After a moment, she said, "Very well, if you think it's best that way."

"Don't mention any of it," she repeated softly aloud, after he had gone into the hall. The words ran round and round in her mind. *Not any of it.*

Nelsing arrived in very short order, but he didn't come in. She heard Todd talking to him at the door, the tones low and grave, the words unintelligible. Sitting in the dusky living-room, her watchful eyes on Harry Gillespie, who seemed to be resting easily under the blanket with which she had covered him, she tried to make her tangled nerves relax. None of the neighbors had seemed curious about the pistol shot; probably in the classic manner, they had thought it was a car backfiring.

Time passed. She was not eager to hurry it, nor to be away.

It was enough for the moment to have the terror removed, to know that even if danger threatened again she had only to call out for help.

Once she dragged herself wearily into the kitchen for a drink of water, and glanced out the window as voices suddenly rose and swelled in the street. There was a knot of people up there on the Devlins' lawn, their heads close together, chattering and gesticulating. She saw Ricky and his parents, and Mr. Frey and Claris, and—yes, even Professor Paev, standing a little aloof from the group, his long bony hand covering his mouth. Georgine supposed they must all have heard of the suicide attempt, and had gathered out there in the twilight to talk it over. The clock said half-past seven; they were all through with their dinners, no doubt. For once in her life she didn't feel in the least hungry.

The group, however, seemed to be looking down the road, past the Gillespie house. Peter Frey's head turned birdlike from one to another, his eyes trying to catch those rapidly mouthed words. There, someone had taken pity on him and was writing. She saw him look up suddenly, and the slip of paper dropped from his fingers. It shouldn't have startled him that much, that there'd been an accident to Harry Gillespie.

The ambulance came at last; it had been delayed by a bad traffic crash downtown. The young intern stood out of sight on the Gillespies' doorstep for several minutes, seemingly talking to someone, receiving instructions. Perhaps it was Nelsing who gave them to him, for when he and the stretcher-bearers took Harry away, they asked no questions.

When she came out into the cool foggy twilight, the group of neighbors had vanished. "What on earth were they looking at down there?" Georgine murmured to herself. She glanced toward the foot of the road but could see nothing more exciting than a number of parked cars.

Surely another car couldn't have plunged into the canyon? She walked down the slope, feeling a curiosity so idle that it was almost a state of inertia. One might as well see…

But there was nothing in the canyon.

At the south side of Professor Paev's house the high shrub-bery rustled, and she imagined that now and then a murmur of conversation could be heard. Not the calf again? Oh, surely they hadn't dug up those ridiculous bones for the second time!

She glanced into Professor Paev's, through the door that unaccountably stood ajar. She crossed the open parking-space and went in. Nobody was about. She found herself going up the stairs and opening the door of her workroom. "What did I come up here for?" said Georgine aloud, in astonishment. Force of habit, she supposed, and the remains of the afternoon's shock, which had carried over into a sort of dreamlike state. She looked vaguely at her desk. Only one or two pages of the notes remained to be typed, and one untidy sheet to be re-done.

For a moment she dallied with the idea of sitting down right now and finishing. *And then I'd be done forever,* Georgine thought, *and I'd never have to come back here.*

No, that wouldn't be practical; she realized that she was too tired and shaken to be capable of decent work. Much better go home and eat something soothing, like milk toast, and get some rest. Todd might have stayed to see her home; she couldn't think why he'd disappeared so abruptly.

There *were* voices down there, in the tall flowering bushes; and the square of late cold light in the window had flashed brighter for a second. What on earth were they doing?

She was in the Professor's bathroom, raising the window. She leaned out, gazing straight down on to the heads of a group of men clustered round that space next to the wall of the house. It had been loosely filled in by Nelsing and Slater before they had left it on Wednesday night. Now the grave was open again.

Nelsing was there; he heard the window go up, and his head tilted back so that the after-sunset light struck cold on his face. For an instant his eyes met Georgine's; he began a violent gesture; and at that moment a photoflash bulb burned, and the grave's contents started into stark clarity.

She found herself backing across the room, gasping, "No!

No!" and pushing in front of her with her hands as if to press away that glimpse of a blackened face and a protruding tongue. No one could have recognized the features in that dreadful swollen globe, and the bright blond hair was dulled and grimy with loose earth; but the white chenille robe was still wrapped about the body.

They had found Mimi.

CHAPTER FOURTEEN

Speaking of Clocks

"**T**HERE IS NO DOUBT** about this one," said Inspector Howard Nelsing soberly. "There was a good chance that Hollister's death was accidental; but there is no way in which Mimi Gillespie could have been accidentally strangled with the belt of her own housecoat and then buried. The same argument applies to suicide."

He paused, and let his eyes travel deliberately round the room: Sheila Devlin's living-room, formal and perfect in its pale green carpeting, its tight upholstery of shining gold and salmon satin, its flower prints and crystal. The impersonal blue gaze dwelt on face after face: John Devlin's, its handsome fleshiness grown loose and flabby; Ricky's, shocked and defiant; Sheila's tightly set mouth and outraged eyebrows; Peter Frey's strained look of intentness, as if he were trying to follow the proceedings from behind a thick wall of glass; Claris's face, every now and then quivering out of control; Professor Paev's, its angry black eyes like coals in a bed of ashes.

He looked last at Todd McKinnon, paler than usual but still impassive; and at Georgine.

Georgine huddled in a corner, drawing her shabby coat tightly around her. In spite of heat from the register, she felt cold to her very bones. She met Nelsing's glance dully. He looked as if he were choosing one from this company; choosing sides for a spelling bee or choosing a victim for the gas chamber, you couldn't tell which from his expression.

One person was absent; but she knew that Nelsing had not forgotten Harry Gillespie.

"At seven forty-five, when she was found," Nelsing resumed "Mrs. Gillespie had been dead for twenty-four hours or more."

Everyone looked at the gilt clock over the cold fireplace. Its hands stood at half-past nine, and before he spoke again it gave out a tiny tinkle to mark the hour. "Twenty-four hours or more," he repeated. "That means she must have been killed shortly after she left her home late yesterday afternoon. It is scarcely credible that she wandered about in negligee for any appreciable time without being seen by someone. I think you will all agree that it's more likely she died almost immediately. I will ask you again, how many of you were at home between four-thirty and six yesterday afternoon?"

There were murmurs; John Devlin had been on his way home from the office, Sheila resting in her room, Ricky working on an airplane model in his basement bedroom. Peter Frey, after his daughter had hastily scribbled the question on his pad, said, "I was," in a tone scarcely above a whisper. Professor Paev had been in his laboratory.

"I was at the movies," Claris added in a defiant voice. "I had a date, and it was a double feature, and I didn't get back till nearly supper time."

"None of you saw Mimi?" Nelsing said. "If you denied this yesterday and wish to change the story, now's the time." He waited. "Could she have crossed to the top of Grettry Road without being seen?"

"Oh, I don't think so," Mrs. Devlin said, as if brightly interested. "I was in my bedroom, and I should have noticed."

"Very well. That bears out the implication of the fur slipper, allegedly left in the Clifton home, under an open window. Someone killed Mimi," said Nelsing without change of inflection, "and concealed her body during the early part of the evening, and, much later that night, took it to the place behind Professor Paev's house of which you all knew; took it there for easy concealment, in earth that was loosely filled in and free of vegetation. It would not have been a difficult task; Mrs. Gillespie was small, almost anyone here could have carried her body. Probably in handling her, one of her slippers fell off unnoticed for the moment; and the murderer, finding it later, decided to confuse the issue by getting rid of it. He or she flung it through the open window of the Clifton house."

"But why, Inspector?" John Devlin demanded harshly. "For God's sake why should anybody want to kill that harmless little woman?"

"I can think of a number of reasons," Nelsing said. "It must have been done on impulse, of course; a sudden fit of rage or apprehension, fingers around her throat in a panic—she could have lost consciousness very quickly; we are told that she was in an advanced state of intoxication when she left the house."

"We are told," Sheila Devlin murmured, and smiled. "The impersonal touch is very good, Inspector Nelsing, but every one of us knows that Mrs. Wyeth was in the house, possibly drinking with her, and was the last to see her."

Georgine said nothing. Let them think what they liked.

"And," Mrs. Devlin continued, reaching for a large sewing bag, "since no one else saw her, isn't it obvious what happened?"

There was a little silence, during which the tiny heartbeats of the clock were quite audible. Then Nelsing said, "I should be interested in hearing your theory, Mrs. Devlin." His courtesy had never been more formidable.

The long face lifted, and Mrs. Devlin looked across the room at Georgine. Her eyes shifted to McKinnon. After a moment she smiled. "Why of course, she ran down into the canyon and met a tramp; and—" Her gesture finished the sentence.

"We searched the canyon yesterday evening, while it was still light," Nelsing pointed out.

"Oh, well, obviously you weren't thorough enough, and simply missed seeing her body." She threaded a needle for her embroidery.

"Then," said Howard Nelsing frigidly, "why was she buried? Mrs. Devlin, could I ask that you give me your full attention?"

Sheila put away the needlepoint, with an impatient shrug.

"She was buried under cover of night," Nelsing went on. "That much is obvious. Did none of you hear unusual sounds during the night?"

Once more there were blank looks. A faraway part of Georgine's mind said, *Most of the bedrooms are upstairs near the street. Nobody would necessarily have heard sounds in the gardens or in the canyon, except—*

"I sleep heavily," said Professor Paev on a sharp bark.

There was another little silence. Everyone looked furtively at the Professor, and then back at the floor. Nelsing opened his lips to resume.

Peter Frey leaned forward violently, as if to thrust himself by force through the invisible wall that surrounded him. His harsh outcry ripped the air. "This damned place! It's a—a sink of danger, I tell you! Our women aren't safe. I won't have my daughter staying here, running this risk. You've got to let her go away!"

"That will be all right," Nelsing said, mouthing the words. Frey seemed to understand, for he fell back in his chair and sat breathing hard as if in relief.

"Couldn't she stay with me?" Georgine said diffidently.

"That might be a solution. How about it, Miss Frey?"

"Oh, yes, I'd like that," Claris said.

"Suggest it to your father."

She scribbled for a moment. Peter Frey read what she had written, and looked at Georgine; his slanting eyelids pulled tight with some expression like fright or horror. "No!" he said loudly, and tore the sheet from the pad, hurling it in a crumpled ball toward the fireplace.

"Let them think what they like," Georgine told herself apathetically. She was still too cold and sick for feeling.

No, not entirely; for with a terrible pang, she remembered Barby. If Barby had to see her mother suspected, dragged through an investigation as a possible criminal—would she be old enough to understand? Or if she were, would there be any way of explaining to her that you had only to hold tight to your own knowledge of innocence, and things would come right in the end?

It's got to be over by the time she comes home, Georgine prayed silently. *If it can only be over and settled, so we can go back to our own quiet life! There are two days more.*

Ricky Devlin was speaking, his face drawn tight with strain. "You haven't said yet, Inspector, why she was killed. It couldn't have been a tramp, like Mother said?" Nelsing shook his head. "Well, then, *why?* Because after all, Mr. Hollister's dead now, and—" He stopped, flushing scarlet.

"You don't know what you're talking about, Ricky dear," his mother told him with a sweet smile.

"Yes, he does, Mrs. Devlin. That is a possibility," Nelsing said quietly. "Jealousy might have entered into the motivation, though it seems unlikely so long afterward. But, when two violent deaths take place in the same neighborhood within a week, and the murdered persons were connected in a way whose details I am not at liberty to give you, it is a not unlikely assumption that the deaths were also connected. The first one, I believe, was premeditated, or partly so; the second entirely impulsive, for no one could have foreseen that Mimi Gillespie would have rushed out—unnoticed, as it happened—to the home of one of the neighbors with something she must tell or ask. I believe"—Nelsing's voice was very smooth—"that she held some clue to Hollister's murder, possibly one she had not recognized before; and that on a sudden impulse she went to the person whom she had vaguely suspected, perhaps with an accusation." He slanted an unreadable glance across the room. "It was Mr. McKinnon who suggested that she might have been killed to silence her, rather than that she had run away to escape questioning."

"Fiction-writer's mind," Todd murmured modestly. He had been sitting motionless on one of the satin-upholstered chairs, his eyes flickering from one speaker to another. Georgine, not far away, could feel even through the dull aftermath of shock that he was more than usually alert and attentive.

"What was it she knew?" said Alexis Paev suddenly, harshly, from his corner. "Mrs. Wyeth, she was talking to you before she made this hypothetical sortie into some neighbor's territory. What did she say?"

"Nothing," Georgine told him wearily. "Just that; nothing. There was a story that—" she caught Nelsing's eye and went on, "that I can't repeat; but it did nothing but remove one possible suspect, and make me think that nobody else could possibly have known what—what was important."

Their eyes were all on her; fierce black ones, anxious light blue ones, incredulous brown ones. The last were Sheila Devlin's. She smiled slowly, and Georgine's own eyes dropped. *Let them think it!*

"This is getting us nowhere," said Nelsing abruptly. "Someone is refusing to coöperate. There is the remote possibility that none of you, here in this room, had any part in Mimi Gillespie's death. I should be glad to think that. You must see, however, that suspicion rests in some degree on every one of you."

Once more his eyes swept about the circle of mute, stubborn faces. "I must ask," he concluded, rising, "that you all stay as close to home as you can for the next few days. We will make suitable arrangements for Miss Frey; if you'd tell your father that?— Thank you for the use of your home, Mrs. Devlin."

The group broke. People got up sighing as if at a reprieve, not yet with the full breath of relief. Sheila Devlin stood uncompromisingly by the door, waiting for them to go, her long horse-face wearing an incongruously social smile, one large hand on her son's arm.

In the doorway, "I've got to talk to you," Todd McKinnon murmured in Georgine's ear. "Will you wait here a minute?" He went quickly after Peter Frey, holding out his hand for the writing pad. Georgine could see them, in the shaft of light from the doorway, one scribbling quickly, the other bending a gray head over the paper.

"Mrs. Wyeth," said Nelsing formally, coming past, "don't go yet, please. I'd like you to ride down to my office with me, I have a report to put in; and then I'll see you home."

"All right," she said, not much caring; and moved a few steps into the darkness. A moment later she thought, with a sort of faraway laughter, *I never was so popular*, for a low voice came from the shadows behind her.

"Mrs. Wyeth," Claris Frey said breathlessly, "listen, quick, before anyone sees me talking to you, Daddy told me I was to go straight home but I can get there before he does. I know where he's going to send me, over to Grandma's. Oh, heck," she added, her young voice breaking plaintively, "if he'd only let me stay with you!" She must have missed the implications of her father's refusal. "Grandma's just ghastly strict!"

"I should be, myself," Georgine told her firmly without looking round. "Seems to me it'd do you good."

"Well, look. If—if anybody asks, that you think ought to know, would you give 'em the address? Her name isn't Frey, she married again, it's Tilton. Mrs. Carrie Tilton on Gough Street, will you remember that *please*, because I daren't try to tell anyone else."

"Yes, I'll remember," Georgine murmured wearily. "How will your father get along if you go over there?"

"He'll be all right. He was happy as a clam when he bached it up on Telegraph Hill when I was little. He only came and got me from Grandma's when he wanted to move over here and paint all these trees, and he couldn't get a housekeeper. I told you before," Claris said, very offhand, "he doesn't care what I do."

Georgine's numbness melted in a warm flood of compassion. "You poor baby," she said in a low voice, "you haven't had very much out of life, have you?" No wonder Claris had flaunted her attraction to men. Their admiring looks provided the nearest thing to family affection that she could get.

"Only Ricky," came Claris's soft murmur out of the shadows. "'S funny, isn't it, I just thought of him as a kind of excitement, at first. You—if you get a chance, you'll tell him where I am?"

"I'll tell him," said Georgine, and heard Claris slip away under the tall shadows of trees. It was neatly timed, for Mr. Frey was still occupied and did not follow his daughter for several minutes.

Beside Georgine, Todd McKinnon materialized from the darkness, making her start nervously. He began to talk at once, in the casual voice that usually calmed her. "I was asking Frey how everybody looked when the news about Mimi came out. They all rushed into the street, you know, and I thought he might have noticed some odd expression; people who can't hear are very quick about picking up visual clues. But he told me they were only shocked, as anyone would be."

"What did you expect?" Georgine said tiredly.

"I scarcely know. Whatever it was, I didn't get it. Look, before Nelsing whisks you off, this is what I wanted to say: we're outsiders in this business, you and I. We have been from the start. Naturally the police didn't confide in us. We'll not know, until Nelse chooses to tell us what progress he's making."

"I suppose that won't be till the case is closed. Well, that seems only fair."

"Perhaps. But it's just possible that you and I could pick up some information that people wouldn't want to give him. We can pass it on right away, but it's up to us to gather it if we can."

"No," Georgine said.

"For your own sake," McKinnon pointed out softly. He was standing a bit behind her, and she felt an unaccountable crisping of her nerves. "You'd be safe asking a few innocent questions. If you should happen to see Ricky Devlin alone, would you find out who put up the signal first, last Friday night—he or Claris?"

"Why?"

"I just want to know," McKinnon said.

"I don't want to ask."

He was silent for a moment. In the band of light flung from the doorway, Nelsing appeared, speaking to a policeman whom he had called in from the street. "How do you feel about Mimi's death?" Todd inquired abruptly.

"That was *bad*," Georgine said somberly. "That was really evil. I couldn't quite see it in Hollister's death, but I do in this. I liked her, Todd. She was loving and pathetic, and she ought not to have died."

"You wouldn't believe any of these people were bad," the half whisper sounded in her ear. "Hollister died because one of them was weak and afraid, but Mimi died because that weakness had gone too deep; there was no difference between it and evil."

She said, "Todd. You've got to tell me—did I cause her death? I mean, by not telling soon enough that she'd disappeared."

A shade too quickly, he said, "No! You mustn't think that. She must have died within five minutes of the time she ran down the stairs, before you'd even missed her."

"How do you know that?" she whispered, and took an involuntary step forward into the light.

"I'm only guessing," he said, surprised. "I haven't a minute's doubt that she thought of something while she was talking to you, and was just tight enough to think of going to check up on it, but not sober enough to realize her danger. And maybe she'd only got out a few words of the accusation, when the person who'd already killed once realized that she knew too much." His voice was only a breath now. "And a pair of hands was ready."

"Will you stop?" said Georgine painfully.

"No. Because you must realize that she was talking to you just before she died; and nobody knows how much she said. It's quite possible that if you hadn't run out into the street when you did, you might have died too."

"But I told them! I told them all that there was nothing! Don't *you* believe that?"

"I believe she told you something without your knowing it, perhaps without realizing its importance herself. If I came by tomorrow morning, would you go over the interview in detail?"

"In the morning," said Georgine grimly, "I am going to be locked up tight in my house, and if I can manage it I'll be fast asleep."

"M'm," Todd said. "I see. Then, good night, Georgine."

As Nelsing came up, he wandered carelessly away.

"Nelse, I'm frightened," she said.

"I can't say I blame you," Nelsing told her surprisingly. He stood by the glass-topped door of his office, looking out into the lighted corridor, his back to Georgine. Outside the big building were the midnight streets, in this quiet town almost empty of life; but in the Hall of Justice there was ordered activity. Officers in neat khaki uniforms and Sam Browne belts came and went; telephones burred briskly.

"What are they doing?" Georgine demanded wearily. "What is it you're waiting for?"

Without turning, he said, "It may not be done tonight, but we're making chemical analyses of the scrapings from under her toenails, and testing the robe she was wearing. Maybe that'll show us where we're going. This time," he added with satisfaction, "we've got something to work on. When Hollister died, his murderer didn't touch him, and there wasn't a thing to be found out from the car; no fingerprints on the steering wheel, except Ricky's. Nothing to go on, d'you see? But you can't strangle someone without personal contact."

Georgine made a small sound, and put her hand over her eyes.

"I'm sorry you had to see her as we found her," Nelsing said remotely. "We thought we had everyone corralled."

"But *why*, Nelse? I know, everyone kept asking you that, but I can't see it yet. Was that true, what Todd suggested, that she knew too much?"

"There's a chance that he was right. The murderer's in a panic now, that much is certain. If we just keep still for a few days, and go on with our analyses, we may get a break."

"Who is it? Do you know?"

"Not yet."

"But—whom can I trust?"

"Nobody, I guess," Nelsing said briskly. "I'll see that you're kept safe, if I can find a man to stand guard. Wish I could do it myself, but—"

"Oh, no. You're going to be busy, of course."

She looked at his broad back in the dark suit, outlined against the lighted inner window, the yellowish finish of wood-work. A man in plain clothes went past in the corridor, not looking at Nelsing's cubicle. *I've got to ask him straight out*, Georgine thought; and got to her feet as if it would be easier, standing.

"You don't know who killed Hollister and Mimi. Please tell me, Nelse, did you suspect me a few days ago?"

His back was still toward her. "No," he said roughly.

"Thank heaven," said Georgine, relaxing. "And did you think you'd get more information out of me if you treated me as a suspect?"

Nelsing turned round slowly. His hands were in his trouser pockets, and she could see the fists straining against cloth.

"Georgine, will you marry me?" he said.

She found herself sitting down, without knowledge of how she had found the chair. Her face felt stiff with astonishment.

There was a brief silence. Outside the glazed partition the plain-clothes man went by again, briskly. She opened her lips, and by sheer reflex out came a remark whose inanity nearly undid her.

"But, Nelse," she quavered, "how can—I mean, this is so *sudden!*"

She would have laughed, but he remained entirely solemn. "Didn't you know why I was so hard on you?" he said harshly. "Good Lord, I talked to you in a way I never used on a witness before, man or woman either. It was all because I—I was afraid of letting my own feelings come between me and justice. I thought you—look, I've got to explain something to you."

He paused, wetting his lips. "I've been waiting for a case like this ever since I was a rookie, and made up my mind I'd try for the homicide squad. I got on the squad, finally, after I'd studied and been trained for years. And what did I get? A few razor battles down in Darktown, and a filling-station robbery with violence, and a couple of dead tramps to identify. And then, after five years, this breaks: the real thing, a chance to use all that science and training, a case that can make or break me." He waited for another minute, looking at her with a bewilderment that was almost dislike. "I never thought that there'd be anyone like you mixed up in it. You didn't try to lie your way out of anything, or flirt with me or drown me in tears so I'd let you off. I've seen plenty of women, but I never—I didn't think there was anyone who—oh, damn it, I didn't want to fall in—to be thrown clear off, like this."

He broke off and stood waiting.

In her wildest dreams Georgine had never got him as far as the altar. She couldn't seem to recover from the vast astonishment of this proposal. *Why,* she thought, *I could stretch out my hand and take him. What on earth is holding me back?*

"Nelse, can't you see what's happened?" she said at last, gently. "You've got me mixed up with the case itself. It's your heart's desire, and getting it at last has—sort of dislocated all your other feelings. It wouldn't be fair to settle this now. Wait till it's all over."

He looked at her thoughtfully. "It should be over in a few days more."

In a few days more Barby would be at home. "Let's not talk about it until then," Georgine said. "But I'll do anything I can to—to hurry it up."

Nelsing nodded and drew a quick breath. With the movement he became once more the impersonal officer of Justice. "If you feel that way, perhaps there's something more you want to tell me?"

"I'm sure you've thought of this already, but—almost the last thing Mimi said to me was, 'Nobody could possibly have heard us.' And then she stopped in the hall, as if she'd thought of something, all of a sudden, and then cried out and rushed for the stairs. Do you think—"

Nelsing, once more seated at his desk, nodded slowly. "Sounds almost as if she'd remembered someone who could have heard Stort telling her about the plan for the first foggy night. But who? She didn't tell you that. If someone did know, the rest of it all falls into line. You're sure Mimi hadn't let out any details of the plan to anyone?"

"I asked her that, and she said *no*; especially not—" Georgine stopped short.

"Not who?"

"T-Todd McKinnon. I don't know why I thought of asking about him, except that he talks to everyone."

"Did she seem to be afraid of him?"

"She wasn't really afraid of anyone, that I could see; and if she had been, surely she wouldn't have rushed out and—"

With a horrid sensation of chilliness, she watched Nelsing's forefinger gently tapping on the desk blotter.

"Just what went on this afternoon between you and Harry Gillespie?"

"I think he was really going to shoot me, except that Todd managed to—to deflect his interest."

"How?"

"He—went off on a flight of fancy, and made Harry think that he, Todd I mean, had been Mimi's lover without anyone's suspecting it; and that maybe Hollister had got in the way. It was all fiction, of course. He said so."

"He thinks fast," Nelsing observed. The finger tapped on.

Georgine nodded. She shuddered once, remembering, among all the other events of the day, that moment when Harry Gillespie had walked slowly across the softness of the figured rug; the other moments when, half-incredulous, she had watched the silent clock on the mantel and had wondered if she had only five more minutes to live.

"Have you been in the Carmichael house?" she asked suddenly.

"Yes. Why?"

"What kind of clock have they?"

"Electric, I believe. It's a modern interior. What made you think of that?"

"For some reason I keep expecting to find a chiming clock."

Nelsing looked up at her, consideringly. "I haven't heard a clock chime in any of the Grettry Road houses."

"Oh," Georgine said, and frowned. "I must be thinking of the Campanile."

"Maybe," Howard Nelsing said, continuing to gaze at her.

The door of the cubicle opened and Slater came in. "Preliminary report on those tests, Inspector," he boomed.

Nelsing leafed through the sheets of paper, and glanced up, frowning at his assistant.

"Nothing there," he said heavily. "We'll have to try again."

CHAPTER FIFTEEN

The Gas Chamber

THERE WAS NO ESCAPING now, no way to pretend that nothing had happened. The papers had the news. For two days the whole populace of the Bay Region rocked with the excitement of Mimi Gillespie's death, and the headlines were secondary only to those about the war.

Georgine had been warned, not only by Nelsing but by a hasty telephone call from McKinnon. "You'll probably be more comfortable if you manage to dodge the reporters. So far they've minimized your part in the case, but if they got a personal interview…"

He let it trail off ominously. "I'll stay close to home," she told him, "and not speak to anyone. I haven't even looked at the papers."

"There's nothing new. The police are supposed to have a clue," said Mr. McKinnon, rather sardonically. "That may be so, and it may be a good story. But they'll get something in time. After a day or so you can come out and resume operations, when the first excitement's blown over. You're not nervous, there by yourself?"

"A little. Nelse said he'd try to find a man to guard me, but that makes me feel rather foolish. Anyway, maybe he didn't do it, I haven't seen anyone."

"I see." McKinnon seemed to be digesting this information. "Well, I think you'll be all right."

Turning away from the telephone, she thought that he'd sounded queer, unlike himself, toward the end. She didn't like any of her thoughts, these days.

There was one bright spot; Barby's hostess had written to say that the homecoming had been postponed for one day. In order to avoid the week-end traffic, the party would drive down to the Bay on Monday, reaching home in time for supper. Georgine could hardly believe that she was glad of this—another day's delay before she saw her own baby!—but it was so. One more day for the police to work, to come nearer to the solution that meant safety.

She thought of it through all of Saturday and Sunday, moving about behind drawn curtains that cast a cream-colored gloom over the three small rooms of her cottage. She cleaned the place from top to bottom, and made Barby's favorite cookies and cinnamon rolls, and listened to the radio: every program from the horridly cheerful wake-up ones of early morning to the last fragment of news at night. By Sunday the local newscasters had almost ceased to mention the "Grave in the Hills Mystery." Did that mean that the excitement had really blown over?

She had been out once, to the grocery three blocks away. She didn't try it again, for the trip had left her with a curious feeling of uneasiness. It had been only discreet to choose the path through the rear gate of the property, and across the weeds and brush of the vacant lot. What she didn't like was the rustling noise among the bushes, that seemed to parallel her progress to the street. It gave her the feeling that someone was following her, even when she came back unmolested by the front gate.

It could have been a dog among the bushes; it could even have been the police guard of Nelsing's half promise. If the latter, however, it seemed a queer way for the police to act.

After that last news broadcast on Sunday night, she thought of this again. She stepped outside the front door, closing it behind her as if she meant to go on down the walk, and then suddenly halted.

Yes. Someone had moved quickly, out there in the darkness, as if to melt into a deeper shadow.

Georgine looked hopefully at the lighted windows of her landlords' house. Nobody would dare do anything to her, surely, with people right here within call. She thought also of challenging the intruder, boldly; and after she had opened her lips found that she couldn't do it.

It would be safer inside the house, with the telephone at her elbow. She went back quietly; she even managed to sleep through most of the night, with all the doors and windows locked and the lights blazing in every room. In the morning, perhaps this would all seem foolish.

Daylight, and coffee and toast, and the sounds of Monday traffic did indeed restore her nerve tissues to an appreciable extent. She remembered uneasily that at 82 Grettry Road she had left a job unfinished, and that Professor Paev had paid her a hundred dollars in advance—which she'd already spent—to insure the job's being done within a specified time.

Georgine cursed her conscience, and her utter inability to suspect anyone whom she liked or pitied. It was no use; she'd have to finish earning that money before she could ever feel comfortable again. She called the Homicide Division, and found that although Nelsing was not in his office, Mr. Slater was.

After inaudible consultation with someone at the other end of the wire, "I think it would be safe enough, Mrs. Wyeth," the startling bass voice said. "Things have calmed down, up there."

"Nothing—going on? You haven't—"

"I can't say anything about that." He had caught her meaning, and the voice took on the patient inscrutable tone of an official. "I believe the Inspector expects to be in Grettry Road later this afternoon."

That should be enough. After all, it was full daylight, and she had lost the sensation of being followed.

Grettry Road looked peaceful and quiet as ever. Georgine stood at the top and once more took one of her heavy breaths as if to work up courage for a plunge into chilly water. She passed the Clifton house, which seemed to be deserted, and swung round the curve toward the lot where Ricky Devlin's jeep had once stood.

Behind her a door closed, not loudly but with great firmness, and Ricky himself appeared, hurrying after her.

"You don't happen to know where she is, Mrs. Wyeth?" he said breathlessly. "I couldn't get near her before she left, and Mother hasn't given me a chance to ask her Dad. Maybe he wouldn't tell me anyhow. And I've got to see her, to say good-by."

"Good-by?" Georgine repeated. It was ridiculous how the least hint of anything untoward brought her heart into her throat.

"I enlisted in the Navy this morning," said Ricky.

"Ricky! You—" Georgine just saved herself from crying out, "You're too young." She substituted, "How'd you manage it?"

"My father gave his consent," the boy told her. Already he looked a shade more mature. "You have to have one parent say you can."

"But your mother—how is she—"

"She kind of went to pieces," Ricky said in a low voice, looking down. "But Dad said she'd—she'd always have him. He said he'd stay and take it. They've been—we've had kind of an upset in the family."

She had to face the truth about the Las Vegas story, thought Georgine. *She's known it all along, in her heart, but they made her realize it. And then John Devlin took the brunt of it so that his son could escape.*

He couldn't have simply—wanted Ricky out of the way?

"So you see I've got to find Claris. I called everybody named Frey that I could find in the 'phone book, and none of them was her grandmother. I've got to see her, Mrs. Wyeth! Is there any way you could find out?"

"Mrs. Carrie Tilton, on Gough Street," Georgine murmured. The young face flamed with relief. "Gee, thanks," Ricky said. "I can't help it if Mother is in bed with a nurse, I got to go over there and see Claris. Gee, *thanks.*"

"Wait a minute, Ricky. I'd like to ask an impertinent question. On the night of the blackout, you and Claris met in the canyon. She told me about it, and about the signal. Which of you put up his signal first?"

Ricky had gone crimson, but he did not drop his eyes. "She did," he said.

"That's—thank you for telling me." Georgine had changed her sentence hurriedly. No use in letting him know...

But he asked her directly. "What did Claris say?"

"She said she saw *your* signal, and answered it."

"Funny," Ricky said, frowning. Then his face gradually took on a queer expression, and he began to back away. "I'm sorry, I've got to go now. Thanks awfully, Mrs. Wyeth. I—good-by, I might not see you again."

"Good luck, Ricky," Georgine said slowly.

She watched the tall young figure going back into the Devlin house; then, herself frowning, she walked down the road. Quiet again now that the boy's voice was silent; more quiet than ever before, she thought, because two of those houses had been emptied by death.

Mr. Frey was gardening at the side of his house, but his back was to her and Georgine passed without his turning round. The sound of her feet was once more, as on a day two weeks before, the only break in the stillness.

It gave her the feeling of re-living a dream, to have Mrs. Blake open the door for her. There was a difference today, though. The woman's ebony calm had been shattered. She was half in tears, shaking with apprehension.

"The P'fessah's gone," she said, white eyeballs starting. "He got took down to the police station this morning, Mis'

Wyeth, and he hasn't come back. I'm afraid it was me that did it. I didn' know what I was sayin', when I told that police officah that the P'fessah hadn't nevah been in Mr. Hollister's house to any of the block meetings, nor anything."

"What did that—" Georgine began, and stopped, the words all at once shaping into a tingling certainty. Everyone in the road had left prints there, Nelsing had said. But that meant the Professor's shouldn't have been there…

The quiet movements in Hollister's living-room, on the night of the blackout; the Professor's return to Grettry Road at an unspecified time, and his lack of obvious surprise when he learned that Hollister had worked for the Fenella Corporation—the smell of burning paper in the house when she went in to get a drink!

She was gazing at Mrs. Blake, and the African Queen gazed back fearfully. "He must have been here," Georgine said aloud, to herself, "and heard the commotion over Hollister in the street, and jumped at the chance to get into his house and go through the desk while we were all occupied outside…"

Had he come back to the Road earlier yet, just before the sirens sounded? Had he guessed about Hollister the minute he realized that the telephone call had been false? Or had he been the one who knew all along that there'd be a blackout that night? It had been the chief point in his favor that he hadn't known… And there was that grave in his own back yard, and the laboratory where Mimi's body might have been hidden till nightfall…

"I don't know what he did, Mis' Wyeth," said the African Queen, her voice trembling, "but my Lordy, the ruckus he raised when he found out that it was me told 'em! I'm mighty near scared to stay heah and cook his dinnah. He tol' me to, but—"

"Oh, please!" Georgine said, panic-stricken, "stay just a little while. I have only a few more pages to type and then I'll be finished. If you want to go, we could walk down together."

The Queen didn't seem to have heard her. She blinked and mumbled to herself, and stalked off toward the kitchen.

Georgine ran up the stairs and attacked the scattered papers on the desk. She hadn't seen them since Friday evening, since she had decided not to work on them, and had instead gone into the bathroom and looked down on an open grave.

She gave one convulsive shudder, and then forced herself not to think any more. One page carefully typed; the second page—be careful to get the carbons in right side up...

There. She had finished, except for that untidy page. She had earned her hundred dollars—probably, thought Georgine bitterly, at the expenditure of five times their worth in mental agony and shock. There were only a few more lines.

Downstairs the telephone rang, and she heard the velvety Negro voice murmuring like a bee. In another moment it was calling up the stair well. "Mis' Wyeth! They called me from the police station and the P'fessah's there yet and wants to have me come down and tell 'em some mo'. I've got to be goin'."

"Wait!" Georgine shouted, frantically typing. "I'll be right down. Ten minutes can't make any difference!"

It was done. She scrambled the sheets together, ribbon copy and carbon and onionskin, and left the three neat stacks beside the covered typewriter. "If the Queen has walked out on me," she told herself grimly, snatching her hat and coat, "I'll have her black hide. But I don't believe she's gone; I heard someone down there half a second ago, when I opened the room door."

"Wait for me, Mrs. Blake," she called, and came with flying feet down the stairs. She hadn't heard the front door close; maybe the Queen had gone out by the basement entrance, toward the canyon path. Down another flight, to the laboratory floor...

Georgine glanced, puzzled, up and down the cement-floored corridor. The door at the garden end stood ajar, but no majestic figure was visible through it. "She couldn't have disappeared like that in five seconds," Georgine told herself, a faint uncomfortable chill running down her back. It couldn't be another case of Mimi? No, because there were sounds behind her, in the garage end of the hall. Of course Mrs. Blake was making her way through the garage.

She was about to call out once more, impatiently, when she paused, twitching her head around. The noise, a furtive sort of rattling, was coming not from the garage, but from the laboratory to her left —from an empty room.

The Queen couldn't be in there.

Lock the door—she snatched the key from the lock—and run!

Georgine whirled, poised for flight, measuring the distance to the rear door; and a voice spoke, with an uncanny hollow boom, from the niche under the laboratory sink.

"Could I interest you," said the voice meekly, "in a Magnificent Combination Offer?"

She began to laugh, so hard that she had to hold onto the edge of the door. After a minute she staggered into the laboratory and let herself down on the high stool, still gripping the door-key. "Todd, you complete goon," said Georgine faintly, "what are you doing under there?" The relief made her feel almost dizzy. Once that had passed, she felt that extraordinary sense of being at ease which seemed to accompany his presence. It was only Todd.

"Come out," she said severely.

Mr. McKinnon emerged, absently dusting himself. "I feel very foolish," he said.

"And look it," Georgine said.

"Now they'll never let me be a detective," he went on, sadly. "I told Nelsing I could keep an eye on you without you seeing me. It's easier outdoors, though."

"It's been you? Following me around for two days?" He nodded. "Well, why in heaven's name haven't you wanted me to see you?"

McKinnon waited for a moment before he spoke, in his quietest tone. "I was afraid it might not reassure you."

Georgine looked at the floor. Her lower lip folded over the upper.

"I'm not quite as insensitive as I make out," he said. "And for the last few days I couldn't have helped seeing that you didn't feel safe with me."

"I've been scared of my own shadow." She looked up at him and laughed. "If I had suspected you, it would've been your own fault. Who made out the Case Against McKinnon? Who's the perfect type of Policeman's Little Helper?"

"Good for you," Todd said, still with that remote twinkle. "Never overlook anyone. If you still feel that way, the door's ajar behind you, and I'll give you a fair start."

"Oh, don't be silly. Wouldn't that be a bit ungrateful, when it was you protecting me, acting the faithful doormat? Did you stay outside my house all night?"

"Pretty much. I didn't think our murderer would make any more false moves, but there was always that chance. Nelse agreed with me that you might be in danger, but the force has been losing men to the Army, and he couldn't dig up anyone to guard you. So…"

"Well, it was awfully good of you. I still don't see quite why *you* had to take on the job."

"Because," said McKinnon in a clipped voice, "what happens to you is quite the most important thing in my life. Must I draw you a diagram to explain that?"

Georgine gazed at him wordlessly, while her heart performed some peculiar evolutions. She felt her temper beginning to spark like the fuse of a firecracker. "You make me tired, Todd McKinnon," she said. "Why do you have to come out with this *now*, when it's—"

"When it's too late?" His face remained impassive. "I'm sorry about that. At least I've had the romantic pleasure of protecting you—from nothing."

"I'm sorry you had to put yourself out," Georgine snapped. "I suppose you think some specific person was after me?"

He nodded.

"Do you know who?"

"I think so."

"Well, who was it?"

He hesitated. His eyes glinted sideways. "I wonder if we ought to be talking here. Where's—where are all the neighbors?"

Georgine considered. "There's nobody at all across the road, of course; and Hollister's house is empty, and so is the next one—unless Harry Gillespie's out of the hospital?"

"Not to my knowledge."

"The Professor's at the police station, and Mrs. Devlin is in bed, guarded by a trained nurse. I don't know about her husband."

"On him I'll take a chance," Todd said. "So we're all right. I hope you don't mind if I go mysterious for a few minutes?" He perched on a corner of the table and fixed her with one of his intent glances. "Look at the pattern of the case. You were attacked because it was thought you might hold the key; Mimi was killed because she knew who was aware, beforehand, that there would be a blackout, and who could plan a little in advance. By the way, did you find out who put up the first signal?"

"Ricky said Claris did."

"And she said he signaled first. See what that means? Somebody wanted those two kids out of the way, either to protect 'em or to keep 'em from barging in on the commission of the crime. That gives us another characteristic of the Nervous Murderer; he's smart enough to make adequate plans, and to conceal his guilt—up to a point; then he can't let well enough alone. All right, we have our type; then combine that with possible motive. It couldn't have been straightforward greed, nobody was the beneficiary of Hollister's will and no valuables were missing from his house. It might possibly have been jealousy, but the only really jealous person is Harry Gillespie and he doesn't fit the classification. You know why?"

Georgine nodded, "He's too simple and obvious, isn't he? And if he threatens to kill people, he does it straight out. Not nervous, I'd say."

"That's it. As to the fanatic—I can't believe this is that kind of crime. The attacks have too much connected purpose. And if it were the Jehovah complex, a nice gal like this Mrs. Gillespie wouldn't have had to be put out of the way. Revenge? Well, the police have gone over Hollister's past fairly thoroughly, and they can't find that he'd done anything very bad—yet. Of course, there's always the chance that the Professor was getting in his revenge beforehand."

"Aside from everything else," Georgine said, "I think he'd be a—what did you call the first type, the Sit-tighter?"

"The Standpatter. Yes. And he was the one person who could not have arranged the booby trap for you, and the only one who knew that you'd be staying in his house on the night of the murder."

"You know, Todd, this character business is all very well, but will it fit all the physical facts of the case? Well, yes, I suppose anyone up here would have been agile enough to jump out of that car when it was going full tilt, and strong enough to choke poor Mimi, But who could possibly have known about the blackout? She said absolutely no one could have heard her."

"Ah," said Mr. McKinnon portentously. "Where were she and Ralphie when they were discussing it?"

"In the canyon, near the kids' meeting-place."

"Couldn't they have been in view from any of the back windows? Then suppose somebody *saw* them, with a pair of opera-glasses, and—didn't have to be near enough to hear?"

"Lip-reading?" Georgine said. "Oh, brother. You don't just do that by instinct, you know. Even Mr. Frey isn't good at it, and he tried to learn for years." A chilly draft swept down the passageway, and she automatically tucked up her feet on the lowest rung of the stool.

"Dear me," Todd said reflectively. "Maybe you're right. Well, skip that for a minute, and get back to motive. I think this crime was motivated by fear. D'you remember our talking about the people who were living lies? One of them was afraid his lie would be brought out into the open. Maybe that's been the key all along, instead of this problematical clue that you might or might not have possessed."

"Seems to me," Georgine objected, smiling, "that's kind of a skeleton key. It'd open anybody's door."

"Oh, no, no!" Todd swung round and gazed with unseeing eyes at the glass-brick wall of the laboratory. "*Think*. Who's living the biggest lie, as a fundamental part of existence? Whose whole way of life would fall into bits if that lie were publicized?"

"Not"—she had a curious aversion to saying the name— "not Las Vegas?"

"Not quite. This murderer didn't have much of a conscience. The nervous ones don't; they make their false steps in trying to protect themselves, not out of remorse. John Devlin's conscience would have given him away long before this. But you're next door to the solution."

"Am I?" She thought hard for a minute. In the pause, the open door swayed gently in the breeze, and on the same gust came a far-off sound of bells. "Great heavens, Todd," Georgine exclaimed, "is that four o'clock? I've got to get home, Barby will be there! I can't stay for any more guessing games. Go on, tell me."

"Name your candidate first. You were supposed to hold the clue."

"Oh, I can't. And I believe I know what my clue was. The Campanile made me think of it. It doesn't strike the half-hours, does it?"

"No," Todd said. He looked round at her, frowning a little. "You mean you've remembered what you heard on the night Hollister died?"

"I think so. And it doesn't mean a thing. I heard a clock chime the half-hour—and it must have been from some-where away off, because Nelse himself said he'd never heard a chiming clock in Grettry Road."

For a moment Todd McKinnon sat as if he had been turned to stone. Only his deep-set eyes changed, with the slow increase of horror. "So you remembered—" he began.

Then his head jerked up, and he looked at the door behind her. "Wait here a minute," he said in a barely audible whisper, and got down silently, quickly from his perch. In three or four soundless steps he was across the floor.

The door slammed behind him.

It startled Georgine, who had been sitting with her back to it. She gave a convulsive jump that nearly dislodged her from the stool, and swung round to look at the door, which seemed still to be quivering from the impact.

She hoped it didn't lock itself, so that she would be imprisoned here... No, of course not; even if those doors couldn't always be opened from the inside, she had the key in her hand.

For the first time it occurred to her to wonder why the Professor had left this room wide open. It didn't seem like him. She looked round quickly. There was something else queer; the filing cabinet, repository of his closely guarded secrets, also seemed to be open. She entertained herself momentarily with a picture of the old gentleman setting a trap for the unwary; after all, just the fact that you had been called down to the police station didn't mean you were to be there forever.

There were muffled sounds in the hall. What was Todd doing out there? She called his name, but there was no answer, and the sounds continued, soft and undefinable.

Frowning a little, she jumped off the stool and went to the door. It was locked, all right. Confidently, she put the key in and turned it. Now the handle moved freely.

The door wouldn't open, though.

Impatiently Georgine pushed at it, rattling the knob. "Todd," she said loudly, "I'm stuck. I'm locked in the laboratory of the Mad Professor!" She pushed at it again. "Todd! Let me out! What are you doing?"

The way he looked over his shoulder at the door, it had seemed almost as if he'd caught sight of someone in the hall; at least, she'd received that impression. Had he gone chasing off somewhere, leaving her locked in so she wouldn't follow and get into danger? He should have known better than that; it would be the last thing she'd do; if told to stay put she would do so until the skies fell.

She became aware that her heart was beating irregularly. A fine business this was, with Barby due at home any minute. "I've got to get out," Georgine said aloud, reasonably. "I've got to be at home..."

What was the matter with that door? She pushed at it again with all her strength, and felt it give a little toward the top. It was at the bottom that it seemed to be stuck. Georgine got down to peer through the thin crack above the sill. There was something just visible, holding it...

She remembered the wedges, covered with corrugated rubber so they wouldn't slip on the cement floor, which always lay about the passage. It looked as if one of these had been forced into the crack. No use pushing, then, she would only imprison herself more firmly.

"*Todd!*" she screamed at the top of her lungs; and then, after a long minute when there was no answer, "Help, anybody! Get me out of here! *Help.*"

Her voice beat impotently against the solid wall of glass brick; her hands were sore from their instinctive battering against the unresponsive door. She dropped back a pace and stood breathing hard. *No matter how I yell*, she thought, *who's going to hear me? There's nobody between here and the top of the road but a stone-deaf man.*

Todd had asked her if anybody were about.

Cold went sliding over her flesh like a snake. Had he seen anyone in the hall, or had he just—wanted to get out? He had looked at her very oddly when she mentioned the chiming clock. She had never been in the Clifton house, and it wasn't impossible that they had such a clock; couldn't one discon-nect a chime so that it wouldn't sound any longer—after it had betrayed one by sounding, through a momentarily opened door, in the quiet of night? And wouldn't one go on hoping that it hadn't been heard—and encouraging the only witness when she refused to search her memory?

"Dear God," Georgine said aloud, in an awed voice of horror. No, it couldn't be! But just the same, she had to get out of here. She had to find some way of knocking that wedge away from the door.

How long had that faint humming been going on? Somehow, the air-conditioning system must have been switched over when the door was closed. Well, that would help; at least she wouldn't suffocate in here. Georgine cast a glance at the louvred openings, high up in the wall, and then started purposefully toward the drawers under the cabinet and sink. There were eight or ten drawers. She jerked them open one after another; rubber tubing—more scrap rubber, like the old tires and pieces of hose in the garage; test tubes, syringes; here was a hammer, that might be of some use—now, if she could only find a thin screwdriver! Papers, an oilcloth apron, more papers. Sundry equipment, but nothing that would be thin enough to go under the door, and sturdy enough to knock out a wedge.

She stood in the middle of the room, her head turning from side to side with nervous intensity. It must be getting late, for the colorless light filtering through the glass brick had imperceptibly changed in quality. How long had it been since the door slammed? Perhaps not more than five or ten minutes, though it seemed very much longer. She'd have to—

Georgine made a sudden dive for the filing cabinet. It was a steel one; sometimes, in those deep drawers, there were removable partitions.

She caught a breath like a noiseless shout of triumph, and pulled out a thin sheet of metal. On her knees beside the door, she slid it against the crack, working it through... Yes. It would go.

She began to tap gently on the outer edge.

Maybe this wouldn't be necessary; maybe at any moment she would hear voices in the street above—or could one hear through these walls? Nelsing was due up here sometime this afternoon. Sometime. That might mean anything...

Something was happening outside; for a moment she ceased her hammering and sat back on her heels.

Another sound, quite near to her, had mingled with the metallic clang: a soft roar and then a steady chugging. That was the Professor's car, in the garage only a few feet away. He must have come home, she hadn't dared hope for that! But why hadn't she heard the garage doors open? They had been closed when she arrived.

"Professor Paev! I'm in the laboratory! Let me out!"

Nobody answered; and on the echo of her cry, a peculiar odor began to steal through the room.

Her hands had gone very cold, and she bent furiously to her hammering on the sheet of metal. She could see in her mind's eye the ancient coupé; its gears locked, but, in the old-fashioned manner, its ignition did not. Anyone could have started the engine, and set the hand throttle. There were those long pieces of hose, in the garage; and an air-conditioning system had to have a cold-air intake, somewhere.

She wondered how long it took one to become unconscious, when exhaust gas was pouring into the room.

CHAPTER SIXTEEN

Final Diagnosis

SHE HAD WONDERED, TOO, while her mind reluctantly built up a case, what good it would do to lock her in here. A fugitive couldn't get far in an hour or two, and surely she'd be out before then, and could tell what she knew.

Now the plan was obvious.

Grimly, angrily, she bent to her work. The wedge seemed immovable. "I won't die here," Georgine told herself between set teeth. She did not dare to think of Barby.

Nobody had ever been such a complete fool: to walk in and sit down happily, with a murderer, and unburden herself of all her secrets including the one that would bring him to ruin if it were known!

She'd mentioned the chime to Nelsing the night before— but she hadn't said that it was what she heard as Hollister's murderer made his escape. Nelsing couldn't have been expected to guess. He was investigating this case scientifically; maybe he'd arrive at the correct answer, in time; but all the science on earth wouldn't bring her to life if she died of carbon monoxide poisoning.

Perhaps he'd come up to the Road before the afternoon was gone; he might hear the engine running, he might come to investigate; but she couldn't count on that, she must get herself out somehow.

The air was growing heavy and acrid, and still the soft chugging persisted. Georgine paused for a moment, looking up, wondering if she could manage to plug those openings in the wall. She got up and climbed on the stool, reaching up. The louvres were a foot beyond her reach. No good.

She got down hastily, dizzily. Better not breathe deeply, nor waste breath on any more screaming; the fumes were beginning to reach her brain, she thought, for they seemed almost visible as they poured slowly into this tightly enclosed room. Back to the hammering; the air might be just a fraction better, down here near the small crack that was her only road to freedom.

Todd, she thought painfully; *Todd McKinnon, soothing and considerate and humorous. Nobody ever suspected a man with a sense of the ridiculous, it was his mask and his armor.*

The hammer clanged, and the sheet of steel moved almost imperceptibly outward. Was the wedge giving way?

Todd. It couldn't be. He had saved her life...

But not until after he had made her tell what she knew, and realized that it did not endanger him.

Todd, playing his sinister little tune on the mouth-organ, like a rattlesnake giving warning before he struck. That must have appealed to his macabre sense of humor.

Who was living the biggest lie, indeed? Who but the person who could tell the exact truth and make it sound like fiction, and who gently implicated her, Georgine, at every turn—but at least that hadn't done any good, Nelse hadn't fallen for it.

The hammer clanged. *The wedge was moving.*

Georgine's head spun as if in slow, regular circles. The chugging had not ceased, but the air didn't seem to be any thicker than it had been a few minutes since. Maybe it reached a certain concentration…

Who was living a bigger lie than the person who pretended to detect, while he himself was the murderer? The motive had been simple enough. He had described it to Harry Gillespie. *Todd.*

"I thought he loved me," Georgine heard herself whisper.

And with a shocking suddenness the metal shot clear through the crack under the door Gasping, she got to her knees and turned the knob, the door opened, and did not strike the wedge again. Fresh cool air poured down the corridor. Georgine struggled to her feet. Her head cleared gradually as she made her faltering way to the door at the end, and stood there, leaning against the wall, filling her lungs again and again.

She looked out dully over the canyon. Far behind her, a heavy step sounded on the gravel of the driveway. There was a noise of battering, and a moment after the garage doors had squawked open, the engine of Professor Paev's car fell silent.

About time the police got here, she thought. She started around the outside of the house, was interrupted by one last fit of coughing, and went on, feeling almost restored. Probably if you didn't get enough monoxide to make you unconscious, it didn't really hurt you. She had a good strong heart.

There, moving about the garage door, was a tall figure with a handkerchief over mouth and nose. It was—yes; it was Nelsing.

She said his name, hoarsely, and he looked up for a minute as she reached the door. She glanced inside, and stopped short.

Nelsing was bending over Todd McKinnon; and McKinnon was sprawled on the floor, near the exhaust pipe of the coupé, his hand clutching an end of rubber hose.

Caught in his own trap, Georgine thought.

Nelsing had the unconscious form out on the grass,

wrapped in a robe from the car. He had straddled it and was beginning artificial respiration, snapping a question at Georgine as he worked.

"Yes, I'm all right," she said remotely. "He didn't figure on my being able to get out of the lab, I guess. At that, you probably would have got here in time."

Nelsing, swinging rhythmically back and forth, grunted that he'd been as quick as possible. The sound of the motor had been deceiving, it was a few minutes before it had dawned on him that it was running in a garage.

Georgine leaned against the wall, looking wearily down at the slight figure. It looked much taller, stretched out like that. She felt nothing but an immense desolation, as if she had lost something beyond price.

"Isn't it funny. I can't hate him even when I know what he did," she said at last. "He never did seem bad."

Nelsing grunted again.

"Nelse, do you—do you have to work so hard, to bring him to? Wouldn't justice be satisfied if you let him die of this?" She heard herself give a forlorn laugh. "It's almost the same as the lethal chamber."

Inspector Nelsing looked up at her, his blue eyes stretched wide. Surprise had made him almost falter in his rhythmic pressure. "Good God!" he said loudly, still swinging back and forth. "You didn't think *Mac* was the murderer?"

Georgine gazed at him stupidly. "He—he wasn't? What was he doing in the garage, with the hose—"

"Pulling it off the pipe so you wouldn't get any more of the gas," Nelsing snarled. "What did you think, that I'd let him stand guard over you if I had any reason to suspect him? Look at that bruise on his head, he must've got caught out somehow and knocked cold—"

"When—when he went into the hall," Georgine breathed.

"—and thrown into the garage. That inside door won't open, it's wedged somehow. I guess he came to, you can see the grease smear on the floor where he dragged himself over to the car—probably couldn't get up to turn off the engine so he grabbed the hose off and the gas began pouring right into his face."

Her body felt as if electricity had been shot into it. She was on her knees beside the limp form, "Nelse, he's not dead? Is he—is he going to die?"

"Dunno," said Nelsing, maintaining the steady, even swing. "Gas might affect him specially. He's only got one good lung."

"One—what did you say?"

"He got hurt—skiing accident, years ago. Broken ribs, punctured his lungs, and by the time they got the rest of him patched up the lung was flat with adhesions."

"Nelse," Georgine said, "get away from him. Let me take over."

"You're groggy yourself."

"*Nuts.* I never felt better, and I'm sick and tired of standing by wringing my hands while somebody saves *my* life."

Her eyes blazed; when he moved it was as if propelled by the sheer force of her look and voice. "It's the right lung," he said gruffly, getting to his feet. "Go light on it. I've got to go—up there. Somebody'll come to help you in a few minutes."

Sure enough, she thought vaguely, there had been some commotion on the Road above them. She could not stop to wonder about it. Press gently; squat back and wait; press forward…

They had taught her in first aid class how to gauge the rests, but she found herself remembering the old-fashioned method of her childhood. "Out gas," you said, pressing, and, "In come the air slowly." She swayed back and forth, frantically intent.

Presently she began to talk aloud, though jerkily, as if the form were awake and listening. "Todd, you utter dimwit, was that why you wouldn't—even get into competition? All those— stories about why you couldn't get into—the war; I might have known how horribly you minded!"

Out gas; in comes the air slowly.

"You wouldn't say you loved me! You said not to take any—"

Out gas…

"—Anything second-rate. Did you mean *that*?"

In comes the air slowly. Had he moved then, ever so slightly? She dared not stop to make sure.

"Why, you poor lug, if I love somebody—d'you think I go around—counting his lungs?"

Out gas…

"S-second rate! What do you think is tops? What do I want with—a man who doesn't like women? Anybody—who married me would get two of 'em to start with."

Out gas…

Her back and arms seemed to be full of red-hot rope, her wrists were shaking. In comes the air slowly… You couldn't call it crying when there were no sobs, when the tears just ran out of your eyes and dripped uncomfortably off your chin; but she couldn't see his face through the blur.

"You come out of that, Todd McKinnon, and start breathing. Todd darling…don't you dare die!"

When the ambulance interne came, she had to be lifted away, expostulating, "I can't stop, you mustn't stop it for a minute. Let me go on, or take it over yourself."

"He's conscious, lady," the interne said. It was the same one who had supervised the removal of Harry Gillespie, and he gave her a curious look. "He's got his eyes open, didn't you see? I guess he's been conscious for three, four minutes."

"He has!" Georgine stood trembling, looking down at the eyes which were now innocently closed. "You mean to say I've been falling on him every five seconds, with that lung of his? I might have killed him!"

The bluish lips moved, and the interne bent over. Then he gave Georgine another penetrating glance. "He says from you it felt good," the interne said.

"Where are you taking him?" Painfully she moved up the drive, following the stretcher.

"Emergency Hospital."

"Can I go with him?"

"You his wife?" He shook his head. "Afraid there won't be room. You can come after, if you like, but he'll have to be quiet for a few days."

"He's not going to die?" She turned to Nelsing, who stood beside the ambulance. "Nelse, he didn't throw away his life for me?"

Nelsing looked at the interne. "Good chance he'll recover, I should think," the white-coated young man said. "Doesn't seem to be any skull fracture." The stretcher slid gently into the ambulance.

"He'll be all right, Georgine," Nelsing said. She closed her eyes for a moment. When she opened them, he was gazing at her intently. "You look a sight," he said.

Not until long afterward did Georgine realize that he had been testing her. She didn't lift a hand to her smeared face and disordered hair. "I suppose I must," she said.

"It's McKinnon, is it?" he said cryptically.

She understood him, and nodded.

There was a murmur from the ambulance. Nelsing swung himself inside, and bent over Todd. She could hear his answers.

"Sure, we knew, as soon as we analyzed the stuff under Mrs. Gillespie's toenails. She lost that slipper in the struggle and her foot scraped the floor. Paint, and—"

"...Almost too late. He hadn't expected us, but he saw us coming, and took gopher poison in the bathroom, with the door locked so we had to break it down. Got a statement, though. They have a few lucid moments even when they're dying of strychnine. Did you see him when he attacked you?"

"...Oh, you guessed. He must have hoped against hope, trying to make it look like a double suicide or something. He'd have the world's best excuse for not knowing that engine was running."

"...Okay, you get well. I'll be in later."

He swung down again, and the ambulance backed slowly round in the space at the foot of Grettry Road. "What will happen to him?" Georgine asked breathlessly.

Nelsing looked down at her, frowning a little. "Nothing! You can't punish a dead man."

"But you said he'd be all right," she insisted wearily.

"Oh. You're still talking about Mac. Don't you know who the murderer was?"

She shook her head dumbly.

"For the Lord's sake, don't you even care?" said Nelsing incredulously.

Again Georgine shook her head.

He gave her a look of despair, of vast scorn, of something very like relief. He turned and set his hat at a jaunty angle on his head, and walked away up the road, whistling a little tune.

It must have welled up from his subconscious, for Howard Nelsing, who had no laughter lines around his eyes, would never have chosen it deliberately: that song whose words ran, "And they sing, oh, *ain't* you glad you're single!"

She sighed and pressed her palms against her face. It must be well after five, and she must get home to meet Barby, like greeting someone out of another life.

Maybe one of the policemen would give her a lift home. She too began to climb Grettry Road. There were men moving about the doorway in one of the small white houses. One of them was jostled against the door-post, and she heard, as if through a night of fog and impenetrable darkness, a single chime. It sounded like a clock striking the half-hour; but it was Peter Frey's tubular doorbell.

"Visitors, Mr. McKinnon," said the nurse brightly, opening the door of the hospital room.

"Ah, Mrs. Wyeth," said Todd, politely bowing. "And Miss Wyeth, I presume?"

Georgine squeezed her daughter's hand, and Barby looked up and smiled at her; the plain, thin little face became luminous with the swift passage of that smile. Then they both looked at Todd.

He seemed perfectly well, he was on his feet to receive them. His face, bent toward Barby, softened and came completely alive.

"How are you, Todd?" Georgine said.

"I could go home this minute," he said, holding chairs for his visitors and himself perching on the high bed, "but they love me here. And besides, who'd nurse me at home?" He attempted to look pathetic.

"Three guesses," Georgine said, "but you're probably afraid I'd be too stern with you. That blond nurse would eat out of your hand."

Barby was looking Todd over, seriously. "Mamma," she said, "is he the funny man you told me about?"

"He's the one, Barby."

"Say something funny," Barby requested courteously.

Georgine had never before seen Todd completely at a loss. He fell back against his pillow, looking at her wildly, reproachfully. "My dear young lady," he said in a feeble voice, "you paralyze me."

A small miracle occurred. Miss Wyeth accepted this as an answer to her request. She tried it over under her breath, "you paradise me," she murmured, and then began to shake with quiet giggles. "He's funny," she said confidentially to her mother.

"And when he's well," said Georgine, exchanging a glance with Todd and drawing a long breath simultaneous with his, "he'll play the mouth-organ for you, I have no doubt."

"*Now,*" Barby whispered, entreating.

"Of course I can," Todd said in answer to Georgine's dubious look. "I've been getting along on half the normal allotment of air for years. What's a little gas?"

He gave her a level look, and added, "I'm glad you're not a lung counter. Dreadful habit, that."

"Oh, you heard all that, did you?" She grinned at him, unembarrassed. "Fine. It ought to save a lot of trouble."

"It will. Okay, Barby, here we go."

Georgine sat relaxed and serene in the hard hospital chair, watching a technique that might have given points to the Pied Piper himself. The way Todd looked at Barby, they might be sharing a private joke; and Barby was succumbing completely.

She must be an instinctive judge of character, thought her mother fatuously.

Todd played *Oh Susanna*, and *Camptown Races* and *La Golondrina*. By the time he'd finished repeating *Jingle Jangle* three times, by request, Barby was smiling. Her thin face had grown slowly radiant, and she had risen from her chair and gone to stand by Todd. Barby the solemn, the reserved and undemonstrative, was actually leaning against a stranger's knee.

The atmosphere of good will, in fact, was all but overpowering.

The concert came to an end. Todd gave the harmonica to Barby, having first thoughtfully wiped it off with alcohol, and watched her retire with it to a corner. Then he looked at Georgine.

"I'd thank you for saving my life," she said placidly, "but it gets too monotonous."

"Saving it, yet!" Todd said. "When I got you into that hole and da—and very nearly killed you?"

"We can cancel that," Georgine told him, "because it turns out I needn't have gone to the Professor's at all that day, except for my ghastly conscientiousness. He hadn't remembered to tell me that there was no hurry any more. The poor old creature had just found out that most of his experiments had been paralleled by some other scientist. I think it was announced that Monday morning."

Mr. McKinnon gave a sympathetic whistle.

"The odd thing was, he didn't seem to mind so much. It was given out, free to everyone, through the Medical

Association; and he's got a few refinements of his own left, so he'll still have the honor. Did Nelse come to see you?"

"He did," said Todd with a subdued groan. "I had to tell him I'd guessed right on everything except who was the murderer. It *ought* to have been Sheila Devlin, you know; willing to go to any lengths to preserve her illusions, Also, when I heard she was in bed guarded by a nurse, I figured she couldn't walk in that back door and listen to what we were saying in the lab. Just a slight miscalculation, da—bad luck to it."

"Barby knows that gentlemen sometimes used bad language, but ladies never."

"Good. Damn it, then. You were on the right track from the first, when you asked about sound perception. I ought to have guessed, I suppose, that if Frey had the genius to put over the rest of his total-deafness act, he wouldn't forget a point like that. He was genuinely deaf for two years or so, you know; a sort of prolonged shell-shock from that industrial explosion. He had plenty of opportunity to start learning the technique."

"But Todd, what made him keep it up after his hearing returned? You'd think he—"

"My dear," Todd said, "he'd never been so happy in his life. He didn't have to work any more, he could live modestly on the pension—some kind of compensation insurance—that was paid him so long as he was disabled. There's no way for an examining doctor to be sure the nerve of hearing hasn't been destroyed. It was a really stupendous feat of malingering, the sort that's got away with once in a thousand cases. The act got better and better as he went on. Pretty soon it was fixed in everyone's mind that he couldn't hear a thing. He never forgot the li'le tricks, saying the wrong thing and looking embarrassed, or making his voice too loud or soft—that was so he wouldn't have to counterfeit that unmistakable flat tone the very deaf use."

"I guessed most of that when I realized that he must have

knocked against his chime doorbell when he stole back into his own house. And then I tried to remember the sound I'd heard, through the blackout, and hinted there was something I might know—standing right outside that hedge of the Carmichaels'. Well, if he attacked me after that—he *must* have been able to hear. All so simple, isn't it, when you know the answer? But I don't quite see about Hollister."

"Hollister knew. He'd known Frey when the divorce went through, which was after the two years of deafness. Maybe the act wasn't so good in those early days, and Hollister tumbled to it and filed away the knowledge for reference. Then Fenella Corporation hired him and gave him the Professor's address. He thought of Frey, who was already on the Coast; he'd kept in touch with him just in case, and he needed to make sure of getting a house as near Paev as possible. I think it was quite by chance that Frey took a fancy to the place and snapped up the other vacant house."

"He didn't mean to kill Hollister from the beginning, then?"

"Not until that last day." Todd sighed and gave her a melancholy look. "Do you know what was the worst blow to me? I was right there while Hollister put the screws on Frey; I was in the kitchen, drying dishes for Claris as part of my good-will tour, and Hollister, twenty feet away, was keeping up the fiction to the extent of writing on Frey's pad, and laughing heartily. But what he was writing was something like this: 'I need a bit of money in a hurry, and I'm sure you'll let me use that cash you'd earmarked for a War Bond'."

"Oh, great heavens. Thirty-seven-fifty, Mimi said. And the Freys never did get around to buying the bond, Claris told us. That unmistakable amount!"

"Uh-huh. I suppose Frey thought of it as the thin end of a lifelong wedge of blackmail. Hollister knew his secret, and could let the insurance company know about the fraud. It'd mean a jail sentence—and beyond that, the loss of the whole way of life Frey had built up all those years, puttering round happily with his paints, letting someone else support him. He sat there in the next room, within earshot of his daughter and me, and took that blow, but he couldn't talk to me afterward, he had to rush down into the canyon to paint, to be alone and decide what he should do."

Georgine glanced at Barby, who was blissfully breathing soft discords into the mouth-organ.

"I'll tone it down," Todd promised. "He swore that he didn't have murder in his heart, not even when he learned about the blackout that was to come on the first foggy night. It was only on chance that he turned on the lighted house-number—playing with the idea, was how he put it; and there was nothing to lose in working that shenanigan with the kids' signals—fixing up Claris's window-curtain, and then rear-ranging it after Ricky had put up his answering signal. Frey had known about that affair for a long time, and hadn't lifted a finger. He was fond of Claris in his way, but he didn't care much about her upbringing. He was still playing with the idea when the blackout came, and when he slipped out to the Jeep, and when Hollister started to cross the road. At any time he could have dropped the plan, and no harm done. But—nothing went wrong, and Hollister got into position—and Frey released the brake. If he'd missed, or the impact hadn't been fatal, maybe he'd have had to go back and finish him off; but he just happened to be entirely successful. And then you barged into the middle of it."

Georgine nodded, biting her lip. "But wouldn't you have thought he'd realize I'd never suspect him? Because the person who tiptoed up the road *heard* me when I called."

"You forget," Todd smiled gravely. "He was the Nervous Murderer. I think he was more concerned about keeping the secret of his deafness than the one about the murder; and as a result he thought about discovery, and feared it, and began to expect it to the extent of mania. Can you guess what Mimi said to him?"

"The last thing she said to me was, 'There wasn't a

soul there who could have heard us.' I suppose"—Georgine looked up—"that Frey was painting in the canyon, and Mimi and Ralph thought of him just as they'd think of a tree. Maybe she wondered if he'd read their lips, or if they'd raised their voices and he could hear just a little—and thought of him not as a murderer, but as a possible witness to Ralphie's good faith!"

"And rushed across to his basement studio," Todd took it up, "in no state to realize implications, and said, 'Mr. Frey, did you know what Ralphie and I were talking about? *Can you hear at all?*" And once he'd panicked and set his hands on her throat, to choke back those damning words, he had to go on. He couldn't afford to revive her, because he'd given himself away. And he could simply," McKinnon sighed, "have denied the whole thing and been a Standpatter. I guess it wasn't in his character."

"Yes," Georgine said slowly. "I can understand all that. I can even feel sorry for him. What I never could forgive is the laboratory business. No, I don't mean his taking another crack at me, that was natural enough. It was his leaving you outside, so I'd think you were the murderer!"

"You'd have found out I wasn't, soon or late," Todd suggested gently. He was smiling again, and his eyes no longer resembled the hardest variety of agate.

She looked at him, and began to lose her train of thought. "But I might have found you myself, and left you to die in the garage—because I couldn't ever have stood it, to see you tried for murder. I'm afraid I—even then, for those five or ten minutes, when I thought—when I—"

"Dear Georgine," Todd said, "please stop talking. I love you very much, and I want to kiss you now."

He swung himself deliberately off the bed, and then halted thoughtfully. "I should like this, at least, to be artistically perfect," he added. "Barby, my dear, I wonder if you would step into the corridor for a few minutes? And if the nurse comes, tell her I don't want her."

"I like it in here," Barby demurred, politely but firmly.

Georgine broke in. "Darling, when Mr. McKinnon asks you so nicely to do him a favor, you do it right away."

Barby, a woman of strong convictions, still hesitated.

"Or," her mother concluded, as pleasantly as before, "I will skin you."

"Oh," said Barby, and was gone with the speed of light.